I HOPE THAT I DON'T FALL IN LOVE WITH YOU

I Hope That I Don't

Fall in Love

With You

HARPER BLISS

CHAPTER 1

"To his credit," Dakota said, "he did ask if I had an orgasm."

Head tilted, bangs covering half an eye, Jamie just shrugged. She was probably tired of Dakota telling the same old story over and over again.

"It's such a shame. He was really cute." Maybe Dakota should berate herself for having high hopes every time she went on a date, but she didn't. She believed in love, damn it. What else was she going to believe in?

"Maybe you shouldn't have put out on the first date," Mac said.

"I firmly disagree." Dakota fixed her gaze on her neighbor. "We had obvious chemistry. He was clearly into me and vice versa. Sadly, he failed where many other men have failed before him. Or maybe it's just me, you know? Maybe I'm the problem."

"You're not the problem," Jamie insisted.

"How do you know?"

Jamie and Mac were an absolute dream couple. Dakota had become friends with them when she'd renovated their house, which they were sitting in right now. Coming here was a real professional thrill because she could enjoy the fruits of her labor while spending time with her friends—and getting dating advice.

Jamie shrugged again, as though Dakota's question didn't merit an answer.

"From what I hear, because of all these apps, the straight dating world is a real minefield," Mac said. "I hope you don't feel too much pressure to sleep with a man on the first date because it's what they've come to expect."

Dakota shook her head. "Trust me, I can withstand whatever pressure there might be. I so wanted to get it on with this guy but then, once we were in bed, it was just the same old wham-bam-thank-you-ma'am again."

"You should have given him a copy of *She Comes First*." Jamie chuckled at her own joke.

"I'm sure that would have gone down well." Mac grinned at her wife.

"I don't mean to sound blasé," Jamie said, "but do you know who doesn't have this problem?"

"Oh, babe, no." Mac actually groaned. "Don't say it."

"But it's true." Jamie's voice went up a pitch.

"It's okay, ladies. You don't have to spell it out for me. I'm well aware that the orgasm frequency among same-sex couples is infinitely higher than among heterosexual ones. I read the *New York Times* as well." It seemed a popular topic to cover in long essays in the weekend supplement of many a newspaper. Fat load of good it did Dakota. All she could do was be happy for those around her. For Jamie and Mac. For her next-door neighbors, Izzy and Leila. And her ex-husband, Chase, and his male partner. Dakota was surrounded by sexually satisfied same-sex couples. Maybe she should hang out with her straight girlfriends more. Or maybe she should move out of the house she shared with Chase and Corey and leave the street she lived on with all these lesbians and their superior sex lives.

"Maybe you should give it a try," Jamie said matter-of-factly.

"Try what?" Was she—rather casually—suggesting Dakota go on a date with a woman? Just like that?

"Swipe for a lady instead of a man." What started as a small smile on Jamie's face quickly turned into a wicked grin.

"Babe, come on." Mac elbowed her wife in the biceps. "Don't be silly. Would you ever swipe for a man?"

"I don't need to swipe for anyone, let alone a man."

"If you were in Dakota's position," Mac urged.

Even though it wasn't helpful, it was amusing to watch Jamie and Mac go through their spiel. Dakota had only popped in for some much-needed venting, not for this kind of foolishness.

"I'm just kidding." Jamie winked at Dakota. "You know that, don't you?"

"Maybe I should." Dakota surprised herself. "The last thing I feel like doing is opening Tinder and scrolling through an endless list of mediocre men again, setting myself up for more disappointment. It's either swipe for a lady or take a break."

"Take a break." Mac nodded at Dakota. "That's probably the best idea."

"I say go for it." Jamie perked up. "Provided you're completely honest about your intentions, what's the worst that could happen?"

"She could break a poor lesbian's heart," Mac said.

Dakota chuckled. Not at the prospect of 'breaking a poor lesbian's heart', but because of the absurdity of the conversation. "What would my intentions be exactly?" she asked.

"Pleasurable sex with another person," Jamie said. "Isn't that what ninety-nine percent of men use the app for? So why can't you?"

"Because I'm a woman?" Dakota offered.

"Why don't we just have a look?" Jamie raised her eyebrows so high they disappeared under her bangs. She rubbed her hands together. "See what's out there?"

"That sounded a little too keen, babe." Mac slung an arm around Jamie's shoulder.

"Aren't you curious?" Jamie looked her wife in the eye.

Maybe they were turning this into foreplay for what would no doubt be an extremely pleasurable night of passion later. The kind of night Dakota would like for herself—the kind of night, if she were completely honest, she'd been fruitlessly chasing for too long.

———

"Are you on Tinder again?" Nico asked Jack. "I need your eyes on that door, partner."

Jack gave Nico an eyeroll instead. The hours she'd given to this job and he was telling her off for some innocent scrolling during down time?

"You can take your own Tinder break when I'm done," Jack replied.

"I don't need a Tinder break." Nico also took his eyes off the door they were watching.

This stakeout was probably a dud, anyway. Jack felt it in her bones. The guy they were after wasn't going to show up tonight. She just knew it.

"But I get it's intimidating spending so much time with a happily married man," Nico added.

"A phone break then, to look at pictures of that lovely wife of yours." Nico had been Jack's partner for almost three years and she still found it hard to believe he had a family. She'd often been a guest at his and Lorna's house and every time she left feeling uneasy, convinced that their kind of marital bliss was some sort of ruse—the kind of happiness not possible for an officer of the NYPD.

"You and your Tinder, tsk. I'll never get it."

Tinder worked just fine for Jack. Her eyes grew wide. *Holy moly.* Tinder was working really well for her right about now.

Jack whistled to get Nico's attention. "Maybe you'll get this." She showed him her phone screen.

"Yeah." Very dramatically, Nico puffed out some air. "I get *that*." He made a dismissive gesture with his hand. "Forget it, Russo. That woman is way out of your league."

"We'll see about that." Jack couldn't swipe right fast enough. She'd soon find out if this gorgeous woman had done the same for her or not.

"She's probably some model they've hired to boost their algorithm," Nico said, as though he was suddenly a Tinder expert.

"In that case, I'm about to private message a model." Jack showed Nico her screen again. *It's a match*, it said.

"Wonders never cease." Nico winked at her. "Good luck to you and your model, partner."

"There are many stages between a match and a date." Jack's heart did a crazy pitter-patter. Nico was probably right about one thing: regardless of the match, the woman in that picture was out of her league. But if years on Tinder had taught Jack one thing, it was that there's nothing more deceiving than a profile picture on a dating app. This woman, Nessie was her Tinder name, probably had a degree in Photoshop. Nevertheless, Jack was thrilled. She wanted to message Nessie immediately but she had some professional courtesy left. She wasn't going to do that while on a stakeout with Nico. It gave her something to look forward to tonight other than watching reruns of unrealistic cop shows on TV.

———

The black-and-white picture portrayed a woman with brooding, smoky eyes. She cast a sidelong glance into the lens, her shoulder-length dark hair falling gracefully onto a crisp white shirt.

"Not bad," Dakota said.

"I'm more than pleasantly surprised with what's on offer," Jamie said.

"All of this is so superficial," Mac said, but her tone betrayed a hint of glee at the proceedings. "It's just a picture. What can you actually tell from just a picture?"

"Well." Jamie examined the picture they had swiped right on a few moments earlier. "She's pretty hot."

"The woman in that picture is hot. I'll give you that." Mac took the phone from Jamie and glared at it. "Excellent hair. Sultry eyes. Sure. But is it real?"

"There's only one way to find out." Jamie held out her hand for the phone. Mac gave it back to her. Then Jamie gave it to Dakota. "Send her a message."

"I never message first." Dakota never had to. The profile picture she used on Tinder drove men crazy. Her blue eyes sparkling. Her blond hair combed back. Just the right amount of tantalizing cleavage.

"It might be different with a woman, and isn't that the whole point of this experiment?" Jamie said.

Dakota stared at her phone. Excitement and trepidation were doing a funny little dance inside her. What the hell was she doing? Sure, dating men had been a succession of letdowns. But maybe she'd just been unlucky. Maybe her profile picture attracted the wrong kind of guy. Maybe how she looked stood in the way of her getting what she actually wanted. But what was it that she wanted, anyway? As if what Jamie had suggested was even possible. As if all Dakota had to do was change her gender preference to female on a dating app and great sex would no longer be a memory from a distant past. *Yeah right.* If only life were that simple.

With a shake of the head, Dakota put her phone on the table. "Let's forget about it, okay? I'm a mother, for crying out loud."

"What's that got to do with anything?" Jamie fixed her gaze on Dakota.

"My kids are already dealing with their dad being married to a man. I can't start dating women as an experiment." Never mind that Dakota's daughters had handled their father's new love interest a whole lot better than she had.

"Just my two cents," Mac interjected. "If you were to go on a date with a woman, don't tell her she's an experiment."

"But it is an experiment. That's what Jamie just literally called it." Dakota was over it already.

"And don't drag your kids into this," Jamie said, ignoring Dakota's last comment. "They've got nothing to do with this."

Peyton and Aubrey were at an age where they couldn't

care less who their mother was or wasn't dating. Thirteen-year-old girls had so many other things to occupy their volatile little minds. Dakota experienced that every single day. Jamie was right. Her girls had nothing to do with this.

"How about I just wait until she—" Dakota checked her phone screen. "Until J.R. messages me and I'll take it from there."

"It's your call," Jamie acquiesced. "It's your love life."

"But do keep us up-to-date of any developments." Mac beamed her a smile. When Dakota had started working with them on their house—after Leila had recommended her architectural services—Jamie and Mac had shared the story of how they'd got together. Just like Dakota and Chase, they'd met in college, at that age when anything still seemed possible. Also, just like her and Chase, Jamie and Mac had broken up in their early thirties, albeit for very different reasons. But now, they were both in their fifties and crazy about each other. Life had brought them back together. That was never going to happen for Dakota and Chase, who was married to Corey now.

"I suppose I can take the first step." Dakota went into Tinder's message dashboard and started typing.

Nice to meet you, she sent to her match. Then she waited.

CHAPTER 2

Just as Jack had predicted, their perp had not shown, and she and Nico had spent the rest of their shift wasting time in the car. Dull hours like that were part of the job. In real life, unlike on cop shows like *King & Prince*, the end of the workday was hardly ever neatly wrapped up by catching a criminal. Being a detective was often more frustrating than rewarding, yet Jack couldn't imagine being anything else. It was in her DNA. It ran in her family. It was her life's purpose, although she had enough smarts to not go shouting that off any rooftops.

She'd closed the Tinder app after matching with that insanely hot lady. If she hadn't, she'd have been checking her phone for messages every thirty seconds, and that was no way for a detective to behave.

But now she was home, in her cozy—which meant tiny in real estate speak—apartment right on the edge between Brooklyn and Queens. She kicked off her shoes, grabbed a beer, and settled on the couch.

She opened the app and her pulse spiked as she saw the message notification.

Nice to meet you, it said. No emojis. No frills. But Jack could work with that. She had a fair bit of experience in this department. She started typing, hoping Hot Lady—it sounded so much better than Nessie, which made her think of the Loch Ness Monster—was up for a chat.

> Likewise. How's it going?

No immediate reply was forthcoming. She supposed it meant that Hot Lady wasn't glued to her phone at all times. That she had a life. Or a busy job, maybe working an evening shift. In a way, this was one of the most fun parts of Tinder dating. All she had to go on were a few pictures and a short bio. Hot Lady's read: *New York state of mind.*

That was it. Clearly, she didn't want to give much away. There was one more picture of her, looking equally glamorous, dressed in a swanky suit and with diamond studs in her ears. Jack could at least deduce that Hot Lady was into dressing up and a moderate amount of bling. And she loved New York. Jack, too, was born and bred in New York. At least they had that in common, because Jack was not into ostentatious jewelry or expensive clothes. The best she could afford on her salary were moderately priced pantsuits and the occasional high-quality shirt.

Jack had been an early adopter of Tinder. She'd been on her fair share of dates. Inevitably, some had been dreadful, especially in the beginning, when she was still learning the ropes. After a few years on the app, Jack had developed a sixth sense about who to meet in real life and who to block. Her system wasn't foolproof, but she did consider herself somewhat of a Tinder expert.

Her phone buzzed in her hand. A rush of excitement coursed through her. But it was only a message from Nico.

> Lorna says you should come to dinner at our house this weekend instead of going on another Tinder date.

Jack might take him and Lorna up on their offer if she couldn't arrange a date. Right now, the odds were fifty-fifty, but they could soon change. Her phone buzzed again. This time it was a message from Hot Lady.

> I'm doing fine, thanks for asking.

Hot Lady was not a chatty Cathy then. She was probably new to Tinder. Or maybe she was messaging ten possible dates simultaneously. Shallow as it may be, with that picture, her matches must be through the roof. Jack was probably just one of many suitors. But she could rise to the challenge. She sent another message.

> Where in New York are you from?

> I've lived in Brooklyn for 15 years, but I grew up in Oregon. You?

> Brought up on Staten Island, but also in Brooklyn now.

They exchanged short purely informational messages for a while, not going into too great a detail—you never knew who was actually texting you. Jack had done this dozens of times before—she could go through this initial phase in her sleep. She was always careful not to give too much away, even when, through some sort of virtual magic, she felt a tiny spark take root. The seed of possibility. But she preferred to not drag out the messaging stage for too long. She had learned the hard way that it was better to meet up sooner rather than later.

She found out that Hot Lady was an architect, was thirty-six years old, and lived in Brooklyn. That was all she needed to know before moving on to the next step. Setting up a date.

———

Just messaging with a woman instead of a man already felt different to Dakota. Maybe because it was new and, perhaps, a little illicit. Dakota felt as though, just maybe, she shouldn't be doing this. That it wasn't entirely fair on J.R. She was all for being honest—while definitely not calling this an experiment out loud—but she couldn't be too honest, not while they were only exchanging vague information about themselves.

What woman in her right mind would meet up with her then? A horny one, perhaps. Dakota chuckled at the thought. But that was one of the reasons why, earlier at Mac and Jamie's, they had all agreed that J.R. could be a good possible match. It was written in her bio in black-and-white: *Not looking for anything serious.*

Dakota was dying to ask J.R. what the general response to that was. If she were to put something like that in her own bio with her preferences set to 'Male', Dakota would be swamped with dick pics. She was curious to find out the reaction to that kind of statement among women. All in all, she was more than intrigued enough to meet with J.R.

In the end, it was just a little bit of time spent in each

other's company, in a public place. What really was the worst that could happen? That they didn't like each other. Or that Dakota changed her mind about all of this—which was still highly likely. Or that J.R. threw her drink into Dakota's face when she admitted she'd only just expanded her search parameters to include women, and that J.R. was the first ever woman she'd gone on a date with. Odds were none of that would happen. Perhaps Dakota would have a pleasant evening with this woman who was not looking for anything serious. She would only find out if she arranged the date. So she did.

Dakota and J.R. agreed to meet at a first-date-friendly wine bar—it said so on their website—in Park Slope on Saturday, which was only two days away. What on earth would she do with herself until then?

For a split second of temporary insanity, Dakota considered going upstairs to confide in Chase but quickly decided against it. She had no idea how he would react and she had enough unknowns in her life right now. Luckily, Dakota was a mom-of-two with a busy job. So she did what she always did. She lived her life and pretended that it wasn't a woman she was going on a Tinder date with this weekend.

CHAPTER 3

Jack was running late. Story of her damn life. She had hoped to arrive first, scope out the place and get a feel of the vibe before Hot Lady arrived.

When she opened to door of the bar, her gaze was instantly drawn to one singular spot. To that table by the window where a spectacular-looking woman with short blond hair was fidgeting with the stem of a wine glass.

In most situations, it was impossible for Jack to turn off her detective brain. Perhaps the only time she didn't feel like a detective was when her mind was sufficiently distracted by a hot woman next to her in bed—one of the reasons she was here. Jack had long ago decided on a life without emotional entanglements, but she was a hot-blooded human and, quite simply, required the occasional roll in the hay. That's what Tinder was for.

There was no doubt in her mind the woman she'd spotted was Hot Lady—or Nessie. Not only because she actually did resemble her picture—*oh, sweet joy!*—but also because of her nervous waiting-for-my-date body language. Shoulders slightly hunched. Foot tapping. Eyes glued to the door.

Hot Lady noticed Jack. Their eyes met. Jack tried to rein in the stupidest of grins—she'd already won the dating lottery tonight, which was ridiculous, because they hadn't exchanged a single word yet.

Hot Lady slid off her stool and drew her lips into a warm smile.

"J.R.?" She tilted her head and a lock of hair fell forward. She tucked it away with the suavest gesture Jack had ever seen.

Holy moly. What the hell was going on with her? Jack took a breath and nodded.

"In the flesh, but call me Jack—short for Jacqueline." She was usually so good at smoothing out the awkwardness of those first few moments. People skills were Jack's bread and butter—but not today, apparently. For some inexplicable reason, she held out her hand and pursed her lips at the same time, making her look like an idiot.

"I'm Dakota," Hot Lady said. Her smile transformed into a grin. She moved in, brought her hands to Jack's shoulders and, gripping with the gentlest of touches, pecked her lightly on the cheek. "Nice to meet you in real life."

Jack inhaled deeply and tried to pull herself together. She took a seat opposite Hot Lady—Dakota.

"Sorry I'm late." Jack wasn't going to start with a lie and claim that was highly unusual for her. "Have you been here long?"

"Just long enough to have a few sips of wine. Can I get you anything?"

"I'll have the same." Jack's heart rate slowed. Her stress subsided. She became herself again. "Thank you."

All Dakota had to do was glance in the direction of the bar for a server to hurry over. She obviously had this mesmerizing effect on everyone, not just Jack. Dakota actually looked better in real life than in her Tinder pictures. That was a first.

"Where in Brook—" They both started at the same time. Jack chuckled; Dakota did the same. Dimples appeared in her cheeks. *Oh, brother.* Jack gestured for Dakota to reply first.

"Cobble Hill," Dakota said. "You?"

"Williamsburg."

A server came over with Jack's wine. She could do with a large sip. Before she indulged, she held up her glass. "To our first date," she said. Jack didn't have many second dates. It wasn't why she was on a dating app. But that wasn't exactly something you started a conversation with.

"It's certainly my first date with a cop," Dakota said. "And with a—" She abruptly stopped mid-sentence. "Sorry. Nothing." Dakota fixed her gaze on her glass.

"I don't want to push, but I *am* a detective." Jack tilted her head. "Being extremely curious is part of the job description." So was putting two and two together, but Jack had nothing to go on just yet.

"I promise to tell you later." Dakota put her glass down. "Let's, um, get to know each other a little better first."

A semi-tough nut to crack. Jack was rather fond of that. "Deal."

"What does a day in the life of an NYPD detective look like?"

"It's not like on television, I can tell you that." Jack was well aware this was her pet peeve. If only she could turn on her TV and not be bombarded with two wise-cracking, trigger-happy detectives once in a while. "It's a lot of long hours and following leads that go nowhere, but I wouldn't trade it for anything else." The profound sense of pride Jack felt about her profession was always hard to convey in words—no matter how many first dates she'd gone on and practice she'd had. "It's busy, stressful, and I'm never home on time." Not that anyone noticed. "But I get to have so many adventures while serving the people of New York." Even though saying that made Jack cringe a little, the line had worked in her favor many a time. "The stories I can tell."

Dakota didn't say anything. She just looked at Jack with narrowed eyes. Maybe she would be an even tougher nut to crack than Jack had first believed. But if she was good at one thing, it was waiting out an awkward silence. Having the patience to let the other person speak first. It could tell you a lot about someone.

"Does your job have anything to do with your Tinder bio? With stating so clearly that you're not looking for anything serious?" Dakota asked.

Dakota wasn't one to mince her words. Jack was growing to like her more with every passing minute.

"It's a deterrent," Jack confessed.

"I don't know what that says about me being here, but sure." Dakota chuckled.

"That you're not looking for anything serious either?" Jack made sure to examine Dakota's face while she waited for her reply.

"True. In a way." Dakota sighed deeply. "You're totally honest in your bio and I appreciate that. Can I be honest, too?"

"Nah, I'd rather you tell me devious lies all night long." Jack grinned, which probably made her look way more confident than she felt. From the moment she'd walked into this bar and laid eyes on Dakota, this hadn't felt like any of the other dates she'd been on. An array of possibilities flashed through her mind. Was Dakota an undercover Internal Affairs officer investigating Jack for something she wasn't aware of? Or was she really a model hired by Tinder—no, that was too ridiculous a thought to entertain.

Dakota grinned back, showing her dimples. "This is my first date with a woman." The dimples in her cheeks swiftly vanished.

"Ah. Right." This wasn't an issue for Jack. It certainly wasn't the first time she'd gone on a date with a possible *latebian*. "I appreciate your honesty as well." She flashed Dakota a reassuring smile. "It's okay. That's what Tinder is for. A little bit of experimentation once in a while." Jack had zero objections to experimenting with someone as hot as the woman sitting across from her.

Dakota burst out laughing. "It's funny that you said 'experimentation'. I was explicitly forbidden to call it that in front of you."

"What else are you going to call it?" The last remnants of stress were retreating from Jack's body. This could all work greatly in her favor.

"I don't know." Dakota's shoulders relaxed a fraction. She was probably relieved to have gotten that information off her chest.

"What made you decide to try… a little batting for the other team?" Jack could so easily guess, even though she genuinely hated being that cynical.

"I've been single for years and let's just say I've been on a lot of disappointing dates since."

"With men?"

"Yes," Dakota said, despite shaking her head. "God, I'm sorry. This makes me feel so silly."

"It's not silly." Jack picked up her glass. "It's a clear sign of intelligence to try something new after trying the same old thing over and over." She eyed Dakota over the rim of her glass. "How's it going so far?"

"Ten minutes into the date, I'd say it's looking promising."

Ooh. A hint of flirting. Jack loved it. This was why she spent so much time on Tinder. For moments like this.

"If I may ask, what was so disappointing about all those dates you went on?"

Dakota shrugged. "I think the kind of man I'm looking for might not exist."

"What kind of man would that be?"

"A beta male trapped in an alpha male's body," she said wistfully.

"I'm far from an expert in men, but from what I can gather, there isn't too short a supply of those." But what did Jack know? She'd worked with men all her life. Some had been assholes, others had been pussycats. Most were somewhere in between.

Dakota expelled a sigh. "If I'm being completely honest…" She briefly fixed her gaze on Jack. "Which I'm not sure I should be, but it must be your detective vibes having an effect on me."

"Go on," Jack encouraged her.

"I might actually be looking for a copy of my ex-husband." She scoffed while shaking her head. "Which would be the most ridiculous kind of man for me to look for, because he's gay."

"No shit?"

"Oh yeah."

"Tell me everything." Jack put her elbows on the table and leaned in.

CHAPTER 4

What must she look like to Jack? *Jack*. Dakota liked the name the woman opposite her went by. This hot cop simply didn't look like a Jacqueline. And although Jack might not appear as glossy as in her profile picture, she sure seemed interesting—and she had the most soulful pair of eyes. That's as far as Dakota could take things at this stage. There was no use in getting any ideas in her head, especially since she had just clumsily confessed that her ideal man was gay.

"Obviously, I'm not looking for a gay man," Dakota clarified. It might be ironic, maybe even a little sad, but Chase had been the most considerate, and definitely the best lover she'd ever had in her life. He was gentle but not too gentle. He was in charge, but not too much. And he was so dreamily handsome. Chase was perfect in so many ways. Except for the gay bit.

"Obviously," Jack said.

"Call me shallow, but I'm drawn to handsome men."

"I don't think that's shallow at all. I'm pretty partial to a hot lady myself." Jack sent Dakota a sly grin.

Dakota enjoyed a bit of flirting. It was why she was here, but she had to set something straight—no pun intended. "For the record, I'm not still hung up on Chase. He's the father of my children and we're still very close." Maybe she shouldn't mention that they all lived in the same house, albeit on different floors. Dakota really wasn't painting a very attractive picture of herself.

"Children, huh?" Jack's eyes widened.

"I have two girls. Twins. They've just turned thirteen."

"Thirteen? For real?" Jack suddenly didn't look like a seasoned detective any longer. "What's that like?"

"Half the time, they're at each other's throats and the other half, they're ganging up on me," Dakota joked.

"You were so young when you had them."

"Fresh out of college," Dakota said. "Yep."

"Wow." Jack looked stumped for words.

"Do you have kids?" It was only polite to ask.

"No." Jack's voice was firm. "No kids. No ex-husband or ex-wife."

Dakota kept her gaze on Jack's face for a few moments. Clearly, the cogs in her brain were churning away.

"I know it's a lot." Dakota finished her wine. "I don't usually share all this information on a first date."

"In that case, I'm honored that you told me." Jack's wine was finished as well.

Dakota pointed at her empty glass. "Would you like another?" *Or have you had enough?* She didn't say that out loud.

"I'd love another." Jack caught her bottom lip between her teeth and slowly let it slide free.

Dakota turned to the bar. The same server as before hurried over, as though all this time, he'd only had eyes for her. She ordered two more glasses of wine and a bottle of water.

"Can I ask," Jack started, then paused—possibly for effect. "What it is you want from this date? Knowing that when you swiped right on my profile, you knew I wasn't looking for anything serious. A womanly chat? A bit of mild flirting? Something else?"

Dakota burst into the kind of giggle her teenage daughters specialized in. "I don't really know, to be honest. I'm—" Luckily, the server arrived with their drinks, buying Dakota some time.

"That guy is so into you, it's a little embarrassing," Jack said.

Dakota shrugged off the comment. She was busy trying to think of a satisfying reply to Jack's question.

"You don't even notice." Jack tilted her head. "Interesting."

Dakota was a good-looking woman—conventionally extremely attractive, Chase had once called it—with a shade of natural blond hair most men couldn't resist. It must stir in them an evolutionary urge to flirt with her. Blasé as it may sound, Dakota was used to it—and equally skilled at ignoring it.

"I'm a little busy trying to answer your rather forward question to notice anything else," Dakota quipped.

"Fair enough." Jack's smile grew wider. "You don't have to answer if it's too forward. I'm like that sometimes, but I'm easy enough to shut up."

Dakota liked Jack, but she wasn't sure she was attracted to her. Not that Jack wasn't attractive—Chase might even call her conventionally attractive as well, even though, with her dark hair and eyes, she looked nothing like Dakota—but she was a woman. Dakota might have chosen to put herself in this situation, but that didn't automatically imply instant attraction to another female. She wasn't used to this dynamic, to this kind of subtle flirting. To how easily she confided in this stranger. To any of this.

"What do you like to get out of your Tinder dates?" Dakota turned the tables on Jack. Why the hell not? That's also what dates were for—experimental or not.

Jack grinned at her, baring her sparkly white teeth. "I'm a one-night stand kind of girl. That's the subtext of my Tinder bio."

"Oh." Dakota could hardly pretend this was news to her—as subtext went, it was pretty obvious. "You never go on a second date?"

"Never is a big word. I have been on second dates. I've had friends with benefits, but…" Jack shook her head. "It never takes long before things become too complicated. I don't want to deal with all that stuff."

"Why not?" Dakota might as well be direct as well. They both seemed to have a knack for it.

"Because I don't want a relationship. Simple as that." Jack held up a finger. "Please, don't ask me why. That's my business."

Dakota was surprised by Jack's defensive response. She could only assume Jack had good reasons for wanting to remain single. Maybe it had something to do with her being a cop.

"Sorry," Jack offered, "if my reaction was too strong, but there are things I don't talk about on first dates."

"We've been here how long?" Dakota pretended to check her watch. "Not even thirty minutes and I already know more about you than about all the men on my previous ten first dates combined." Men loved to talk about themselves, but to actually find something out about them, something vulnerable and truly fascinating, was either a skill Dakota didn't possess, or something most men didn't do. Most men who weren't Chase. She had also shared a lot more private information about herself than she usually would. "I don't have to know everything."

"But…" Jack leaned in again. "You still haven't answered my question from earlier."

"I thought we'd agreed it was too forward?" Dakota slanted toward Jack. The ice between them was well and truly broken. Attraction or not, she was starting to get a feel for this date, and she hoped it would go on a good while longer.

"I conveniently forgot." Jack locked her gaze on Dakota's. "Just for the record, and at the risk of being too direct again, I totally get why that server can't keep his eyes off you. He's probably waiting for me to leave so he can make a move." She followed up with a crooked grin—it suited her well.

Dakota tilted her body even farther forward. "I'd best make sure he doesn't get any more ideas in his head then." This was taking a quick turn. Dakota wasn't entirely sure what had just come over her, but she enjoyed the sensation.

Jack played along. She bridged the last remaining distance between them and brought her lips close to Dakota's ear. "This should do the trick," she whispered. Her breath was warm on Dakota's skin, and it made her think, for the first time tonight, that she might actually, at the very least, want to kiss a woman—that she might want to kiss Jack.

"Also for the record," Dakota whispered softly, turning her head so her lips were less than an inch removed from Jack's. "I don't want you to leave."

"Thank fuck for that." Jack lingered for a few seconds before retracting her head.

"Maybe, um…" Was Dakota really doing this? Even though this decision now didn't necessarily mean that more would happen later. She had many more decisions to make tonight, and she would take her sweet time doing that, but she felt at ease with Jack. They had a rapport that was new to her in the context of a first date. It wasn't only easy friendliness between females. Jack was very clear about what she wanted—no more subtext required—and Dakota was still here. "After we finish this glass of wine, we can get out of here together."

"I would like that very much." Jack stared into her wine glass, then took a couple of very obviously hurried sips.

Dakota grinned and did the same. "Before we do, to avoid any awkwardness later, would it be possible to go to your place instead of mine?"

"Sure," Jack said. "Are your kids home?"

"They're with their dad, but Chase and I share a house. We live on different floors, but the kids tend to float between." More inadvertent sharing. Dakota could just have said yes to Jack's question and that would have been that. It wasn't as if Jack was flashing her badge at her. Maybe it was a subconscious thing when sitting opposite a cop.

"How long ago did you say you divorced this man?" Jack narrowed her eyes.

"Seven years." And he divorced me, Dakota thought. "We wanted to remain close for the girls."

"Okay." Jack just nodded.

"It's not as complicated as it sounds. Chase and I

would have stayed friends regardless and the house was more than big enough for two generous apartments."

Jack looked at her with what Dakota interpreted as a should-I-even-ask expression on her face.

"You and your gay ex-husband are still good friends? And he lives in the same house as you?" Jack shrugged. "Why the hell not? When you've worked for the NYPD all your life, you've seen it all."

This specific nugget of information was not something Dakota revealed to someone she was seeing until they were a few good dates in. She didn't have to tell Jack. Yet she had. Again. Had that eager server put something in her wine that made her want to emotionally unburden herself?

"What I find hardest to wrap my head around is the size of that house. This is New York. Real estate is exorbitantly expensive. Yet you managed to transform your house into two generous units, with rooms on each floor for your daughters. What kind of architect are you that can magically add space like that? You must be in extremely high demand with the people of New York City."

"It's just a really big house." Dakota had drafted the plans for restructuring the property, but she had little to do with its size. She wasn't sure she should divulge this next piece of information, but Jack had that effect on her. "Chase's family is wealthy. Like, really loaded, as the girls would say. He's a Van Ness."

Jack whistled through her teeth. Most New Yorkers knew the Van Ness name and the extent of generational wealth it stood for. "A billionaire, gay ex-husband." Jack twirled the stem of her wine glass between her fingers.

"But what I'm really dying to know is how you reacted when Chase Van Ness told you he was gay?"

Dakota held up her hand. "That's where I draw the line. Like you did earlier. I so don't want to go there right now." Dakota was having a good time. She didn't want to relive one of the most devastating moments of her life.

"Of course." Jack leaned back, as though physically taking some distance from Dakota. "Ah, Nessie. Now it makes sense. You kept his name."

"It's a hard name to let go of," Dakota admitted.

"Is it?" Jack asked, her tone a touch sharper than before.

The frisson that had sparked between them minutes earlier was changing into something else. Dakota got an inkling of what it must be like to be in the interrogation hot seat with Detective Jack. She didn't much like it.

"What was your name before marriage?" Jack's voice had softened considerably, as if to cancel out the sharpness from before.

"Gallagher," Dakota said. "Yours?" High time to flip the conversation back to Jack.

"Russo, hence J.R."

"Russo? Is that Italian?"

"Very much so."

"I gathered." Dakota was ready to take things up a notch again. "And again for the record, or should I say for the benefit of the tape"—she threw in a smile—"you are a very hot Italian cop, Detective Russo."

"*Grazie*," Jack said, and promptly finished her wine, her gaze firmly fixed on Dakota.

CHAPTER 5

Uncertainty filled Jack's mind. She'd been honest about her intentions. Dating was all about one-night stands for her. About getting mutual sexual gratification with a like-minded soul. With someone who was after approximately the same thing as she was.

Dakota was easy on the eye—a grave understatement of fact—and wonderful to talk to, but she was not a like-minded soul.

Even though Jack wanted to, she wasn't sure she should go there. Dakota had so much emotional baggage and while Jack had zero moral objections to being a curious woman's experiment, she couldn't be sure of Dakota's intentions. For all her experience as a detective, she couldn't read her sufficiently well. Or maybe she simply didn't want to. Maybe something else was at play here—something Jack was unwilling to admit to herself.

Yet, here they sat. They'd both finished their wine. Dakota had insisted on paying and was currently making their server ecstatic by simply tapping her credit card against his portable machine—as though she was doing something else entirely.

"So?" Jack said when they were standing outside the bar. "Are you sure you want to come back to my place? It's all the way in Williamsburg."

Dakota chuckled. "It's really not that far." She paused. "Unless you don't want me to go with you, of course."

"I do, but let's agree that getting into a cab together doesn't automatically imply… other things. We can just go back to mine for another glass of wine, or some Italian coffee, if that's your thing."

"Is that a euphemism?" A wild grin broke on Dakota's face, displaying those irresistible dimples in her cheeks, and erasing a hefty percentage of Jack's doubts. She hailed a cab and they headed to her tiny apartment.

———

"When I say humble abode"—Jack slid the key into the front door lock—"I mean that quite literally."

Dakota shrugged in response. She stood behind Jack, towering over her. God, that woman was tall. If she hadn't become a rich New Yorker's trophy wife, Jack was convinced Dakota could have been a supermodel. What was wrong with the men Dakota had mentioned she'd gone on all those dates with? Didn't men know how to treat a lady anymore? Or were they too intimidated by her looks? Both were options. Tinder had changed the dating world forever—at least Jack knew all about that.

"Do you only design houses for the ultra-rich?" Jack caught herself babbling. She pushed the door open.

"I don't live in a bubble. I'm well aware what New York real estate is like." Dakota followed her inside.

Jack flipped the light switch. She cast her gaze about her living room, trying to see it with Dakota's eyes. She always tidied up before going on a date. Her place was compact but cozy—in the real sense, not real estate lingo. Modest, but comfortable.

"I didn't come here to evaluate your home." Dakota shouldered off her leather jacket.

"That's right." It wasn't the first time tonight Jack threatened to lose her cool with this gorgeous woman. It flustered her because she wasn't used to it. "You're here for the Italian coffee."

"I'll take a glass of wine, if you have one."

Jack took Dakota's jacket and threw it over a chair. On second thought, she carefully draped it over the back rest, because god knows how much it cost. This woman's children were Van Ness heiresses. Thank goodness Jack was only into one-night stands because she wasn't exactly dying to meet those particular teenagers. No relationships. No entanglements. And most certainly no children. Thank you very much.

Jack took the few steps to the kitchen. She filled two glasses with Vernaccia, a crisp, dry white from Tuscany.

"Your place is lovely. Very warm and inviting." Dakota sank into the plush couch where Jack spent most of her down time—and a fair few of her nights, if she was honest. Often after a late shift, she fell asleep in front of the TV and couldn't be bothered to make it to the bedroom. An affliction she wasn't suffering from tonight. Not with such a gorgeous woman in her home. The doubts she'd had earlier were quickly evaporating. The next step had been taken. They were here now.

Jack handed Dakota a glass and made sure her pinkie finger brushed against her hand as she did. Just as a little feeler. To see what a spontaneous little touch like that would feel like. She hadn't expected to break out into goose bumps.

"Thank you." Dakota waited for Jack to sit before holding up her glass, as though they were here for a formal occasion instead of the next stage of a very promising date. "For your hospitality."

"I am a little bummed I'll never get to see your mansion." It would be a piece of cake for Jack to find out where Dakota lived—with her kids *and* her ex-husband— in Cobble Hill. Not that she would.

"Maybe, um, we can move on from that. I used to be married to one, but I'm not a Van Ness." Dakota chuckled. "Although, admittedly, my name suggests otherwise."

"You're a Gallagher." Jack tilted her glass in Dakota's direction before taking a sip. Part of her wanted to inquire further. To ask whether Dakota had any siblings and what her parents were like. The other part of her just wanted to gaze into her big, dreamy eyes. To find out whether they were blue or green—it was hard to tell—or an intoxicating blend of both. Jack was also really interested in finding out whether Dakota was a natural blond. She had her ways, although they were hardly foolproof. Yet, she very much looked forward to trying. Maybe she should start by sitting a little closer. She had a trick for that as well. "Let me put on some music." Jack rose to turn on the speaker behind the couch. She shuffled the playlist on her phone reserved for bringing back a woman to her place. Jack really was a player with all the tricks. But she wasn't ashamed of that. She was what she was, and she had her reasons. That was good enough for her.

When she sat again, she made sure not to leave too much space between them.

Glass in hand, Dakota leaned back a fraction, looking at Jack expectantly. That's what it felt like to Jack. She was the experienced dater of women. The participant in many a one-night stand. The next move was up to her. Jack knew this, but something stopped her.

Was she not ready? Or worse, was she scared? If so, scared of what? That her lips might never want to stop kissing Dakota's once they'd had a taste? That Dakota might get under her skin? Nah. She shook off those ridiculous thoughts. Her mind was just playing tricks on her. She was only human. A little nervous, and exceedingly excited. Because twist or turn it any which way, Dakota was not your average Tinder date. At least she wasn't Jack's average Tinder date—she was an eleven in a world of sevens. But that didn't mean Jack couldn't handle it. Rising to every possible occasion was part of her job description.

"Are you okay?" Dakota pulled Jack from her useless reverie. "You've gone very quiet. Are you having second thoughts about me being here?" Dakota didn't look as though, if that were really the case with Jack, she'd bolt right out of there. She didn't look as though *she* was having second thoughts at all. In fact, she came across as very comfortable on Jack's couch.

Jack shook her head. "On the contrary. I'm glad you're here."

"This wine is excellent, by the way. You have good taste."

"Hence you being in my apartment tonight."

Dakota smiled, and her cheeks dimpled again, and Jack reacted by scooting a little closer. Maybe they should talk more. Maybe they should at least finish their wine. Maybe she should give Dakota more time to adjust to this new-for-her situation. But Jack banished all thoughts from her brain. All but one. She was a cop, after all. And a decent human being.

Jack looked into Dakota's eyes. From this angle, they were definitely blue. "Can I kiss you?" she asked.

"Yes. I think you should." Dakota flicked her tongue over her lips.

Jack took their wine glasses and put them on the coffee table. She shuffled closer. She leaned in and when she inhaled, Dakota's luxurious perfume drifted into her nostrils. Everything about her was intoxicating. Dakota's skin was smooth and luminous. Her eyes looked more green than blue again. How was that even possible? The dimples in her cheeks were to die for.

Jack waited for Dakota to tilt her head toward her. She did ever so slowly—as though this special moment before their first kiss was happening in slow-motion, just so they could enjoy the thrill a little longer. Jack had no problem with savoring this moment. She parted her lips and bridged the last of the distance between them. She put her hand on Dakota's shoulder and let it slide gently up her neck, relishing the feel of Dakota's soft skin on her finger-tips. Their lips touched. Then Jack lost track of what was happening.

CHAPTER 6

Jack's lips were so soft against Dakota's. So incredibly gentle, yet so sensual. Not a bad start at all. Dakota slipped the tip of her tongue into Jack's mouth. Jack's fingers rested against the side of her neck. As they drew closer to each other, not a hint of scratchy stubble around, Dakota could only conclude that this was great fun. More than fun. She could kiss Jack for quite some time longer. They had only just begun—and who knew where it would end? But Dakota couldn't think about that just yet.

She was kissing another woman. That was enough for her brain to deal with. Jack was making it very easy, though. And extremely enjoyable. Her hand slid upward until her fingertips reached the edge of Dakota's jaw.

Jack leaned in a little closer, deepening their kiss.

With their lips firmly locked, Dakota let go of the last tension in her body. She drove her hands into Jack's hair. She surrendered to the kiss and moaned into Jack's mouth —a low groan originating deep in her core. As far as experiments went, this one seemed to be working out a-okay.

Jack pulled back a little, not too much, but far enough to break the kiss. "Are you okay?"

Dakota swallowed hard. "Yeah." It was only a short word, but she barely recognized her own voice. She gazed at Jack's face. That was one hot cop, indeed.

"Excellent." Jack painted on a smirk—one that promised so much more than an amazing first kiss. "Because it's damn good to kiss you." Jack moved in a little closer, pressing her body against Dakota's. Without further ado, she kissed Dakota again.

This kiss was much less tentative than the previous one. It was full of intention without being forceful. It conveyed a message and Dakota was getting it loud and clear. If she wanted to, this could be much more than an experiment in kissing. As the kiss progressed, and Jack's tongue grew bolder, her teeth catching hold of Dakota's bottom lip for a split second, Dakota was very much inclined to accept the unspoken invitation.

She had nothing to lose and, unlike with most of the men she'd dated the past year, she had an inkling she might stand to gain at least one orgasm. Dakota wasn't going to turn down that opportunity. Something about Jack screamed extreme proficiency in the bedroom. Maybe it was her cop swagger. Or the way she was kissing Dakota, so soft but intense at the same time. Dakota wouldn't mind some more of that. She wouldn't mind going all the way.

She pulled Jack as close as she possibly could, just to get her point across. Although, with a woman as straight-forward as Jack, Dakota could probably just tell her. There was no need for hints, let alone games. Jack had been nothing but direct about her intentions, and that suited Dakota just fine. As far as what they both wanted from this

Tinder date, there couldn't have been a more perfect match.

The best proof of that was what they were doing—and the effect it was having on Dakota. With every second that ticked by, she wanted Jack more. She wanted to undress her. She wanted to run her hands all over her smooth skin. She wanted to kiss her in many other places than her lips. But, most of all, she wanted Jack to do whatever she was going to do to her.

Maybe Dakota was being naive because she'd experienced so many ultra-promising first kisses before. A couple of guys had managed to swiftly sweep her off her feet—quite literally—because they were such spectacular kissers, their kiss promising fireworks once they got naked, all for it to fizzle out disappointingly—and frustratingly—in the next hour or so. It wasn't all the guys' fault, of course. That would be too easy.

Dakota could be hard to please. A small detail could make her lose her sexual appetite. A wrong word. A misinterpreted glance. For her, casual sex perhaps wasn't so casual. The problem was that, when push came to shove, it was all far more delicate and easily ruined than she hoped it would be. Sometimes, because the guy was too rough or selfish. Other times, because he treated her like a porcelain doll. Most times because, despite decades of feminism, he had no clue where to find her clitoris, and if he did, he didn't know what to do with it. Not a problem Chase had ever had—and Chase was gay, for crying out loud.

Jack's kiss was exhilarating. Her fingertips skating along the skin of Dakota's neck thrilling. But it could still all turn out to be a dud.

There was only one way to find out.

Dakota pulled Jack even closer, so her lips hovered over her ear. "I want you," she said. Jack was definitely the type who would ask her later for clarity's sake, anyway, so she might as well get that out of the way. "Take me to bed," Dakota breathed into Jack's ear. "If you want to," she just managed to add, realizing that she had to take Jack's desire into account as well. Although, to be honest, Jack's desire was very much on display.

"Oh, I want to." Jack's gaze on Dakota was just as intense as her kiss had been moments earlier. The playfulness of her smile had morphed into something else. Dakota was looking at the very picture of desire. "You take my fucking breath away," Jack whispered. She maneuvered off Dakota and rose. She held out her hand, and Dakota took it.

———

Dakota stood in Jack's bedroom. She cast a quick glance at the room, but she really only had eyes for the spectacular woman in front of her. Jack was unbuttoning her shirt and Dakota couldn't look away from her nimble fingers. Could it really be this easy? And if so, how come she'd never felt this before for another woman?

Probably because she'd never let herself. Because it wasn't an option. Even when Chase had told her he was gay, Dakota had never questioned her own preference. Why would she? She loved her husband with every fiber of her being. He was the one for her. She'd known that since the very first time they'd exchanged hellos at Yale. It had been confirmed after their first kiss, and even more solidified once they'd gone to bed together. Chase was a dream of a man. Although, in the end, all he turned out to be was a mirage. And that was the real reason why Dakota was standing half-naked in this hot cop's bedroom, watching her take her shirt off.

No wonder none of the men she'd picked up on dating apps, and sometimes other places, could satisfy her. They didn't stand a chance—because they weren't and never could be Chase Van Ness. Of course it was foolish for Dakota to assume just because her date was a woman, things would be any different that way. But she wasn't feeling very foolish right now.

Jack slid her blouse off her shoulders, revealing a black lace bra. Dakota swallowed hard. Jack was the epitome of sexy. There was no point in asking herself why she reacted to her in this way right now. She'd have plenty of time to do that later. Right now, Dakota's only concern was how quickly she could get that bra off Jack so she could lay eyes on her breasts.

Jack took a step toward her. She slipped her hands underneath Dakota's top, her fingertips setting her skin on fire. Dakota couldn't wait any longer. Her hands snaked up Jack's back and she unhooked her bra. Jack gazed up at her with a grin on her face. Her hands followed suit and she undid Dakota's bra. Dakota suppressed a chuckle. Was this what it was like with another woman? Like looking in a mirror but not seeing yourself reflected. Every action leading to the same reaction with the other person. What would Jack do next if Dakota removed her bra? But Jack beat her to it. She hoisted Dakota's top over her head and, unlike Dakota's jacket that she had carefully draped over a chair earlier, she tossed her top into the room somewhere. Decorum didn't matter any longer. Something else had taken over.

Dakota was overcome with the urge to kiss Jack again.

She was taller than Jack and had to bend her knees a little to kiss her on the lips when standing. But there was an easy solution for this. Dakota drew Jack near and walked them both to the bed. It only took a few small steps. Dakota's bra slid down her arms. She took it off and treated it the same way Jack had treated her top moments earlier.

Gently but with a definite aura of command, Jack pushed Dakota's shoulders down until she was sitting on the bed. Then she took a small step back and, tantalizingly slowly, let her bra glide down her arms. Her tongue flicked along her lips. In response, Dakota's skin broke out in goose bumps. This was more than promise now. The thumping between Dakota's legs already required so much more than that. It was all so slow and sensual. Not the usual hurriedly getting her clothes off and quickly hopping into bed. Maybe because Jack was an expert in one-night stands, she'd learned to take her time. To enjoy every single second of them. To draw them out for maximum extended pleasure.

Jack bridged the distance between them again and pushed Dakota's knees apart. This time around, Dakota was looking up at Jack, stretching her neck in order to kiss her. Jack glanced down at her and, her touch light as a feather, skated a fingertip from Dakota's belly button up to her breasts. Dakota's nipples ached for Jack's touch. It was a little unsettling how much she wanted Jack. But she did. Oh, but she did.

Dakota skimmed her fingers along the waistband of Jack's jeans. She opened the button and unzipped them. Jack's panties matched the bra she'd taken off earlier. The black fabric contrasted deliciously with her skin. Jack wriggled out of her jeans and stood in front of Dakota in just a flimsy pair of lace panties.

Dakota couldn't help herself. She cupped Jack's ass in her hands and pulled her close. Slowly undressing each other was sensual, sure, but it was also terribly arousing, and the thrum between her legs was escalating.

Jack pushed Dakota onto her back on the bed and climbed on top of her. She bent over, her hair cascading down, tickling Dakota's cheeks.

Jack gazed into her eyes and as she did, another kind of grin appeared on her face. It was sexy and confident and promised so much more than the single orgasm Dakota was hoping for. Instead of kissing her lips, Jack lightly pecked Dakota on the cheek. She feathered kisses along her jawline, down her neck. Just as Dakota was bracing for the heavenly touch of Jack's lips on her aching nipple, Jack kissed her way up again. This woman was such a tease. But Dakota could hardly complain. Everything Jack did turned her on.

Jack hovered over her, peering into Dakota's eyes again, holding herself up on strong arms just high enough that her rock-hard nipples brushed against Dakota's breasts. Jack bent at the elbows, pressing her breasts against Dakota's. The hardness of her nipples against all that soft flesh was an extra turn-on. Then, Jack lowered herself all the way down, and slipped her tongue between Dakota's lips.

Dakota had no idea when she'd lost her jeans, but she was only wearing panties now. When Jack had started kissing her, with their breasts pushed together, Dakota had lost herself in the abundance of soft, smooth skin. In the divine sensation of having another woman's body draped all over hers. In how it was all totally, absolutely, about her —and why couldn't it be, just this once?

Jack kissed her way down again and, this time, her

kisses traveled all the way to her breasts. She flicked the tip of her tongue over Dakota's nipple and Dakota could only groan low in her throat, like a hungry animal that had just caught sight of its juicy prey. Because even though this whole experience was soft and gentle and sensual, there was something animalistic about it as well. Something instinctual that went beyond Dakota's logical mind. Something that connected deep inside of her. Something that reminded her of being with Chase—and surely something she hadn't experienced with anyone else since Chase.

Jack wrapped her lips around Dakota's nipple, and her breath stalled in her throat. What the hell was happening to her? Dakota was starting to get a little worried, but, luckily, she knew better than to give her worry any more attention. The sensations crashing through her body were too thrilling, too arousing, too mind-boggling. In the back of her mind, the next stage of this experiment was already being prepared. Was it only this particular woman that made her feel like this? Or could other women have the same effect on her? And she hadn't even climaxed yet. That was another big difference Dakota was floored by. A person's climax was, in a way, always their own responsi-bility—and Dakota didn't always excel at taking that responsibility. But here, in bed with Jack, she didn't have to spend an ounce of brain power on this. Because Jack was all over her and her intention was clear even in the tiniest of her actions. Jack wanted to make Dakota come. She was going to take her sweet time doing so—that much was also crystal clear—but there was no doubt in Dakota's mind that she would.

So she let Jack take her time. She surrendered to the shudder in her flesh when Jack sucked her nipple deeper into her mouth. She reveled in the sparks that ran up her spine when Jack moved on from Dakota's breasts and started to kiss her way farther down. She sank deeper into the mattress, safe in the knowledge that, when Jack finally took Dakota's panties off, it was with only one single goal in mind.

But Jack wasn't taking off her panties just yet. She ran her fingertips over them, expertly avoiding Dakota's throbbing clit. Dakota pressed her nails into Jack's flesh. She dug her heels into the sheets. She braced herself for that electrifying moment when Jack would finally get those wretched panties off her. Instead, Jack hooked a fingertip underneath the gusset, exposing her swollen center to the air, which made Dakota lose the power of breath altogether. That wasn't just a groan emanating from her throat. It was a desperate cry for more. A plea for release. Oh, the fun Jack must be having. Although Dakota could hardly complain. The thrum of her heartbeat resounded not only in her chest but everywhere a pulse could be felt. And Dakota knew this wasn't a fleeting sensation she had to latch onto before it disappeared forever—like she'd had to so many times before. Most arousing of all was knowing for certain where all this exhilaration was leading. To more exhilaration culminating in deep satisfaction. To something elusive that she'd been searching for in vain for too long. To, very simply, coming at the hands of another person. To share that intimacy she had started to believe was not achievable with someone she didn't have a deeper relationship with. Yet, she had no relationship with Jack. She'd only met her a few hours ago. They'd chatted. Flirted. Drunk some wine. Took a cab back to her place. That this was the result, Dakota at the cusp of orgasm, was so unlikely, it only heightened her pleasure—and Dakota was already beside herself with joy.

The moment had finally come. Instead of slowly guiding the garment off her legs as Dakota had expected, Jack couldn't get rid of it fast enough. Maybe she'd reached the next level of arousal as well—no small thrill to Dakota, either. To drive another woman crazy like that was sexy as hell. Jack wasn't some random guy with a one-track mind. Dakota might not know her very well at all, but she could easily glean that Jack was intelligent and, above all, really good fun. And her hotness only increased when the clothes came off which, in Dakota's vast experience, was not always a given—oh, the surprises a well-tailored shirt could hide.

Jack positioned herself between Dakota's legs. Before she bowed down, she looked up into Dakota's eyes. Hungry didn't even come close to describing the desire on her face. It only increased Dakota's own desire. Jack folded at the waist and kissed Dakota's inner thigh. Immediately, all her senses switched to high alert. The patch of skin Jack had just kissed burned in the most delicious way. Jack's kisses inched closer and closer to her clit. Until, at last, her lips touched against Dakota's pulsing bud.

"Oh, fuck," Dakota muttered under her breath, as she surrendered to the moist heat of Jack's tongue. To how utterly on top of the world it made her feel. To how, in a matter of seconds, Jack released all the tension that had been building in Dakota's muscles for far too long. To the strange but delightful sensation that everything about this joyous moment was meant to be.

A powerful wave of pleasure swept through Dakota, followed by another, even stronger one. Her pelvis bucked up against Jack's mouth. Dakota no longer had any control over her body whatsoever and it was the best

feeling in the world to surrender to this glorious woman—
and the unbelievable prowess of her tongue.

"No fucking way," Dakota whispered to herself,
because she couldn't believe this. What had just happened
here?

"Sorry? What?" Jack looked up at Dakota from
between her thighs. "Are you okay?"

Dakota shook her head, realizing too late that her
gesture of disbelief would worry Jack. In Dakota's
defense, her brain was only operating at about three
percent of its capacity.

"Hey." Jack crawled up to her. "What's wrong?"
Worry shone in her dark glance.

"No, I'm sorry. Nothing's wrong." Dakota could at
least smile again. "Sorry if I gave you that impression. I'm
just... astounded." Dakota cupped Jack's cheek in her
palm. "I wasn't expecting that, although I guess that I was.
I mean, I kind of knew it was inevitable, but..."

Jack grinned at her. "If that's your way of saying
thank you, it was my absolute pleasure and, just so you
know, that was just the appetizer."

Dakota burst into a chuckle. "Nu-huh. I don't want to
burst your bubble, but there's just no way you can make
me come like that again."

Jack drew up her eyebrows. "Correct. The next one's
not going to be anything like the appetizer orgasm you just
had. It's going to be much more satisfying."

Had Dakota been beamed into a different dimension
of multiple orgasms that only increased in intensity? Jack's
confidence was such a turn-on. Despite herself, Dakota
couldn't help but believe in what she'd said just a little.

"Please don't take offense. This really is a case of 'it's

not you, it's me,'" Dakota confessed. "I'm simply not a multiple-orgasm kind of woman."

Jack held out her palm. "Wanna bet?"

It was Dakota's turn to arch her eyebrows all the way up. The audacity of this cop threw her, but it also excited her. Because this kind of confidence looked so completely different on a woman than it did on a man. Many a man had promised Dakota nothing short of paradise in the bedroom but only a few of them had ever come close to delivering on that promise. The biggest difference was that Jack had already given her an earth-shattering climax, yet she kept on promising more.

"You seem very sure of yourself, so why not?" Dakota shook Jack's hand, which was a ridiculous thing to do under the circumstances, but this entire evening was already so out of the ordinary.

"Challenge accepted." Jack leaned in closer and gazed into Dakota's eyes. "But promise to let me know if anything makes you feel uncomfortable. I only want you to feel horny. Nothing else."

Dakota could only nod. Who was this creature? Was this how Jack spent all her Saturdays? Giving curious women like Dakota the night of their lives? Making them doubt all the previous choices they'd made in their hetero-normative lives? She looked into Jack's dark eyes and another brand-new sensation washed over her. The desire to make another woman come. Men were easy—too easy, really. But what would it be like with Jack?

CHAPTER 7

Dakota peered into Jack's eyes, as though she was trying to unearth some secret from their depths. Jack didn't have any secrets, except, perhaps, that Dakota turned her on to an extent she wasn't too familiar with. It made her feel shallow, but then again, Jack's propensity for one-night stands invited exactly this kind of shallowness. Why would she even spend one single moment questioning her powerful attraction to Dakota? It was the whole point of the evening. And Jack had already made her come once. She hadn't been able to stop herself from promising more. Suggestion was a powerful force. Just planting the seed in the back of Dakota's mind could get her halfway there. But it wasn't as though her first climax had been a challenge—on the contrary. In her head, Jack could take all the credit for that she liked, but she knew damn well it was only partly up to her. It did tell her that Dakota was very much enjoying her first date with a woman. To think Jack had hesitated before jumping into that cab together, but healthy hesitation was a big part of this game she liked to play.

"You're so sexy," Dakota said. "In a way I'm not used to."

Way to make Jack melt. "Keep going," she whispered, because it was a massive thrill to be the first for this stunning woman.

Dakota brought her hand up to Jack's face and traced her jawline with a fingertip. Jack felt the touch reverberate between her legs. Dakota's finger dipped down, ever so slowly, until it reached Jack's nipple. With the same soft touch, Dakota circled Jack's nipple, and the softness of her touch stood in stark contrast to the hardness of Jack's nipple.

Dakota cupped Jack's breast in her hand and leaned in to kiss her. Her tongue slipped deep into Jack's mouth from the get-go. As exhilarating as making another woman climax was, Jack was even more fond of what was about to happen next. Her skin buzzed with energy. Her muscles vibrated with anticipation. She wasn't entirely sure she wouldn't come just as quickly as Dakota had minutes ago, because she was so turned on. Her skin a live wire off which sparks might fly with every single one of Dakota's touches. Their tongues danced and Dakota's grip on her breast intensified. Their lips remained locked while Dakota maneuvered on top of Jack. When they did break for air, both of them breathless, Jack took the opportunity to check in—the impulse so ingrained within her.

"Are you sure?" Jack asked.

"Sure of what?" Dakota grinned at her as though she didn't have a single doubt in her mind.

"It's your first time and I wouldn't want to assume."

"Assume away." Was that a hint of cockiness in Dakota's glance? Jack was rather fond of that, too.

"Gladly." Jack pulled Dakota to her again and kissed

her like there was no tomorrow—this was a one-night stand, after all.

Next time they came up for air, Dakota kissed her way down, leaving a moist trail on Jack's neck. Her lips trailed lower until they locked around Jack's pulsing nipple. Jack swallowed hard. She wasn't sure how much more of this she could take—again, not something she experienced often. Jack knew what she was. A player. Someone who, at all costs, always protected the softest, most vulnerable part of herself. Usually, this translated into her physical reactions as well—because how could it not? Jack had perfected the art of always holding something back. Of not succumbing fully to how enchanting certain women could be. But tonight, with Dakota, whose tongue was skating along her nipple in the most delicious manner, she felt a little weaker than usual. She felt less like the player she liked to be and more like a woman looking for something else—something more. It wouldn't last long, though. She wouldn't let it.

But first, she had a surefire spectacular climax to enjoy. Dakota's first time or not, it didn't matter. Jack's clit throbbed so hard, there was no other outcome possible. Still, she couldn't wait for the first touch of Dakota's tongue between her legs. She ran her hands through Dakota's hair, dug her fingertips into the muscular flesh of her shoulders. Then, another surprising thought flashed through her mind. For a second, Jack considered that she wouldn't mind getting to know Dakota better. To find out what an average day looked like for her. How she was with her kids. To know if she'd run home to her swanky house after tonight and tell her rich, gay ex-husband all about it.

Jack shook off the thought and focused on her body and the state of supreme arousal it was in. It was only normal for an intrusive thought to pop up once in a while when in bed with a beautiful, intriguing woman. Jack was only human, after all. And her job only heightened her natural curiosity about other people.

Oh. Dakota was taking things up a notch. She glanced up at Jack from under her lashes—long and blond, like she was—while she kissed a farther deliciously moist path south. Jack's heart hammered so hard, she feared it might jump out of her chest altogether. Her physical response to Dakota was a little out of control. It was all a bit more than she could handle. But for now, she would enjoy it. She'd see about pulling back later.

With a gesture full of intention, Dakota pushed Jack's legs apart. She dotted long, slow kisses on her inner thighs. Every time Jack felt the tip of Dakota's tongue against her skin, her clit pulsed harder. She didn't need to put a hand between her legs to gauge how soaking wet she was. How ready for this gorgeous woman who was, quite frankly, sweeping her off her down-to-earth seasoned-detective feet.

Jack might be fond of one-night stands, but it wasn't because the women she took to bed were interchangeable. That had little to do with it. Firstly, because every woman was unique in some way. Every single woman Jack had been with had delighted her in different ways. But no matter how special the night had been, Jack never had any qualms about kissing the woman goodbye in the morning. Now, for some silly reason, as Dakota's divine lips were approaching her center, part of her was already dreading something that was still a few hours away. And that was not what one-night stands were for. On the contrary. They were all about being so in the moment, only maximum pleasure was the outcome. And Jack was on the way to feeling extremely pleasured. Something about this particular woman got to her. But again, it didn't matter. Jack was in her most defenseless state. She'd regroup soon enough. Still, she wished her mind would stop playing tricks on her like that.

"Aargh," Jack groaned. Dakota's tongue skated against her clit and all her muscles tightened. When Dakota wrapped her lips around Jack's clit, the delicious tension in her flesh almost became unbearable. She screwed her eyes shut because if she caught even the tiniest glimpse of Dakota's smooth skin—or worse, her mysterious green-blue eyes—she'd come just like that. For some reason, Jack felt she needed to hold on. To what she wasn't sure. Why didn't matter. She just had to. Maybe to prove something to herself. Dakota lightly dragged her fingernails over Jack's belly and—oh god—her other hand darted along her wet nether lips.

Ever since she'd walked into that bar, Jack hadn't stood a chance. Everything about Dakota was irresistible. Although embarrassing, Jack fully understood their server fawning over the gorgeous blond stranger he'd never met before. She'd basically done the same, the difference being that Dakota had swiped right for her. And now here they were. Dakota was doing a lot more than swiping right. Her tongue danced over Jack's clit. Her nails dug into the skin on Jack's belly now. Her fingertips hovered against Jack's pussy and, for the second time that night, Jack didn't stand a chance. She let it all go and surrendered to the climax that rolled through her body, that seized her muscles and shook loose everything she'd been trying to hold on to.

———

Wow. Dakota's cheeks felt flushed. Her chin was moist. She could still taste Jack on her tongue. Her head was spinning, as though she'd had one glass of wine too many and was a little tipsy. This wasn't just any moment in her life. It was significant in quite a few ways. And that blissful grin on Jack's face made her feel mighty good about herself as well.

Jack held out her hand, beckoning Dakota closer to her.

"You have a natural talent," she whispered, while tucking a strand of stray hair behind Dakota's ear. "It would be a shame to let it go to waste." Dakota wasn't sure whether Jack was cracking a post-climax joke or not. Her lips were pulled into a grin, but her voice sounded more solemn than witty. Her dark eyes were a little watery. "Sorry." Jack caressed Dakota's cheek. "Was that okay for you?"

What was she saying sorry for? Jack looked a little discombobulated, which was perfectly understandable after the orgasm she'd just had—the orgasm Dakota had given her. In her belly, a tiny butterfly flapped its wings. Even though Jack had experienced the physical climax, it had been a profoundly satisfying experience for Dakota as well.

"More than okay." Dakota licked her lips, tasting Jack again. "This experiment is really working out for me." She flashed Jack a toothy grin.

"Good, because it's far from over."

"Just so you know, I'm not really used to my one-night stands going on for hours." Dakota snickered.

"We can sleep all day tomorrow," Jack said while suppressing a yawn. "Sorry." She giggled like a schoolgirl. "I just need a moment after… *that*."

Maybe it was silly, but pride bloomed in Dakota's chest.

"You're very lovely," Dakota said, leaning in to kiss Jack on the cheek. "And hot," she whispered after tracing a path of kisses to Jack's ear.

"You're not too bad yourself." Jack pulled her close again and soft pecks on the cheeks quickly transformed into deep kisses on the lips. Dakota enjoyed the silky-soft sensation of Jack's skin against hers. The gentle press of her lips. The tender caress of her fingers. She hadn't been lying earlier, nor had she been joking. This experiment really was working out extremely well. She dug her teeth softly into the flesh of Jack's shoulder, but quickly followed it up with a sweep of her tongue. She wanted to feel so much more of Jack again already. The hardness of her nipple in her mouth. The scent of Jack's arousal in her nose. Dakota had come this far. There was no point in doing things by half anymore now. She was more than ready for her *entree orgasm*.

Jack must have quickly recovered because with the authority befitting a police officer, she flipped Dakota onto her back. She gazed down into her eyes. Ever so slightly, Jack shook her head, then expelled some air from between her lips. Dakota didn't know what it meant, but everything Jack did, every tiny flick of her fingers, every tiny motion of her hand, turned her on.

Before she bowed down to kiss Dakota again, Jack sent her a smile so gentle but sexy at the same time, Dakota felt her heartbeat pulse everywhere in her body. With their lips all over each other, Jack's hand drifted naturally, as though it were the only place it belonged, reaching until it lay between Dakota's legs.

Dakota spread for Jack, also as though that was all her

legs were ever meant to do. Maybe the biggest difference with previous one-night stands was that the intensity of this one didn't fade. It only increased. Dakota might have mentioned mere minutes ago that she wasn't a multiple-orgasm kind of woman, but boy, was she willing to prove herself wrong. In fact, she had no doubt that she would. Jack had that effect on her—and it wouldn't take very long either. Dakota could try to explain this night all she wanted—and she undoubtedly would, later, over a bottle of wine with Mac and Jamie—but right now, she could only think of how sexy Jack was. How brazen and gorgeously confident. In the end, it was a matter of pure luck that she'd happened on Jack's Tinder profile, and that they'd both swiped right. Most of her life, luck had been on Dakota's side, until it wasn't. She knew she had to take the bad with the good and right now, she was drifting on a cloud of good. Because Jack's fingers were growing more insistent—and claiming entrance.

Jack pulled back from their kiss as she pushed inside. Dakota gazed up into her dark, smoky eyes. Was there really no end to the delightfulness of this woman?

Her breath stalled as Jack's fingers slipped deeper inside her. Jack bridged the distance between their lips and kissed Dakota again. Dakota surrendered to the kiss and to the sensation of Jack's nimble fingers inside her. Heat prickled on her skin. Pure pleasure traveled through her flesh. All the dates she'd gone on and all the times she'd taken the leap to go home with a man because she'd felt a spark that she wished to explore, she'd never felt like this. Dakota had no idea that what it really took for her to feel like this, to have an appetizer and an entree orgasm—and who knows, maybe a dessert one as well—was to go on a date with a woman.

A wide smile broke on her face as the orgasm washed over her, because how could she not smile at this? How could she not burst into a fit of silly giggles at the sheer pleasure her body had just experienced? At the unlikeliness but inevitability of it—because Jack had told her. And wasn't that the most exciting of all?

CHAPTER 8

"Have mercy, officer, please. I'm orgasmically exhausted," Dakota said while looking into Jack's eyes.

"That's a new one." Jack couldn't help but stare right back. She could gaze into the bottomless pools of Dakota's eyes for a good while longer. In the darkness of her bedroom, they were more blue than green, but no matter their color, they sure were sparkling with all kinds of delicious mischief.

"Really? Isn't that what you do?" Dakota grinned at Jack.

"What do you mean?" Jack narrowed her eyes. "Or are you talking nonsense because your brain can't process this much sexual satisfaction?" Jack nodded. "I would understand *that*."

Dakota snickered in response. "God, you're just too much."

"In what way?" Even though they were joking around, Jack was keen to find out the answer.

"You're worse than most men I've been with."

"What?" Jack had no problem sounding offended. "Keep talking like that and I'll have to cuff you."

"You're so cocky." Dakota said it on a high-pitched giggle and Jack felt that wall around her heart crumble a little more again. "But in the absolute best way possible. It's irresistible."

"First of all, it's not called cockiness when, you know, no cocks are involved. Nor is it cockiness when one over-delivers on one's promises." Jack's lips were swollen from all the kissing they'd been doing. Her tongue had Dakota's most intimate taste all over it. Her fingers ached with the desire to be inside this gorgeous woman again. But they were catching some much-needed breath—and cracking lame jokes while at it.

Did Dakota just roll her eyes? "The word cockiness has nothing to do with the kind of cock you're referring to."

"That may be so but, either way, there's too much talk of cocks in my bed tonight. I guess I asked for it, what with bringing home a straight girl." Jack arched up her eyebrows. "And for your information, I do have a silicone cock I can pull out of that drawer over there for you." Jack pointed at her well-stocked nightstand.

"I think it's going rather well without the breaking out of any kind of cocks." Dakota treated Jack to a brand-new kind of smile. It was warm and dazzling and simply too sexy to resist. Jack had to lean in again, had to press her lips to Dakota's again, had to taste her skin on her tongue again. They kissed and kissed and Dakota dragged her fingernails along Jack's back in the most divine way. In no time, Jack was all fired up again.

"Actually," Dakota said when Jack's lips had drifted to

her neck. "I was just thinking." Beneath her, Jack could feel a different kind of tension in Dakota's body.

"Yes?" Reluctantly, Jack pulled her lips away from Dakota's skin.

"Well, um, this being an experiment. Could I, um… use that silicone cock on you?"

"Who's the cocky one now?" Jack's skin broke out in goose bumps at the mere thought of Dakota doing what she had just suggested. "You want to strap it on?"

"I'd like to try." Dakota shrugged, as though this wasn't a big deal to her. "I might as well, now that I'm here."

"No one can blame you for wanting to try *all* the attractions in the big old lesbian theme park." Jack grinned.

"I also really want to make you come again."

"Who am I to say no to any of that?" This far into the evening, it was no longer Jack's job to question Dakota's intentions. They were both enthusiastically consenting—and horny—adults. Jack would never have suggested any of this herself with someone as inexperienced as Dakota. She kept the toys for dates with women who didn't need to be made aware that a strap-on actually existed and most likely lurked in Jack's drawer. Jack pointed at her nightstand again. "Your most coveted contraption is right in there."

Dakota sank her teeth into her bottom lip. "Yeah?"

Jack nodded slowly, trying to keep a lid on her overflowing excitement. That this woman had even come home with her was already a miracle. That they were having such an amazing time in bed was the second miracle. And now she was going to fuck Jack with a strap-on?

This was the kind of stuff that dreams she didn't even dare to have were made of. But it was all real. Dakota's flesh under her fingers was real. The groans that had filled her bedroom when she came were loud and hot and definitely not a dream. Every single second of this evening was a million times better than any dream Jack had ever had.

Dakota rolled over, displaying her shapely backside to Jack, and opened Jack's naughty drawer.

Aside from a bottle of lube, a medium-sized dildo and a not-so-medium-sized one, the drawer also held the obligatory fur-lined handcuffs—Jack had learned years ago that more than a few people who went home with a police officer really liked to be cuffed to the bed post—and her trusty Hitachi Magic Wand, mostly for when the one-night stands weren't working out, and sometimes for that little extra when they were.

Dakota looked back at her with a perplexed expression on her face. "Wow," was all she said.

"Pick whatever tickles your fancy most."

"I have a Hitachi at home and, really, we have no need for that." Dakota turned her face—and attention—back to the sex toy drawer. "I'm not saying it wouldn't be a thrill to handcuff you, but I'll forego that small pleasure for a bigger one." Her voice was growing in confidence. She looked over her shoulder at Jack again. "Do you want the big one or the slightly smaller one?"

"You choose." That kind of choice could tell you a lot about a person.

Dakota chuckled. "Okay." She rummaged in the drawer and first put the lube on the nightstand. Then she unearthed the biggest of the two toys and the underwear that would hold it in place.

"Interesting," Jack said, trying to keep her voice level. Between her legs, she went wet like a river.

"Is it?"

"There's nothing wrong with being a size queen."

"Am I?" Dakota looked incredibly hot just holding that toy in her hand, Jack barely registered what she was asking. Even if Dakota choosing the bigger toy told her anything about her character, Jack could no longer process that information either. She only had one thing on her mind.

"Put it on." Jack's voice had grown hoarse.

Dakota got off the bed and it gave Jack another chance to take in her long, glossy limbs. Her perfectly shaped ass. Her soft, smooth skin. It only increased her anticipation for what was about to happen. Dakota stepped into the black briefs with the opening in the front. She found Jack's gaze and shot her a wink. She was enjoying every single minute of this experience, that much was clear. What was harder to believe was that this woman, who was about to position a silicone dildo in her underwear, had never been with another woman before.

Jack watched Dakota like a hawk as she figured it out —it was hardly rocket science, but it could be intimidating. But Dakota was one of those women who grew an inch when they strapped it on—and she was already so tall. The next time their gazes met, no more winks were exchanged. The atmosphere had changed. Things were a little different now. Jack, for one, had not expected to be topped like this. Not tonight. But one-night stands were unpredictable, and this one was chock-full of surprises.

Jack held out her hand and helped Dakota onto the bed. She pulled her on top of her and just feeling the toy wedged between their bodies was already such a turn-on. Jack couldn't wait for what was to come.

Dakota kissed her and, again, it felt like the tables had turned—in the most delicious way possible. Dakota was the kind of woman Jack would let get away with anything. She was the kind of woman who had waiters fawning over her at bars. Surely, she was the kind of woman that turned heads everywhere she walked down the street. She was definitely the kind of woman a rich guy took as his wife to hide who he truly was. Who would even think twice about a man with a woman like Dakota by his side? It was cruel but effective—until it wasn't, Jack guessed. She had never lied about her sexual preference. She wouldn't know where to start if she had to.

With the dildo firmly in place, Dakota kissed Jack differently—not the first time Jack had experienced this. The dynamics between them had changed because something inside Dakota had shifted when she'd put it on. Jack was convinced some clever Gender Studies PhD must have conducted a study into this, but she wasn't that interested in the psychological, nor the scientific reasons, why that might be. Jack was far more focused on the physical outcome. On the pulse between her legs. The heat beneath her skin. Her blood beating hard in her veins. She had conducted many a private study in the matter, and the conclusions were pretty damn positive across the board.

Dakota's tongue danced with hers more intently. Her hand embraced Jack's breast more resolutely. Jack could feel, in every cell of her body, how Dakota's desire for her had multiplied as well. Perhaps it had only been a seed of an idea to try on a strap-on, but now that she had, now that she was about to use it on Jack, it had already become so much more than that. Just like, perhaps, it had only been a silly notion to go on a date with another woman, and now here she was.

The dildo pressed into Jack's thigh as Dakota's hand wandered down, leaving another trail of goose bumps in its wake. Jack couldn't remember a time when she'd been this turned on, this on edge and, quite frankly, this ready to let someone she'd just met, a newbie in every aspect of the game, fuck her with a strap-on. But life could be funny that way—and oh-so sexy. Because Dakota was the very epitome of sexy. Not even in the glossiest magazine—not that Jack was a frequent reader of those—had she seen a woman more sexy than Dakota. Or maybe Dakota was just sexy to Jack.

Just like Dakota had said she liked handsome men; Jack really got off on super-hot women. And sure, real beauty might be on the inside, but Dakota's model looks weren't hurting this date, this time they had together in Jack's bed, the slightest bit. On the contrary. Although, obviously, they wouldn't be here if Dakota wasn't also fun to be around, easy to talk to, and intriguing to get to know.

Dakota's hand dipped between Jack's legs. Instinctively, Jack spread wider, and the tip of the dildo pressed deeper into her thigh.

"No lube required yet," Dakota whispered, as though she gauged other women for sufficient wetness on the regular. With every second that ticked by, her confidence grew. Without further announcement, she took Jack's breath away and gently slipped her fingers inside.

Dakota fixed her gaze on Jack as her fingers moved inside her, as she started tearing at that rigid wall around her heart again. But Jack knew how to build a solid defense around her emotions. She excelled at two things in life: being a detective, and protecting her heart. Or no, make that three. She was a pretty good date, even if she said so herself. She knew how to show a woman a good time, such a good time, in fact, that the women she spent time with, in turn, excelled at giving her a good time. As though they learned by osmosis and all it took for them was to spend some time in Jack's company. Dakota must be the best and fastest learner of all the women Jack had been with, because her fingers were undoing something in Jack. Or maybe it was the promise of what was to come—and all that had already come before.

"Are you ready?" Dakota whispered, her voice deep and low.

Jack could only nod.

Dakota slanted forward to kiss her as she slid her fingers out of Jack. It was a tender but short kiss, because Dakota had some maneuvering to do—the kind she'd probably never done before.

Jack didn't think it was possible to get even more turned on, for Dakota to look sexier than she already did, but when she squirted lube into her palm and spread it over the toy jutting out from between her legs, she reached new, breathtaking heights of sexiness.

Jack swallowed hard. Already, she felt undone—not a sensation she was familiar with. Jack had no issue relinquishing control in the bedroom, but she was under a different kind of spell tonight. Dakota looked like some kind of goddess who had descended from the heavens for one night only and had, for some reason, chosen Jack to spend that time with—to unleash all her sexiness, in the span of one evening, on none other than Jack. Jack wasn't entirely sure her defenses, no matter how carefully constructed, would hold against all this mind-blowing hotness.

Dakota squirted more lube into her hand and gently rubbed it all over Jack's pussy, the tips of her fingers wet and slippery and everywhere.

She fixed her gaze on Jack one last time before focusing her attention on what she was about to do. The tip of the dildo skated briefly along Jack's clit, and she nearly lost it. Just like before, she had to find a way to hold it together. Dakota wasn't making that easy on her.

"Oh fuck," Jack groaned, as the tip of the toy spread her wide.

"Are you okay?" Dakota's voice was so sweet, so gentle and sexy, it made a few more bricks of Jack's defensive wall crumble, just like that.

"Yeah," Jack whispered, her voice barely audible.

"This is so incredibly hot," Dakota whispered back. She cut her gaze to Jack as she pushed inside a little deeper.

Jack wanted to close her eyes, because her precious wall was being rocked by a severe earthquake, but she couldn't look away from Dakota. She was too beautiful. What they were doing was too intimate and joyful.

Dakota slid farther inside, spreading Jack wide, sending sparks of pleasure into the very tips of her toes and fingers. She pushed herself forward, their upper bodies coming together, their breasts soft against each other, until she was deep inside Jack, and her lips hovered over Jack's.

Jack was the kind of person who scoffed at silly notions like love at first sight—or love at first one-night stand—but she had to admit, as Dakota started moving inside her, that perhaps, even she could be wrong about matters of the heart sometimes.

Jack pulled up her knees, allowing Dakota and her toy to move deep within her. But it wasn't just the toy that moved something deep inside her. The mortar holding the bricks around her heart together suddenly appeared to be made up of nothing but water because, as wave after wave of inexplicably profound ecstasy washed over her, in those moments when this ravaging climax touched her the most, she was convinced that Dakota was someone she not only could, but also should, love.

CHAPTER 9

Jack looked stricken, a little pale even. Her eyes were moist and she appeared to be all out of wisecracks. It was one of the most beautiful things Dakota had ever seen in her life. Slowly and gently, she guided the toy out of Jack. Unlike many of Dakota's former dates, Dakota didn't have to inquire if she'd had an orgasm. It had reverberated loud and clear between the walls of her bedroom.

She wanted to get the wet contraption off, but more than that, Dakota wanted to cradle Jack in her arms. She looked as if she needed to be held.

"Are you okay?" Dakota asked as she folded one arm over Jack's belly and slipped the other underneath her neck.

Jack's chin bumped against her shoulder but no other communication was forthcoming. She probably just needed a minute to get her bearings, her breath, and enough energy to speak after the climax Dakota had given her.

What a night this had turned out to be. Never in a million years had Dakota expected to do what she had just done. She'd certainly never have believed it would feel so damn good. So powerful. So incredibly arousing. The briefs that held the dildo in place were soaked with Dakota's wetness. On any other date, the thought wouldn't even occur to her, but on this one, she really wanted to come—again.

Dakota caressed Jack's belly with the back of her hand. Jack had just completely surrendered to her and Dakota hadn't missed a single second of that most divine spectacle. To go from sipping wine in a bar to this in a matter of hours was special, and not something Dakota experienced often on Tinder dates.

"I've regained the power of speech." Jack's voice sounded gravelly and low, as though she'd had to hunt deep inside of her to unearth it.

"It was just so nice and quiet in here," Dakota joked, before pressing a long, soft kiss onto her cheek.

"Granted, you managed something few people do. Shut me up for longer than five minutes." Dakota had expected Jack's tone to be full of snark, but she sounded serious.

"Is that a good thing or a bad thing?" Dakota pushed herself up so she could see Jack's face.

"Good," Jack said, although she didn't sound entirely convinced.

"Are you sure you're all right?" Jack's face had become unreadable.

"I'm fine." She managed a smile but, again, it didn't reach her eyes. "How about you?"

"That was, um, a pretty exhilarating brand-new experience."

"Another tick in the box of your big Tinder experiment." Ah, there it was. The snark was back in Jack's voice. "I'd say it's an enthusiastic three versus a big fat zero for same-sex dates."

"Make that four to zero if you count all the orgasms between us." Speaking of, Dakota thought, acutely aware of the throbbing between her legs.

"It's hardly a fair way to count, or an honest means to conduct an experiment, but who cares?" Jack smiled up at her, and it did reach her eyes this time. "I most certainly don't." She went silent and looked into Dakota's eyes. "Are you ready for number five?"

Dakota nodded. "I'm so turned on right now. I had no idea doing that would make me feel like this."

Jack's smile turned into a knowing smirk. Her eyes suddenly sparkled. "Let's get this off you." She hooked her fingers under the waistband of the briefs and tugged them down. Dakota gave her a hand.

"Do you want to use it on me?" Dakota asked, holding the toy between them, her clit throbbing wildly at the prospect.

"No." Jack shook her head. "I want you to show me exactly how turned on you are."

Dakota wasn't sure what Jack meant. Jack held out her hand and Dakota handed her the dildo and briefs. She put them on the nightstand—out of sight, but not yet entirely out of mind for Dakota. Although she certainly didn't need it to come again. So much had changed since Dakota had assured Jack she wasn't a multiple-orgasm kind of woman.

"Touch yourself," Jack whispered. "I want to see."

Dakota drew up her eyebrows. She could touch herself all she wanted when she was alone. Then a bolt of lightning coursed through her at the thought of doing so while Jack watched. It would make the sensation completely different. Dakota chuckled. She would give Jack a show all right. Jack's attraction to her was glaringly obvious. Even though Dakota had just fucked the hot cop with a strap-on, she was more than ready to push her—and herself while she was at it—right to the edge again.

The instant Dakota spread her legs, Jack's gaze was transfixed. Dakota brought her hand to her pussy. She couldn't recall a time when she'd been wetter, which was logical, because she'd never strapped it on before. This evening might be an experiment, but Dakota already knew one thing for certain: she would be doing that again. It had been too hot, too glorious, the look on Jack's face afterward too stunned—perhaps that had been most surprising of all. For a moment there, Jack had been different from the Jack she'd seen all night. It wasn't just how doing that, moving inside another woman, had made Dakota feel. What it had done to Jack was a large part of it as well. Dakota would have to figure out if it would be the same with another woman who wasn't Jack. But right now, Jack was still very much here. The clock might be ticking, although Dakota had no idea of the time, but their one-night stand just kept on going. Could it last an entire weekend? Dakota wasn't sure her body was up to that, to be honest, although she was eager to find out.

A shudder ran through her as her finger touched her clit. *Oh my.* This was nothing like masturbating in the privacy of her bedroom.

For starters, Dakota was so much more excited, so much wetter, than when she was alone. And Jack's gaze was sizzling on her skin, despite the distance between them. Dakota couldn't keep eye contact for much longer. All the memories they'd already created this evening swirled together in her mind into a whirlwind of excitement impossible to withstand. She'd barely touched herself and she was already getting sucked in. So much for giving Jack a show. It was pretty much the theme of the evening.

Dakota was intrigued by Jack. She'd love to take her out again, if only to process their one-night stand. She'd love to find out what had made her into the person she was tonight. She'd give a lot of money to see Jack so vulnerable again, so totally at Dakota's mercy, but Dakota also knew there were things money simply couldn't buy. Like a second date with this hot cop. So she'd better make the most of this first and only date. That was the thing about making such a bold but clear statement from the get-go. It certainly spurred them on to make the most of the little time they had together—and they certainly hadn't neglected a single second since they'd entered Jack's bedroom.

"Jesus," Jack muttered under her breath. "You're the most beautiful woman I've ever seen."

Underneath Dakota, the mattress shifted with Jack's movements. Was she touching herself? Dakota opened her eyes, delaying her own pleasure—although it would only be more intense if Jack was mirroring Dakota's actions.

"You drive me crazy," Jack said. "Keep touching yourself."

Dakota had no problem following Jack's instructions. Her finger edged along her clit, but it was no longer just her own hand down there. Jack's fingers circled her entrance. Dakota looked up into Jack's eyes as her fingers slipped inside. She could try holding back her climax a few more seconds, but why waste energy on that? If Dakota had learned anything tonight, it was that her climaxes were in far greater supply than she'd always believed.

Bucking against Jack's fingers, Dakota surrendered to another orgasm. Jack's fingers inside her made it all the more intense and gratifying. She reveled in the glorious warmth spreading through her muscles, in the joy that bubbled in her flesh. Dakota couldn't remember a time, since her divorce, when she'd felt more abundantly alive than tonight, in Jack's bed.

CHAPTER 10

It was after nine in the morning when Jack was woken by a noise outside. She stretched her limbs. Her muscles were tense with the kind of delicious stiffness only an amazing night of sex could bring. She turned on her side to get a look at Dakota. It was warm in Jack's tiny bedroom and Dakota had thrown off the covers. One of her breasts was bared and Jack had to stop herself from taking that scrumptious nipple into her mouth. But she could content herself with just looking at Dakota. She should, now that she still had the chance. Soon enough, they would say their goodbyes, and their paths would, most likely, never cross again. They both lived in Brooklyn, but the borough was vast, and they didn't travel in the same social circles. And Dakota wasn't even gay. She'd come across as plenty gay last night, though. Delight rushed through Jack's body at the memory of Dakota strapping it on.

In the throes of passion, Jack might have had a foolish notion of asking Dakota on a second date, but that was to be expected. In the morning light, Jack was her usual levelheaded self again. Although, admittedly, she wouldn't mind if Dakota slept for a while longer, so she could feast her eyes on her model body and photogenic face for as long as she liked. Those sculpted cheekbones. Those long eyelashes. And oh, that perfectly shaped breast. Fuck it. As far as Jack was concerned, as long as Dakota was in her bed, the one-night stand had not yet ended. Jack bent over and touched the tip of her tongue against Dakota's nipple. A surge of heat traveled through her flesh. Apparently, all those orgasms last night—Jack had lost count after five—hadn't quenched her thirst for Dakota yet. Jack sucked Dakota's nipple between her lips and found Dakota's other breast with her hand.

"Hmmm," Dakota groaned low in her throat. "Best alarm clock ever."

Reluctantly, Jack dropped Dakota's nipple from her lips. It would be rude not to say good morning. "Hey, Sleeping Beauty," she said, not caring about how utterly cheesy that sounded.

"Hey, yourself." Dakota pulled Jack toward her. "Did you sleep well?"

"Impossible not to after a night like that." Oh, fuck. Looking into Dakota's face while she was awake, and smiling that angelic morning smile, proved far more difficult than lusting after her sleeping body. "You?"

"Not bad." Dakota stretched her lips into the warmest smile.

"Despite the low thread count of my sheets and the lumpiness of my mattress?" Jack joked.

Dakota just chuckled in response, then kissed Jack lightly on the cheek. "I will never, ever forget your bed—and not because of the mattress or the sheets." She kissed

Jack again, a little closer to her lips this time. "Thank you for last night."

"It was my absolute pleasure. Thank you for *experimenting* with me." Jack found Dakota's lips and another wave of lust crashed through her. Dakota held her close, and it was so easy for Jack to lose herself in their morning kiss—too easy. She shouldn't. As much as she wanted this date to never end, it had to. Dakota was too alluring. Too dangerous. Too much of everything that made Jack lose control of herself—and in control was the only way for Jack to live her life. It was the sacrifice she made for being a police officer.

Even though every single cell in her body worked against her, Jack pulled away from the kiss—their last one, ever. It had to be.

Dakota gave her a funny look when their lips parted, but it only lasted a split second. "It's also an experiment I will never forget."

"Are you planning to keep experimenting?" Damn it. The question had just come out. Jack held up her hand. "Sorry. That's really not my business. Forget I asked."

"That's okay." Dakota ran a fingertip along Jack's hip. "I don't have an answer to that question just yet. I have no idea what I'm going to do next."

"You'll figure it out." Jack tried to pull her lips into a smile, but it must have looked more like a grimace, what with her trying to will her body not to respond to Dakota's touch. If she wanted to get out of this scot-free, she had to get Dakota out of her apartment pronto. But she didn't want to be a bitch about it.

"Would you like me to…" Dakota paused to fix her irresistible blue-green gaze on Jack. "Keep you posted about the evolution of my experiments?" Dakota's finger had reached Jack's belly.

Jack swallowed hard. She bit the inside of her cheek so she would feel something that hurt instead of the desire coursing through her veins.

"That won't be necessary." Speaking those words hurt far more than biting her cheek. Jack scooted to the side of the bed, away from Dakota. "I hate to be rude, but…" Jack had no choice. "Maybe it's time for you to go now."

"Oh." The sparkle in Dakota's gorgeous gaze was replaced with a shadow. "Okay. Of course. The experiment has reached its conclusion. I get it."

Jack watched Dakota gather herself—the shadow in her eyes turned into something steely; her shoulders squared—and clamber out of bed. For a minute there, she had to wonder what was wrong with her. It was Sunday and she didn't have any plans until tonight. She could spend the day, or at least a few more hours, with this woman who had given her so much pleasure—who had made her smile from ear to ear. But it was in Jack's nature to pull the plug on it. She knew the reasons behind her decision, and that was all she needed.

———

Talk about a rude awakening. Although, up until a few minutes ago, it had been sensual and sweet. Dakota had woken with her nipple in Jack's mouth, for heaven's sake. And now she was being kicked out of her apartment, with no further ado. Maybe it was for the best because Dakota could do without Jack blowing hot and cold like that. She had two teenagers at home who had an advanced degree in that particular discipline, she didn't need that kind of fickle behavior from her thirty-something one-night stand.

She considered asking if she could take a shower first, but she'd seen Jack's bathroom. Dakota could wait until she got home to her own swanky shower. So what if, on the way there, she smelled like sex—mind-blowing, amazing sex, she had to hand that to Jack. She collected her clothes, took them into the tiny bathroom, and put herself together.

When she caught a glimpse of herself in the mirror, she had to look twice, but it was really her. Her short blond hair was disheveled, her eyes looked tired, but her skin had a healthy glow about it, which was no wonder, because this felt so different from any other one-night stands she'd had over the past few months—possibly years. Jack might be asking her to leave, but Dakota was smart enough to see that for what it was, and to not have it reflect on the amazing night they'd had.

Besides, Jack had been nothing but upfront about it all. This was entirely within expectations. Although, a night like that might put ideas into someone's head—but clearly not into Jack's. Nor Dakota's. As far as she knew, she was still straight. Or maybe bi-curious. Or just curious in general. Or, as her daughters would suggest, there simply was no need to label it. A night of passionate sex with another woman didn't instantly change who Dakota was.

Jack was dressed in just her panties and a white tank top, and the sight of her made Dakota stop in her tracks. She wasn't just going to quickly skulk out of Jack's apartment. She was going to say a proper goodbye.

"Come here." She opened her arms wide and beckoned Jack over.

At first, Jack arched up her eyebrows. Yet, she didn't

hesitate very long before she bridged the distance between them.

Dakota wrapped her arms around Jack and held her tight.

"You're amazing," she whispered in Jack's ear. Dakota also wanted to say she hoped they would run into each other again sometime, but she didn't.

"I hope you find what you're looking for on Tinder." Jack curled her arms around Dakota a little tighter.

For just one night, Dakota believed she already had.

CHAPTER 11

Mac's eyes grew wide like frisbees. "You strapped it on?"

After a long, hot shower, Dakota had texted her neighbors and demanded what they liked to call a 'lesbian processing meeting'.

What was this weird kind of smugness that bubbled up inside Dakota? Was it a lesbian thing? She had a lot of questions, some of which she could put to Mac and Jamie, but definitely not all. She did tell them about the strap-on, though. It was impossible not to.

"Who is this woman that you went on a date with?" That wasn't just curiosity in Jamie's tone of voice. There was something else in there as well, but Dakota was too busy telling them about her amazing night to figure out if it was awe or envy, or something else.

"Her name's Jack. She's a police detective. And her main pastime outside of work is picking up women on Tinder for one-night stands."

"So you're not going to see her again?"

"No. That was the deal from the start. You know that."

"If I know one thing," Mac said, "it's that intentions you have before a date can change drastically once the date is over. Especially after the spectacular date you just had."

"That's not the case here." Dakota shrugged. "She basically kicked me out this morning." *After waking me up by sucking my nipple in her mouth,* Dakota thought, trying to suppress the flush in her cheeks. "Also, I'm not going to suddenly start dating only women," Dakota added.

"Your loss," Jamie said, sending her a huge smile.

Despite the smile, and the obvious irony of her comment, Dakota rolled her eyes at her friend anyway.

"But fuck," Dakota had to admit. "The orgasms. I didn't expect that. At all. I'm so satisfied, I don't think I'll be opening any dating apps for weeks to come."

"Damn." Jamie looked at Mac. "Is there anything we could call the cops for so we can meet this sexy detective?"

"Excuse me?" Mac tilted her head. "Why do you want to meet the sexy detective?"

"Don't you want to meet the person who had this effect on our dearest neighbor? How long have we been listening to her tales of disastrous dates with mediocre men? Then, along comes this woman and shows her what it's all about… I'm just curious, babe."

"What district does she work in?" Mac asked.

Dakota shook her head. "I have no idea."

"You have her full name. We can google her," Jamie said.

What was it with these two? Dakota had come here to process, not to fan the flame of something impossible.

"We're not going to google her. Let me repeat myself: it was a one-night stand. I won't be seeing her again."

"Fair enough," Jamie said. "Are you staying for lunch? Leila and Izzy are coming over."

Maybe lunch with friends was exactly what Dakota needed because she wasn't entirely sure that if she went back to her house she'd be able to stop herself from googling Jack. Aubrey and Peyton were at their grandmother's birthday celebrations with their father and stepdad. She might as well stay and get her mind off other things.

———

Jack scrolled through Tinder. Her thumb ached from swiping left-left-left. What was she doing, anyway? She didn't want to go on a date tonight. She couldn't even if she did want to—her body reminded her of that, in the most delicious way possible, every time she moved. Either way, she had Sunday dinner with her mother tonight. The truth was she didn't know what to do with herself. On any other Sunday, after staying up half the night with a beautiful woman, she'd be relaxing on the couch, shouting abuse at unrealistic cop shows on Netflix—one of her most-practiced hobbies—but Jack's butt wouldn't stay put in the couch. She tried playing some music, but it reminded her of the songs that had played in the background last night. She considered going to the gym for an exhausting session of weight lifting, but she didn't trust her muscles today—not that she would find the required focus to lift heavy. Maybe she should call Marley, but what would she even say? Jack could easily predict the conversation they would have.

"Oh, please," Marley would say, "stop pretending you're not human like the rest of us and don't want what we all want. Some good old L.O.V.E."

Jack didn't want love. She just had to find a way to get through the day. Tomorrow, she could focus on work again. She'd put all her energy into making the streets of New York City safer for everyone. That's what she wanted more than some good old L.O.V.E.

If only Dakota hadn't been so damn enchanting. She had a hard face to forget. Jack remembered how peaceful and still that gorgeous face had looked this morning, when Dakota was still sleeping. How extremely kissable her lips had seemed. Then she remembered everything they had done last night and Jack couldn't take it anymore. She had to get out of her apartment. She needed to get some air. She needed to go for a long walk—all the way to Cobble Hill.

———

"You do have that self-satisfied, I-fucked-all-night look about you." Leila never minced her words and Dakota's one-night stand with Jack was *the* topic of conversation at lunch.

"But seriously, though," Izzy, who—probably because of the life she'd lived—was always much more sensitive, said, "how does it make you feel to have spent a night like that with another woman?"

"Confused," Dakota admitted.

"We don't have to send Jack a toaster oven just yet," Jamie interjected.

Dakota spent enough time among lesbians to know what that meant.

Mac elbowed her wife in the arm. "Let Dakota speak, babe. This is a big deal."

Was it a big deal? Dakota wasn't sure. Maybe it was a bigger deal to them than it was to her. They had convinced her to go on a date with a woman and they'd selected Jack's profile together. Dakota didn't hold it against her friends that they were a little giddy with how things had turned out.

"Can I ask you something?" Izzy continued, unperturbed by what Jamie had said.

"Shoot." Dakota flashed Izzy a small smile.

"What if this Jack wasn't only into one-night stands? Would you see her again?"

"That's completely beside the point." Was that a touch of defensiveness in Dakota's voice? She had to check herself. "I wouldn't have gone on a date with her in the first place if she hadn't made it clear in her Tinder profile that she wasn't looking for anything serious."

"Sure." Izzy smiled back. "But purely hypothetically. Just to humor me. What if she changed her mind after the night you had together? Trust me, it happens." Izzy shot a quick wink in Leila's direction. "What if she asked if you wanted to go out again? What would you say?"

Dakota had not been willing to spend energy on this scenario because there was no realistic chance it would happen. "I don't know. I truly don't." She raked her gaze over her friends one by one. "Would it be nice to not have to sit here with the four of you as the only single person for once? Yes. Will it be with Jack? No chance in hell. Will it be with another woman who is not Jack? I have no clue whatsoever."

"Let's dig a little deeper into that." Leila loved to

always dig a little deeper. "Are you saying that you'd go on another date with a woman?"

Dakota held her hands up, displaying her palms. All these questions she didn't know the answer to. "I'm going to have to get back to you on that."

"Just for your information, I know quite a few eligible bachelorettes who wouldn't mind taking you out." Leila nodded at Dakota, as though all she had to do was ask. "Especially if you have experience with a strap-on." Apparently, this was really funny while, to Dakota, the memory of using that toy on Jack was far more exhilarating than comic—in fact, there was nothing comical about it. It had been the biggest highlight in a night of many.

Later, when Dakota carried a stack of plates into the kitchen, Leila followed her.

"Seriously, though." Leila sidled up to her. "Was it really that special?"

Dakota could only nod. It had been special. Unexpected and out of the ordinary. "It was."

"All jokes aside." Leila smiled one of her warm Leila smiles. "I'm really happy you had that experience."

"Me too." Dakota was pleased, not only for taking the leap, but also because she hadn't gotten in her own way and had let the evening run its course. It would take a few more days for her brain—and body—to process her one-night stand with Jack. But tomorrow, Aubrey and Peyton would be home, and she'd go back to work, and life as she knew it would resume. Dakota didn't expect to forget about Jack—or about the possibility of dating women—but she would give the 'experiment' its rightful place in her life and take things from there. No need to rush into anything—or draw any more conclusions just yet.

CHAPTER 12

J ack walked and walked. It reminded her of her time on patrol, although most of those years were spent in a car—and she had never patrolled the streets she was walking down now. This was where she lived, not where she worked. Since she'd been promoted to detective, Jack had been working out of midtown Manhattan.

Her glance skittered from here to there, always taking in as much of her surroundings as she could. That was how she was trained, and that was how she lived her life. She inhaled deeply, trying to shake off some of the unease that had crept up on her since she'd asked Dakota to leave. She got a hit of the usual blend of food smells, exhaust fumes, and a hint of garbage. Twist or turn it any way you wanted, that was how New York City smelled. Most of the time Jack didn't notice, but she was trying to be mindful about her breath—and this was how she was rewarded. Time to try something else.

What would Dakota be doing right now? And did she also have trouble filing away their night together as something that had happened in the past—as opposed to something to look forward to again in the future? *Damn it.* Reminiscing about last night was not what this walk was for but, if that really were the case, Jack should have walked in a different direction. She should have strolled to her old stomping ground in Queens, where she'd been stationed as a rookie, and where she'd met Marley, her training officer and closest friend to this day.

"If I failed at anything with teaching you," Marley liked to say, "it's that you're a police officer first, and a human being second."

Jack always thought that was a load of bullshit, because every single minute of every single day, she felt plenty human, and it wasn't as if carrying a shield could actually protect her from anything civilians went through.

Jack was approaching Brooklyn Heights and was getting a little too close to Cobble Hill. Instead of turning around, she grabbed her phone and called Marley. If this walk wasn't going to set her straight, she needed her friend to do so.

"I was just going to call you," Marley said instead of hello. "Invite me to dinner at your mom's tonight, please."

Jack's mother always made enough food for triple the number of people present—and Marley invited herself about every other week. "You're always welcome at Mama Gina's. Invitation officially extended."

"Can't wait to see you. What's going on? Just checking in?"

"Just checking if you wanted to come to dinner tonight," Jack stalled.

"And?" Marley wasn't born yesterday.

"And… I had a date last night."

"What else is new? Don't you have a date every Saturday night you're not on call?"

"Hardly." Jack rolled her eyes.

"What do you need to tell me about this date that you can't say in front of Mama Gina tonight?" Marley asked.

Jack kept on walking. She must be pretty close to where Dakota lived, as though she was being pulled by an invisible thread. "Don't tell my mother about the date. You know how she gets."

"Aw, you know I love nothing more than ganging up on you with your mother when it comes to you and your dates."

"Please don't. Not tonight." Jack kept her eyes peeled for extravagantly big townhouses, but there were quite a few of those in Cobble Hill. Certain parts of Brooklyn had changed so much in the past two decades, she might as well be on the Upper West Side.

"Why not? What's really going on here?"

"I can't get this woman out of my head," Jack admitted.

"Well, duh. It's only Sunday afternoon. Give it some time. I'd say it was a problem if you'd already forgotten about her. That would say certain things about you that would make me question our friendship."

Marley had a point. "It's different than after other dates." Jack sighed into her phone. "I'm walking toward where she lives, like I'm a stalker or something."

"What? Where are you?" Marley's voice went into police officer mode.

"Cobble Hill."

Through the phone, Marley made a whistling sound. "The money part of Cobble Hill?"

"Oh, yeah."

"I didn't know you were looking for a sugar momma."

"I'm not. I don't know what I'm doing here. I don't

even know where she lives. It's just the fact that I'm here and that I walked over an hour to get here."

"What happened on this date?" Marley asked. "That this woman has you stalking her like that?"

I'm not stalking her, Jack protested in her head. "It was a *really* good date," she said instead.

"You've had plenty of good dates. Or at least so you tell me. You also don't have a stalker-y bone in your body. Are you on something? Do I need to come and get you?"

"I think that… I'd like to see her again." There. Jack had said it out loud. It was neither rocket science, nor revolutionary. Still, in Jack's life, an admission like that was pretty seismic.

"Then ask her on a second date, even though it's not really your M.O. It's okay to do something different once in a while. In fact, it's what makes life fun and surprising."

"It's not that simple. She's, um, straight. It was just an experiment for her." For the first time since last night, and maybe ever, Jack didn't feel so good about being someone else's experiment.

"Was she in bed with you all night?" Marley asked. "Were you licking each other's pussies all night long?" Marley always had to add something extra, it was her style.

Jack chuckled. "Pretty much. Yes." The ear she was holding her phone against turned red-hot.

"Then she's not straight. You know who's straight? I am. You know what never even occurs to me? Going on a date with another woman and licking her pussy all night long. You're a lesbian and, as far as I know, dating a man —let alone sleeping with one—is not an option for you. To each their own and everyone should do whatever they like, but that does not sound like the behavior of a straight woman to me."

"It's a little more complicated than that."

"Either way, if this woman is so damn straight," Marley ignored what Jack had just said, "doesn't that make her an ideal candidate for a second date? There's no risk of her falling for you."

"It's not her falling for me that scares me." Jack stopped walking. She'd turned into a street with the fanciest houses she'd seen so far.

"Oh," Marley said. "Ooh. I see. You're afraid you might fall for a straight girl. Isn't that a big gay no-no? That's what you've always told me."

This whole thing was ridiculous. What on earth was Jack doing in Cobble Hill? What was she even implying to Marley? At least she knew she had made the right choice in calling her friend. In her unique way, Marley was setting her straight—no pun intended.

"Absolutely," Jack said. "I need to get out of here."

"I can get you a police escort," Marley joked. "Or you could hop into an Uber."

"As soon as we hang up, I'm ordering one."

"Sure, but listen to me," Marley had lowered her voice. "Having feelings for someone may not be what you want, because of that long-ass list of reasons you keep coming up with, but Marley's here to tell you there's nothing wrong with feeling something for another person once in a while. It's totally normal. It's what makes the world go round. It's human and guess what, my friend, you're human too, whether you like it or not."

"I got a little carried away. Quite literally, actually." Jack looked at her feet in disbelief, as though they had

91

betrayed her and were solely responsible for bringing her here. "But I've pulled myself together. Thanks, Mar."

"I got you, girl. You good?"

"I'm good."

"Okay. Get into that Uber and I'll see you tonight."

Before she could change her mind, Jack ordered a car. While she waited, she cast her gaze along the brownstones in the street she'd ended up in. Maybe Dakota lived in one of those, with her rich, unconventional family, or maybe she didn't. In the end, it didn't matter. As Marley had pointed out, Jack had a long-ass list of reasons why it didn't matter. The top one being that she didn't do relationships. And Dakota was a straight-ish woman who had openly admitted to being on the lookout for a replica of her gay ex-husband. As if Jack would break her precious rules for someone like that.

CHAPTER 13

Peyton and Aubrey hunched over their phones, as though the secret to life itself was displayed on their screens, and they couldn't get enough of it.

"Five more minutes, girls," Chase said. "Then it's phones away." Neither one of their daughters looked up or acknowledged what their father had said. One day, Dakota was certain, they would appreciate Chase for the amazing dad that he was. She certainly still appreciated him for the amazing husband he had been to her—maybe still a little too much. Although, at least, she wasn't jealous of Corey any longer for taking her place.

Dakota's phone beeped. It was another Tinder message. They'd been coming in thick and fast since she'd changed her preference back to men earlier today. Dakota had zero inclination to read them. She should just remove the app from her phone altogether. But then Corey sidled up to Chase, who was cooking vegan burgers on the grill, and kissed him gently on the cheek, and Dakota was hit by a longing so fierce, a desire to have what Chase and Corey had, that she couldn't bring herself to do it.

She hadn't told Chase about her little Tinder dalliance with a woman. Dakota cringed when she thought about what she had—so readily, it seemed—admitted to Jack about the kind of man she was looking for. The kind that didn't exist. Chase had been far from perfect as a husband. He had lied to her. He had hidden his true self. He had married Dakota and had kids with her while he knew he could never love her the way she loved him. Yet here she sat, in their communal backyard, with their kids and his new spouse. It wasn't an ideal situation, but it was how it was and, most days, Dakota wouldn't have it any other way—except for the part where she never brought anyone to family dinner.

Corey had a real knack for asking Dakota about her dating escapades at the most inopportune times, meaning when the girls were around. He was the one who'd encouraged Dakota to use dating apps. He was walking toward her, holding a bottle of champagne.

"Top you up?" He sat next to Dakota.

"Why not?" She held out her glass.

Her phone beeped again.

"Is that your Tinder blowing up?" Corey asked.

"I should put it on silent."

Corey shook his head. "Chase and I were just talking about you last night. About how we cannot believe you're still single. You are such a catch."

Here we go again, Dakota thought. It was as though Corey was somehow trying to assuage any guilt he might feel about being in Dakota's life by telling her, every time he had the chance, how much he couldn't believe she hadn't found a new partner yet. As though that would finally absolve him of whatever he believed he had done wrong. Even though Corey hadn't done anything wrong.

He'd met Chase more than a year after Chase had told Dakota he was actually gay. But even though he had nothing to do with Chase leaving Dakota, he was the person that brought it all to life. He was Chase's husband. He was their daughters' stepdad.

This made him an easy target for Dakota's frustration about everything she felt wasn't going according to plan in her own life—although she'd abandoned the notion of any 'plan' for her life not long after Chase had told her he was gay. How could she plan for anything? She, who had no idea her very own husband was gay. How could she not have known? How could she have been so utterly and stupidly blind?

If there had been hints, Dakota had chosen, consciously or not, to ignore them. She had two young children and a job she insisted on keeping—not necessarily a given for women in the conservative Van Ness family. And she and Chase just worked. She had nothing to complain about in their marriage which, in hindsight, should have been the first hint. Chase was kind, considerate, extremely handsome, and so very attentive in bed. Also in hindsight, he was clearly overcompensating, but how was Dakota supposed to know that when all she could see was her wonderful husband? It had been the perfect ruse that fooled everyone, Dakota included. And now she had to explain—again—to Corey why she was single? Maybe because she didn't know whether she had it in her to ever trust a man again, Corey! Maybe because his husband had made her believe she was the most amazing wife-slash-mother-slash-woman on the planet, only to reveal it was all a big scam ten years down the line.

Dakota sipped from her champagne. She looked at Corey who was, physically, also a dreamboat of a man. He had a full head of salt-and-pepper hair. Sleepy brown eyes. Always—somehow—the perfect length of stubble on his chin.

"Come here." She beckoned Corey closer with her finger. "I'm going to tell you something."

Corey's eyes widened in anticipation.

Dakota found his ear. "Don't tell Chase, but I slept with a woman last night, and it was fucking spectacular."

Corey nearly dropped his champagne flute on the wooden deck. He just caught it, then stared at Dakota with his mouth agape. It only took him a few seconds to regroup. "You're yanking my chain, right?" Corey whispered.

Coolly, Dakota shook her head.

Corey's eyes grew to the size of saucers. "I'm sorry. I need a moment." He cast a quick gaze at the girls. Dakota checked on them as well. She was being reckless, telling Corey with her daughters only a few feet away—but only a bomb going off right beside them could pull their focus away from their phone. Corey looked as though something had just exploded in his brain.

"Take all the time you need." Dakota wasn't sure why she felt so smug about this. Maybe because part of it felt like the ultimate payback. No, that was silly. It just felt good to see Corey a little upset. He was always so obnoxiously levelheaded and had a gift for knowing what to say in the most awkward circumstances. A gift that escaped him at the moment, though.

"I wasn't expecting that." Once again, he regrouped quickly. "But good for you. Especially if it was—quote-unquote—'fucking spectacular.'"

Dakota just shrugged now.

"Was it a Tinder date? I didn't know you were looking for women."

"Neither did I. Mac and Jamie talked me into it."

"And you let them?"

Dakota wasn't going to explain to Corey how dating men could be incredibly disappointing. Nor was she going to go into detail about her night with a woman. She'd just wanted to shock him, really. The thrill of doing so had been quite short-lived—and she should have known better.

"Burgers are ready," Chase said. "Girls. Phones away, please."

While Aubrey and Peyton launched into their usual protests, Chase looked over at Dakota and Corey.

"What are you two whispering about?" He beamed them an unwitting smile. "Not me, I hope."

"No, babe," Corey replied. "Definitely not you."

"Don't tell him," Dakota whispered before heading to the table. "Let's not make a thing of it."

"It's a thing already that can't possibly be unmade," Corey said. "But your secret's safe with me."

———

"Come on," Nico insisted. "Tell me about your date."

"We don't have that kind of relationship." Jack wasn't going to confide in her partner about how she couldn't stop thinking about Dakota. Or about how all she'd done since Sunday afternoon was swipe left on Tinder, because none of the women she saw appealed to her.

"Since when?" He put his hands on his hips. "I don't want details, you know that. Just the usual vague lowdown on how it went." He arched up his eyebrows. "Especially since you were all smug about snagging a date with that model."

Maybe Jack should bite the bullet and swipe right quickly again. Jump back into dating, the way she always did. Maybe it would be a disappointment, or maybe it wouldn't. Maybe it would set her straight. Maybe it was exactly what she needed to pull her out of this funk. Because this was no fun. This was not the point of casual dating—quite the opposite.

"It was okay," Jack lied, because she didn't want to talk about Dakota. She needed to forget about her. "She was very pretty and she looked even better than her picture, but you know how it can be with pretty girls."

"Who do you take me for? I'm a Detective Second Grade, on the cusp of being promoted to First. Do you really think I can't tell when my own partner is lying through her teeth?" Nico held up his hand. "I can only assume you have good reason to do so."

"I do. And I'm sorry. I just don't want to talk about it."

"Fair enough. I shouldn't have pushed." Nico looked straight at Jack. "You're all right, though? Nod to confirm." He flashed her a grin.

"I'm fine." Jack finished her coffee. "Come on. This witness isn't going to question himself."

As they walked to the interview room, Jack's phone beeped. For a split second, her heart leapt. Could it be the impossible, meaning a message from Dakota, asking for a second date—against all odds and despite everything Jack had told her about herself and her dating preferences? She quickly checked. It was a message from Marley, inviting her to dinner at hers and Curtis's tonight after her tour. Jack accepted the invitation because, as she had learned when she got home from her mother's on Sunday, everything in her apartment still reminded her of Dakota. It would take a few more days—and perhaps a few more dates—before Jack could forget about Dakota, but she would. She always did. It was just a matter of not indulging herself too much—and Jack was an expert at that.

CHAPTER 14

"I need to get back in the saddle," Jack said. "Pronto."

Marley rolled her eyes. Curtis was putting the final touches to dinner in the kitchen.

"I think I've earned the right to tell you how I feel about this." Marley fixed Jack with a stare that didn't invite any room for protest. "Because I know you better than most. Hell, better than anyone. Even better than your own mother when it comes to certain things."

"Just say what you're going to say. No need for all the drama."

"Ask this woman on a second date, already. *Please.* Stop torturing yourself. Stop denying yourself what every single one of us craves, just because you're so damn scared."

"Damn. A lecture. You could have warned me." Jack craned her neck and tried to look into the kitchen. "Curtis, we're going to need more wine over here. Marley's lecturing me."

"Coming right up!" Curtis shouted back.

"I'm not scared," Jack said. "I'm just cautious with my

heart." Jack had said it so many times, it didn't sound so ridiculous anymore out loud.

"And the difference between the two is what?" Marley asked.

Curtis walked into the lounge with a bottle of wine. "Here you go, ladies." He refilled their glasses. "Dinner will be ready in fifteen minutes."

"Thanks, boo." Marley blew her husband a kiss. He shook his behind in response.

Watching Curtis and Marley and how they were with each other reminded Jack of Dakota telling her about her ex-husband. Although not necessarily streetwise, Dakota had struck Jack as intelligent. How did she not know her husband was gay? Wasn't the wife usually the first to suspect? But she shouldn't judge a situation she didn't know anything about, nor should she be thinking about this. But, in the extremely unlikely event of a second date, she might ask Dakota that question. She'd put it differently, of course—Jack knew a dozen different ways to get information out of someone, particularly the tidbits they weren't keen on sharing.

"Anyway," Jack said. "As I told you. She's straight."

"And I told you that was bullshit."

"Curtis is such a lucky man to have a wife like you. Someone who truly knows everything. Just like I'm so fortunate to have you as my best friend," Jack joked. "You have the answers to all of life's questions, big and small."

Marley tsked. "Mock me all you want, but I'm no fool. I've seen a thing or two in my life." She pointed at the kitchen. "And if I know one thing, it's that that man in there is the best thing that ever happened to me."

"Curtis is a gem, and you're a wonderful couple, but that doesn't have anything to do with me."

"I'm a police officer too, Jack. That's what this is really about."

"You're the captain now. You spend most of your time behind your desk." And at boring meetings, Jack thought.

"Yet I married Curtis long before I became captain."

"I'm not going to have this discussion again, Mar. There's no point."

"Fine, but how about a challenge?" Marley's eyes brightened. "As your best friend, I challenge you."

Jack sighed in response. Marley wasn't going to let this go, yet her friend's insistence wasn't a good enough reason for Jack to ask Dakota out again. Nothing was a good enough reason. Except, maybe, that stubborn sensation that had lodged itself somewhere deep inside Jack. That inexplicable, foolish, good-for-nothing desire to simply see Dakota again.

"Being my best friend doesn't automatically give you permission to challenge me."

"Of course it does. It's one of the unspoken rules."

"That's the first I've ever heard of that rule."

"Because it's unspoken." Trying to win an argument with Marley was like trying to explain to a child why candy before dinner was a bad idea. Marley pulled her face into its most angelic expression. She batted her long lashes. "I can't reason with you on this," Marley said. "You're too stubborn. So I have to do it this way. It's your own fault."

"What you call stubbornness, I call common sense," Jack said.

"I know, and that's exactly the issue." Marley took a sip of wine. "Anyway, here's my best friend challenge. Before you leave this house tonight, you will invite this woman who rocked your world on a second date. That's it.

That's all I ask, as your best friend who only has your very best interests at heart." She pulled her lips into the widest smile.

"Mar, please. You don't even know the half of it. This woman has children. Teenagers."

"I'm not challenging you to prepare a meal for her and her kids. All I'm asking is that, for once in your life, you're not too chicken to take that next step."

"But what for? What's a next step for if not to lead to the one after? That's the very reason I don't do second dates, even if I really want to sometimes."

"There's no need to think so far ahead. It only messes with your head."

Jack shook her head. "She also has a gay ex-husband who she still idolizes. And who happens to be Chase Van Ness."

This stunned Marley into momentary silence. "Are you kidding me?" Marley took a big sip of wine. "She's a Van Ness?"

"Who's a Van Ness?" Curtis walked into the lounge.

"The woman I'm trying to get Jack to go on a second date with." Marley's tone had gone from excited to dejected in a matter of seconds.

Curtis huffed out some air. "You don't want any dealings with the Van Nesses. They're the one percent of the one percent. Best to stay away from that particular crowd."

"Seriously?" Jack couldn't believe this. "You're doing a massive U-turn on this because of who Dakota used to be married to?"

"Yes," Marley said. "You should have told me who she was from the get-go. I would have left you alone and told you to move on straightaway."

"Wow." This unintended case of reverse psychology was doing a number on Jack. At the very least, it made her want to defend Dakota. "She's only a Van Ness by name, not by blood." *And you haven't met her. You haven't spent a heavenly night with her. You haven't looked into her eyes and*—Jack stopped her train of thought.

"Makes no difference," Marley stated.

"How about reserving some judgment? How about not assuming that you can't be rich and a good person at the same time?" Granted, Jack had spent less than twenty-four hours in Dakota's company and she didn't really know what she was like, but she considered herself an excellent judge of character, and Dakota struck her as a decent person.

"I'm not saying it's impossible," Curtis said. "But too much money does funny things to people. You're both police officers. You've seen it time and time again."

"Not really." Jack dealt with the other 99% most of her time on the job.

"I'm sorry for pushing you, Jack," Marley said. "I didn't have all the details. In hindsight, it's obvious that your date was just some rich bitch trying something new just because she can. Did she pay for everything?"

"What the fuck, guys? You're acting as if Dakota is the devil incarnate just because of who she used to be married to."

"The Van Ness family isn't just rich," Curtis said. "They're rich-rich. You don't gather that much wealth without taking advantage of a lot of people across multiple generations."

"You're both massively overreacting to this," Jack said. "Take a chill pill already."

"Dinner's ready." Curtis pointed at the table.

Jack and Marley got up. As they headed to the dining area, Jack whispered to Marley, "You know what, Mar? I might just take you up on your challenge."

———

"Mom! Corey's here," Peyton yelled. "For you," she added.

Dakota was getting ready for a date. She'd matched with a handsome man on Tinder and had decided to take the leap. The girls were supposed to be getting ready to stay at their dad's and Corey's, although that just meant walking up the stairs. It was the whole point of Dakota still living here.

"Knock, knock." Corey whistled through his teeth. "Hot damn, girl. Your date won't know what's hit… *them*."

"Him," Dakota clarified. She tried to ignore the flat feeling running through her at the prospect of her date. But you just never knew. This could be The One. She'd only find out if she actually went on the date.

Secretly, Dakota had hoped to hear from Jack. Even if just to say hello. A short, polite follow-up. A little something to acknowledge the amazing night they'd shared. But she also understood why Jack hadn't been in touch.

Dakota could have messaged Jack herself. She'd come close more than once, but she'd always managed to stop herself in order to respect Jack's wishes. Was Jack getting ready for a hot date tonight as well?

"What's *his* name?" Corey asked.

"Jack," Dakota said on a sigh she couldn't possibly suppress.

"What's wrong with Jack?" Corey held out his hand.

"Can I see his picture? Let's be honest, we do have the same taste in men."

"Ha ha." Dakota put down the mascara she was applying. "Very funny."

"Hey?" Corey approached her. "Are you okay? Should you be going out when you feel like this?"

"I'm not really in the mood, but I feel like I should go regardless."

"Why?" Corey crouched down next to her.

Dakota ignored Corey's question. "That woman I went out with the other week. She was called Jack as well, short for Jacqueline."

Come to think of it, Dakota might well have swiped right on 'male Jack' not only because he was adequately handsome, but subconsciously also because of his name.

"Was she now?"

"Mom!' Aubrey appeared in the doorway of Dakota's bedroom. "I can't find my charger. Do you have it?"

"There's plenty of chargers at ours, sweetheart," Corey said. "Give me a minute with your mom, please."

Aubrey gave them a once-over, then turned on her heels.

"Are you trying to say," Corey focused his full attention on Dakota again, "that you'd rather go on a date with female Jack than with male Jack?"

"I certainly wouldn't mind seeing female Jack again." Dakota didn't have nights like the one she'd had with Jack frequently. Fragments of it snuck up on her when she was with clients—and every time she saw a police car in the street, which was often in a city like New York.

"Then why don't you?"

"It's not her thing." Nor is it mine, Dakota thought, although perhaps that wasn't totally true.

"What do you mean?" Corey let himself fall onto his backside and stared up at Dakota from the floor.

"Jack made it abundantly clear she's only into one-night stands."

"Oh." Corey nodded. "I get that. I suppose you have to respect that, but... I also suppose one short little message never hurt anyone. Have you texted her?"

"Of course not."

"Did you tell her you were, um, straight?" He grinned up at her. "Although we should probably talk about that later."

"I told her... a lot." Too much. Another reason Dakota hadn't texted. She'd been too mortified about certain things she had admitted to Jack.

"How about we text her now. Here. Together. If she replies, ditch male Jack."

"What?" Corey could be so unbelievably straightfor-ward, a quality Dakota mostly admired him for.

"Just do it. Trust me. Go for it. You literally have nothing to lose. If she doesn't reply, that's that. If she does, you take it from there."

"Before I can do that, I need to switch off quite a few good-girl buttons in my brain."

"Give me your hand." Corey held out his.

Dakota didn't know what he was up to, but she might as well. She put her hand in Corey's.

He grabbed her thumb and pressed the tip. "Good-Girl Button Number One switched off." He did the same with all her fingertips. "There you go. Now, where's your phone? Let's get this done."

CHAPTER 15

J ack narrowed her eyes. She'd been on Tinder when the message came in, trying to find the impetus to swipe right on someone, but everyone still paled in comparison to Dakota.

The message read:

> Hey. How are you? I've been thinking about you. xo

Dakota had been thinking about her? And what was with the 'xo'? Jack's palms went instantly clammy. Her pulse quickened. In the end, after dinner with Marley and Curtis, she hadn't messaged Dakota. It wasn't the right kind of reply to her friends' judgment of the wonderful woman they'd never even met. Marley and Curtis could say whatever they wanted, but none of that changed how Jack felt about relationships—and conducted her life accordingly. What did change matters was this text from Dakota.

Because as soon as it rolled in, Jack had no choice but

to reply. That choice was taken away from her immediately by all the memories from that night, by clasping eyes on Dakota's gorgeous Tinder profile picture again, by all the feelings Jack had tried to pretend she didn't have for the sake of all the rules she lived by. But this message, these dozen or so words, changed everything. They gave Jack the permission from herself that she so desperately craved. She texted back promptly.

> I've been thinking about you too. You left quite the impression. x

Heart pounding in her throat, Jack waited for a reply. Even though Marley had been a pain in the ass about rich people, she'd had a point before she'd turned on Dakota. This sensation, this hungry, nervous waiting for a simple text message was everything right now. It narrowed Jack's attention to one thing only. To the very thing she'd tried so hard to forget. Her phone beeped and her heart nearly jumped out of her chest.

> I'd love to see you again. Will you go for a drink with me?

"Yes!" Jack shouted into her empty living room.

Then, she took a breath. What was she saying yes to? But no, she wasn't going there. Dakota messaging her was some sort of sign that, just this once, Jack had to ignore her rules and go by her instinct, which, from the moment they'd said goodbye—before Jack had asked her to leave, even—had been to see Dakota again. It took a lot of energy to ignore an instinct like that. A desire that rumbles through your bones late at night and wakes you up, all rattled, in the morning. Jack had passed whatever test she'd set for herself, but she was done resisting. Because the simple truth was that she wanted nothing more than to have a drink with Dakota again—whatever that was code for.

> Sure. When?

No need to come across too keen, although Jack hoped Dakota wouldn't choose a date so far in the future it gave her too much time to change her mind.

> I'm free as a bird tonight. xo

Tonight? Damn. And with the 'xo' again. Jack wasn't doing anything more exciting than fruitlessly scrolling through Tinder and yelling at cop TV shows. She could hop in the shower and be ready to go out in less than twenty minutes.

> Tonight it is. Same place? I can be there by 8:30.

The response came quick as lightning:

> Can't wait. ;-)

Jack nearly tripped over her feet hurrying into the bathroom.

———

"Oh my god." Dakota held onto Corey's hand. "I need to cancel my date with the other Jack."

"Male Jack will no doubt be heartbroken, but alas, female Jack has won." Corey pushed himself up from the floor in one swift movement. "Don't change a thing about what you're wearing, by the way. You'll knock her socks right off." He tilted his head. "Can I see her profile pic now? You've left me rather curious about this stranger we've been texting."

Dakota's head was spinning. Was this really happening? She felt bad for the man she was supposed to go on a date with. She knew what it felt like to get all dolled up only to have your hopes dashed by a last-minute cancellation.

She handed Corey her phone.

"Now that you seem to be in charge, can you let male Jack down easy, please?"

"You got it." Dakota had needed many years, countless bottles of wine with friends, and hours of therapy to be able to accept Corey in her life. But she had. Not only because she had no choice, but even more so because— luckily—he was a more than decent guy. A man she'd learned to trust to take care of her own flesh and blood. So it was easy enough to trust him with her phone now— just as it was earlier, when he'd coaxed her to finally text female Jack.

"Oooh, yeah. I totes get it," Corey said, sounding like one of the girls. "You should bring her to the house. We can all have brunch tomorrow morning. I'd love to meet her."

"Don't push it." Dakota watched Corey as he messaged male Jack. What a guy her ex-husband's new spouse was, really. "And not a word of this to Chase. It's too soon."

"My lips are sealed." Corey gave Dakota back her phone. "All taken care of. Or do you want me to handle follow-up as well?" He had the kind of photogenic crooked grin that would make many a male and female Tinder user swoon.

Dakota shook her head. She could take it from there. Butterflies were doing a funny dance in her stomach. In a little over an hour, she'd be seeing Jack again.

"If you want to bring her here, I can make sure the girls stay upstairs."

Dakota wagged her finger. "That won't be necessary. It's too risky." She remembered Jack saying she was sorry she'd never get the chance to see where Dakota lived, but she'd have to be sorry a bit longer—possibly forever.

Dakota inhaled deeply. "I can't believe she said yes."

Corey took a step toward her and put his hands on her shoulders. "Of course, she said yes. Have you looked in the mirror?" There was that grin again. "Plus, you did say your night together was 'fucking spectacular'."

"It *really* was." Funny how Dakota had just said that to wind Corey up, and now she stood here with him like this, as if he was her closest confidant.

"Text me if you change your mind about needing the house." He gave her shoulders a squeeze and dropped his hands.

"Hey, Corey. Thanks for… all this. I—"

"It's okay. We're family. I've got your back. Always."

"Does it not annoy the hell out of you that we all live in the same house?" Dakota asked, kind of out of the blue. But the entire last hour had come totally out of left field. Dakota would need some time to wrap her head around it all—and her second date with Jack was yet to start.

"Of course not." Corey looked her in the eye. "Never. Not for one second. You're the girls' mother. That comes before everything else."

As if on cue, one of them shouted from the hallway. "Mom, we're going to Dad's now."

"Not without saying goodbye to me properly," Dakota yelled back.

She heard them trudge down the hallway and, before they stumbled in, Dakota shot Corey a conspiratorial smile. For better or worse, they were in this parenting gig together now, and it certainly wasn't all sunshine and roses, but it was damn handy to have Chase and Corey so close by.

CHAPTER 16

Was she early? Jack couldn't believe it. She checked her watch. As expected, and frantically calculated in the cab, she was seventeen minutes late, but she didn't see Dakota at the bar. It was busier than last time they'd met here—when her gaze had been automatically drawn to the hot blond by the window. Just as Jack headed inside to find a table, the door opened behind her. She turned around as if in slow-motion, like in one of those saccharine romantic comedies she hated as much as cop TV shows, and looked straight into Dakota's gorgeous face. Holy smokes. She was even more beautiful than Jack remembered. How was that even possible? Wasn't it usually the other way around?

"Hey." Dakota smiled at her, and Jack felt as though her heart might burst right out of her chest. "Sorry I'm late."

"I, um, just got here myself." Jack barely managed to squeeze the words out of her throat. She had to get her bearings—quickly.

"Good evening, ladies." The same server who had fawned over Dakota last time greeted them. "Welcome. Let me get you a table." He only had eyes for Dakota, as though she was there alone. "*Miss* Van Ness, isn't it?" The guy had gained in confidence since last time. Maybe he'd been practicing holding his nerve just in case Dakota returned to his place of work so he could make a quick and smooth move. "Or do you go by Gallagher these days?"

What a creep. Jack was about to bust out some tough cop speak, when Dakota turned to her and curved an arm around Jack's shoulders. "I might go by Russo soon." She winked at Jack, then looked at the waiter again, perfect eyebrows arched all the way up, as if to say, "I'm here with my woman so back off already."

A shot of pure liquid heat burrowed its way through Jack's flesh. *Holy smokes to the nth degree.*

"Oh. Of course. I'll be back in a flash to take your order." He slinked off like a dog with its tail between its legs.

"Sorry about that." Dakota rolled her eyes. "Sometimes, it's the only way."

"Dakota Russo has a nice ring to it," Jack joked, speaking too quickly. *Argh.* "Sorry. I didn't mean to sound as creepy as that guy just did." Just like the first time they'd met, being with Dakota made Jack lose every last ounce of her cool. It even made her able to empathize with that waiter, but only for a split second.

"You didn't sound creepy at all." Dakota fixed her ethereal blue-green gaze on Jack. "If anything, I put my arm around *your* shoulders, implying things I had no idea you'd be okay with."

"Me?" Jack chuckled. "You basically outed yourself."

"Oh. Right. I hadn't even thought about that yet." Dakota pursed her lips before speaking again. "Surely, it's a frequently used trick among women to scare men off?"

"Sure," Jack agreed, not because she actually did, but because she wanted to leave the incident behind them. "It's great to see you again."

A female waiter approached and, very matter-of-factly, took their order without any hint of flirting or inappropriate banter.

"Cards on the table." Dakota leaned over the table as though she meant something entirely different by cards.

It was hard for Jack to keep her focus on Dakota's face with that amount of spectacular cleavage on display.

"I wanted to text you much earlier, but I was anticipating a hard no if I asked you out again," Dakota said.

"Understandable." Jack sucked her lips into her mouth. What could she possibly say? But she had to say something. "After all my preaching about only doing one-night stands."

"What made you change your mind?"

"Sometimes I have two-night—" Jack started to say, but reconsidered. She didn't want to banter with Dakota like that. She'd already given up her most important rule for her. "To be honest, it was you who made me change my mind. And our night together. Turns out, it's a tough one to forget."

"Who says you need to forget about it?" Dakota smiled again. "Do you always forget your one-night stands? That sounds kind of sad."

Jack chuckled. The dynamics between them were very different this time.

"Forget is the wrong word." *Fuck.* Jack was searching for words now. Dakota messed with her head. To be honest, the way she sat there looking at Jack, with her chin tilted, a small smile on her lips, her eyes blazing all sorts of mischief, it was no wonder Jack had trouble stringing a coherent sentence together. Jack might as well forget about trying to find the right words. Instead, she sighed, and said, "I haven't been able to stop thinking about you. It's been driving me crazy because that's not something I usually suffer from."

The small smile on Dakota lips transformed into a wide grin. "Thank you for meeting me tonight."

"Oh, it's my absolute pleasure." Jack had to suppress a giggle in order to not sound like a smitten schoolgirl.

The female waiter brought over their drinks. Jack and Dakota clinked rims.

"To our second date," Dakota said, narrowing her eyes.

"I'll drink to that." Jack's brain was trapped in a whirl-wind of emotions. She was glad she was there, sitting across from Dakota. But she was also afraid she might have opened Pandora's box. Additionally, lust was one thing, but Jack wasn't entirely sure pure desire was the only thing she felt when it came to Dakota. Maybe the only logical next step for Jack was to open up to Dakota the way she had opened up to Jack on their first date.

"I had a date planned with another Jack tonight," Dakota said.

Jack tilted her head.

"I reset my Tinder search to male after, um, you." Dakota was so open and unselfconscious when it came to certain things.

"Because you wanted to end your experiment?" There

was no need for Jack to open up about herself just yet. Dakota was probably one of those women so in touch with her own emotions, she carried her heart on her sleeve. She had messaged Jack. She had taken that step.

"I thought I did, but… here I am."

"Other Jack's loss is most certainly this Jack's gain." No matter how many covert deep belly breaths Jack took, she could not control the crazy pitter-patter of her heart. Dakota didn't just make her brain swirl, she had a very pronounced effect on Jack's other body parts as well—so much for protecting her heart. By simply coming here, Jack had never left it more exposed.

"Corey, of all people, was my emotional support through all of it," Dakota said.

"Corey?" After the night they'd had, Jack had not remembered all the names Dakota had mentioned.

"Corey is Chase's husband." Dakota chuckled. "It's all very woke and complicated."

To think that Marley and Curtis had blown their tops over Dakota being the ex-wife of a Van Ness.

"One of the people you share a house with."

"Even though it sounds odd, it's also terribly convenient at times." Dakota smiled and Jack's world momentarily stopped turning again.

She was a seasoned cop, for crying out loud. She knew all the ways of the world and how it could thoroughly screw you up, yet here she sat, grinning from ear to ear at another woman, as though falling in love with someone was actually something she did. She tried to remind herself that she didn't, and that referring to herself as falling in love was ludicrous—because it was way too soon for that—but that it was even an option, despite all her best and most stubborn efforts, threw her the most.

"I didn't tell Chase about you, but turns out I can talk to Corey about it." Dakota sounded a little gleeful, as though she hadn't expected to be able to have that conversation with her ex-husband's husband. Jack could barely wrap her head around the whole arrangement, so she understood. "Anyway, here we are and my experiment's clearly not over yet."

While it was becoming increasingly clear to Jack that she could develop feelings for Dakota, it was equally clear why she shouldn't. Nothing had really changed, yet Jack wanted to niggle at the status quo a little.

"I'm going to tell you something I never tell any of my dates," she said.

"I'm all ears." Dakota really should have been a model, what with all the different emotions she could put into a single smile.

Jack took another sip of wine before continuing. She didn't have to explain herself, but Dakota made her want to. It was a good and a bad thing rolled into one.

"I come from a long line of cops. My father was a cop. My grandfather was a cop. My aunt is a retired cop. Although my brother, that asshole, is a defense lawyer." Jack shook her head. "But let's not get into that. The point is that law enforcement is a big thing in my family. It's who we are and what gives us pride and honor, but we also know the risks. Being a police officer is not a safe desk job and it can be dangerous." Jack paused. Even after more than twenty years, it wasn't a given to just come out and say it. "My father was killed in the line of duty when I was in high school." Jack would never forget the day she got pulled out of class. "It didn't stop me from becoming a cop, because it's all I ever wanted to be, despite the risks. But when I started on the job, I promised myself I would never put anyone I loved at risk of feeling the way I did when my father died." Marley had quoted the statistics at Jack so many times, Jack didn't even hear them anymore. Statistically, there was only a very small chance of her getting hurt on the job, but statistics didn't matter when your father had died. Experience trumped statistics every single time. "That's why I'm not looking for anything serious. Because I can't."

"I'm so sorry about your father," Dakota said. "That must have been dreadful."

Jack just nodded.

"Thank you for telling me." Dakota slid her hand across the table. Jack looked at it as if she didn't know what to do with the gesture. Even though it would be easy enough to ignore Dakota's outstretched hand, Jack didn't want to. She snaked her fingers closer, until they touched Dakota's. For someone who wasn't into any of that touchy-feely stuff, it sure felt good.

"We all have our story, right?" Jack curled her fingers around Dakota's.

"I won't pretend to know what that feels like, losing a parent like that, but I can understand why you choose not to get attached." Dakota's smile was different again. It radiated a kindness that was reflected in her eyes as well.

"That's why friends with benefits is the most I can offer."

"I'm not exactly in a position to offer a whole lot more than that myself, but I will gladly accept your friendship and I'm pretty enthusiastic about the benefits," Dakota said.

"I'm glad we understand each other." Jack wasn't sure it was just relief coursing through her. Why should she feel relieved, anyway? Because she shared something private that she preferred to keep to herself? Once again, under Dakota's gaze, Jack wasn't sure what or how she felt—all she really knew was that she didn't want her time with Dakota to end, hence the pretty out-there suggestion of being friends with benefits.

CHAPTER 17

Most second dates Dakota had been on since she'd discovered Tinder had not gone like this. Another big difference when dating women, she presumed. Although it wasn't just that. The whole setup was different —for starters, Dakota didn't call it an experiment when she dated men. But she was very much on board with Jack's friends with benefits proposal. Dakota would love to get to know Jack better, and she couldn't wait for the benefits to materialize later tonight—she sure hoped they were also on the same wavelength about that.

By how Jack held her gaze, and didn't let go of her hand, it seemed like it.

As far as the friendship part was concerned, they'd already taken a giant step. Jack had just offered Dakota a large piece of her complex personality puzzle by confiding in her about her father. For that reason alone, Dakota didn't want to retract her hand. Although they were in a bar not far from where she lived, and Jack had made that comment about Dakota outing herself to the obnoxious waiter earlier. But Dakota didn't much care about things like that. She might have married a Van Ness, but the only reason she had done so was because her love for Chase didn't give her any other choice. She hadn't married into the Van Ness family to become a New York socialite—far from it. She'd married for love only. It had brought her riches and status and a whole lot of other things Dakota could do without. Such as heartbreak, humiliation, and endless doubts about herself. So what did Dakota care if anyone saw her holding hands with another woman in a bar? Her ex-husband, who was an actual Van Ness, had married a man. For all of those reasons, Dakota was well aware of what really mattered and what didn't. Right now, laying a foundation for this friendship was much more important than what a stranger might think of her.

She swiped her thumb gently over the side of Jack's hand.

"How old were you when your father died?" Dakota considered her girls receiving news like that. She quickly quashed the thought because she didn't want to imagine it for a second longer.

"Seventeen," Jack said.

Dakota gripped Jack's hand a little tighter.

Jack picked up her glass of wine and tipped it to her lips. After she'd set it back down, she found Dakota's gaze, and asked, "Do you want to get out of here so we can get to the benefits part of our newfound friendship?" Jack shot her a crooked, devilish grin. "I feel like we've done a lot of friendship-ing already."

"Yes. Definitely, but…" Dakota tightened her hold on Jack's hand. "I don't take what you've told me lightly."

"I know, that's why I prefer to keep it to myself." Jack chuckled nervously. "But thank you for saying that." She pulled her hand from Dakota's grasp. "Also, I'm paying for the drinks."

"Be my guest." They might have shared an extremely intimate night, but Dakota hadn't even begun to scratch the surface of Jack's character. On top of irresistibly hot, it made her even more compelling to Dakota.

Jack didn't wait for a server to stop by. She hopped off her chair and sauntered to the bar. Dakota grabbed the chance to ogle her from behind. Jack had a natural swagger—maybe you needed an authoritative walk when you were a police officer—and her ass looked mighty fine in those jeans.

A frisson of desire ran up Dakota's spine as she imagined the next part of their date. The anticipation coursing through her was so instant and adamant, that she made a decision she might come to regret but, under the influence of this kind of heady lust, she made it anyway. She'd deal with any consequences later.

———

"It's surprisingly tasteful." *Oh Christ.* Jack had reverted to lame, possibly even hurtful jokes again. But only one hour into this second date, the evening had taken many surprising turns already. Jack was usually much more in control of everything, even on first dates, which were always a masterclass in improvisation and interaction with a complete stranger—both a large part of her job description, hence her superior skill level at it.

With Dakota, half the time, Jack had no clue what she was doing. She'd already told her about her father. And now she stood in the living room of the humongous Cobble Hill town house Dakota shared with her kids, her ex-husband, and her—Jack didn't know what the term was to best describe Chase Van Ness's husband in relation to Dakota.

"Did you think it was going to be tacky with golden statues dotted around the place?" Dakota smirked, her immaculate eyebrows arching all the way up.

"I'm sorry. I didn't know what to think. I'm a little overwhelmed and not playing it cool at all." Jack took a beat. She raked her gaze over Dakota, who was dressed in that understated yet luxurious fashion the extremely wealthy excelled in. Nothing about her looked cheap, but nothing looked extravagant either—apart from her smile, and those dazzling eyes of hers. "Thank you so much for inviting me to your most humble abode."

"What can I get you?" Dakota led the way into a kitchen that was about twice the size of Jack's entire apartment. "I have a beautiful white Burgundy open." In her own house, Dakota came across as more glossy, more cultured—more rich. Anyone would look rich in a kitchen like that.

"I'll have what you're having."

"Coming right up." Dakota took two glasses from a cabinet and poured them some no doubt very expensive wine. "Excuse me for a second. I'm going to text Corey to keep the girls upstairs until further notice."

"Sure." Jack had happily accepted the invitation to Dakota's house. She'd only been a few streets removed on her silly odyssey to Cobble Hill last Sunday. She took a sip from the wine. It was crisp and a touch fruity, but Jack was no connoisseur—and she preferred Italian wine, either way.

"All done. Although I do expect a witty gay reply."

Dakota chuckled at the prospect. "Or an invitation to brunch tomorrow."

Jack had tried her hardest to not obsessively start googling the Van Nesses since meeting Dakota. She'd only given in once, and had put a stop to it before she could do a deep dive on who's who. She had glimpsed a picture of Chase's dreamy husband, however.

"Come." Dakota held out her hand and they went back into the spacious living room.

After they sat, Jack found Dakota's gaze. "Can I ask you something personal that's really none of my business?"

"Sounds ominous." Dakota stared back at her over the rim of her wine glass.

"How did your daughters react to their dad marrying a man?"

Dakota huffed out some air. "They were still so young when Chase and I separated and, at first, they were just really sad. Chase met Corey about a year later, and by then he'd had plenty of time to explain to the girls why he'd left me—their mother. And although kids are far more intelligent than we give them credit for sometimes, there's only so much about adult romantic relationships that a child's brain can absorb." She paused and stroked her chin—was it a tell for something? Lingering pain, perhaps? The kind that never really goes away? "Even though it was a hard thing to do back then, it was important for me to be positive and enthusiastic about their dad's new partner. So they could see Corey in a positive light and make the transition as easy as possible. They had a few tantrums, as you can imagine, and so many questions." Dakota shook her head, but a smile grew on her lips. "The number of questions eight-year-olds can come up with. Times two, that is, because they're twins." A softness descended on her face. "Half of which I didn't know the answer to." Dakota narrowed her eyes. "It was difficult for a while, for all of us, but then it got better. Because they were still so young, it was easy for them to take for granted that their dad was with a man now. For the past five years, that's what they've grown up with. It's what they know. What they see every day. It helps that Corey is such a lovely man, although it took me more than a few years to fully appreciate that." Dakota's phone beeped. "Speak of the devil." A grin appeared on her face even before she'd checked the message. When she read whatever witticism was displayed on her phone screen, Dakota's lips widened into the loveliest smile. "And, of course, never a dull moment in this house, what with two teenagers and two gay men living upstairs."

"What did Corey say in his message?" Jack was curious.

Dakota shook her head. "It's a little too forward to share." Her chuckle was infectious—and made Jack only more curious.

Jack tilted her head and painted on her most wounded expression. "I think I can take it."

Dakota pursed her lips, as though she was giving sharing Corey's message a great deal of thought, although her eyes sparkled with delight. "He asks if he needs to make an emergency run to the sex shop to get us some lesbian supplies." Dakota rolled her eyes.

"I think I *will* stay for brunch tomorrow," Jack replied. She wouldn't mind meeting Corey. After all, he'd made a fair point in his message. But first things first.

"Chase doesn't know about you or my, er, little experiment," Dakota said.

"How about we forget about the guys upstairs?" Jack took another sip of wine—it was growing on her, but she put her glass down regardless. She shuffled closer to Dakota, but this couch was so annoyingly long, it made Jack feel like a cartoon character engaging in a futile chase. Luckily, Dakota met her halfway. Because this was real life and it wasn't a chase. It was something very different. They weren't friends yet, but Jack was about to reap some big benefits already.

CHAPTER 18

Dakota opened her eyes to find Jack's gaze on her. A smile bloomed on her lips. Jack responded in kind. They stared into each other's eyes for a few moments, wordlessly. Images of last night unspooled in Dakota's mind. Often, in her dating history, going back for seconds turned out to be a disappointment. The spark was gone. Or the guy was less fun, or less considerate, than she'd remembered. Not so with Jack.

Dakota crawled closer to Jack's warm body.

"These billion thread count sheets agree with me," Jack said, her voice soft and low, as though she was whispering a sweet nothing in Dakota's ear. "I slept like a baby, when you finally let me."

"I'm sure it's all down to the sheets." Dakota caressed Jack's cheek with the back of her fingers. "Not to all the times I made you come." Could she still consider this an experiment?

Jack chuckled. "Waking up next to you isn't too bad either." She slipped her knee between Dakota's thighs.

Dakota pushed herself closer to Jack and brushed her

lips against hers. "Good morning, by the way." She kissed Jack again. "Coffee?"

"Oh my god, yes please."

"Hm. You sound more enthusiastic about a cup of coffee than about your final climax last night."

Jack shook her head. "Never." She narrowed her eyes. "Although you'd completely exhausted me by then and, admittedly, I was ready for some sleep."

It was late when they'd finally drifted off, but Dakota had slept like a baby. Her brain was as relaxed as her body. Maybe because she'd finally got what she'd wanted all week. Although, this morning, in the bright light of day, she didn't really know what to make of it. Oh yes, they were friends with benefits.

"Let's lie here for a few minutes longer." She snuggled up to Jack, sliding in between her arms, and resting her head in the crook of her shoulder. "Then we'll have coffee. I promise."

"This is better than the most exquisite cup of brew." Jack wrapped her arms around Dakota and gently kissed her on the crown of her head. "Even better than the coffee at Nika's around the corner from my place, and that's saying something."

"You'll have to take me there some time," Dakota said, without thinking. But it was no longer inconceivable for Jack to do so.

"I'd be happy to," Jack said.

They lay in silence for a few minutes longer, wrapped up in each other, neither one of them ready—or willing—to move an inch.

"Do you want to join me in the shower or is your need for caffeine too great?" Dakota asked, breaking the blissful silence.

"I would absolutely love to join you in the shower." Jack dug her fingertips into Dakota's flesh. "I seem to have come down with a curious affliction." She found Dakota's cheek with her lips. "For the life of me, I can't keep my hands off you."

"I can see how that might become a problem in your daily life." Dakota pushed her cheek against Jack's lips. "I know some really good doctors. We can ask them for advice."

Jack's body shook against Dakota's as they both chuckled. The sheer pleasure of indulging in silly banter like this, in a conversation that only existed for the sake of them lying here in each other's arms—after a night of red-hot sex—was divine. But not as divine as the prospect of dragging Jack into the shower with her.

"Come on," Dakota said, but her body didn't cooperate.

"Whatever you've planned to do to me in the shower, I'm sure you can do here as well." Jack's lips traveled lower down Dakota's cheek, until they reached her lips. Dakota craned her neck so she could fully kiss Jack. Instantly, she was back where she was last night. Deep in lust with Jack Russo.

———

They'd finally made it into the shower. Jack stood with her back against the wall, one leg draped over Dakota's shoulder. Dakota kneeled between her legs and the touch of her tongue on Jack's clit was infinitely better than the powerful water flow from what was probably the most expensive shower head money could buy. Jack glanced down at Dakota's wet hair, at the water cascading off her perfect shoulders. It was pretty obvious Dakota couldn't get enough of her—and the feeling was entirely mutual.

Despite one particularly obstinate fantasy Jack had indulged in the past week—of strapping it on for Dakota —toys had not been required last night. Just their bodies, together, were more than plenty to provide climax after climax. Dakota turned her on beyond belief—beyond the rules she so desperately clung to.

Dakota's tongue skated along her clit and Jack's standing leg trembled. She feared she might crash through it when her next climax came. She sought support against the wall, planting her palms firmly against it. Because more pleasure, more sexual satisfaction at the hands of this gorgeous, addictive woman, was about to thunder through her. Jack didn't know her body was even capable of so much gratification in such a short time span. She'd never put it to the test like this. Her body could take it— her mind, on the other hand, she wasn't so sure of. Not to mention her heart.

Jack curled her toes against the wet marble of the shower floor. Dakota's tongue elicited the most delightful sensation from her body. Damn. This was exactly why Jack wasn't into second dates or foolish notions like being friends with benefits—what did that even mean? But Dakota was utterly irresistible. And Jack was in big trouble.

She threw her head back as the climax tore through her, making a beeline for her inexperienced heart.

"There you go." Dakota looked up at her, a wide grin on her lips. "All clean."

The best option, as with so many things in life, was to laugh it off. Another thing Dakota made easy. She wasn't just incredibly attractive, she was so much fun to be around—and, apparently, also very easy to confide in.

———

"This coffee's even better than Nika's." Jack made a spectacle of inhaling the steam coming off her mug. "Pity this place is too far to make it my local."

"Only the best beans for you." Dakota held Jack in her gaze, and it made her go all fluttery inside. She was dressed from head to toe in denim and Jack had no earthly idea if that was fashionable these days or not, but either way, it made Dakota look like a supermodel—one of those ultra glamorous ones from the nineties. And she was just wearing jeans, for heaven's sake.

"So, friends with benefits," Jack said. This whole situation was a little surreal, like Jack shouldn't be here. Like she'd been dropped into the wrong house somehow. "How do you see that? On a practical level?" *On a practical level? Oh Christ.* Was she losing her marbles again? It was starting to occur more and more when she was around Dakota, that she said something completely silly like that, and it was starting to worry her. Although the solution was simple. Stay away from Dakota. That might be simple in theory, but it seemed totally undoable at the same time.

"Booty calls, I guess." The skin around Dakota's eyes crinkled ever so slightly when she grinned. "A lot of them."

Jack grinned back. Her lips gave her no choice. "But seriously, though." She tried to pull her features into a more demure expression. If they were going to do this, they needed clear boundaries. "Have you ever had a friend with benefits? Aren't you supposed to be friends first, with the benefits coming later?"

"I think you might be greatly overthinking the concept." Dakota tilted her head. It made her shirt, which she hadn't buttoned very well, slide down, offering Jack an exquisite view of the swell of her breasts. "I'm experimenting with women; you don't want to commit to anything. But we do want to sleep together. So that's what we do. That's it. We don't have to call it friends with benefits if the term is freaking you out so much."

"Just sex then." Jack barely managed to squeeze the words out of her throat.

"Just uncomplicated, straightforward, mind-blowing sex." Dakota put her mug down. "Can we pencil in a date for next time already?" She beamed Jack the widest smile. "It'll keep me from wondering if I'm ever going to see you again."

Music played on some invisible sound system. The song changed. Despite Jack barely being aware of any music, because her thoughts were too preoccupied with everything Dakota, her eyes filled with tears when she heard the intro.

"Oh, no." She held up her hand. "Can you change the song, please?"

"Hm. Yeah." Dakota furrowed her brow. "Are you okay?"

"Please, just change the song." *Before it rips me right open in front of you.*

"On it." Dakota fumbled with her phone and a few seconds later the music stopped. "Not a fan of Art Garfunkel?" Dakota's voice was soft and sweet.

"'Bright Eyes' was my dad's favorite song. I haven't

been able to listen to it since he died. I just can't bear it. Music is funny like that."

"I'm so sorry." Dakota hopped off her stool and bridged the distance between them. "Are you okay?" She gently caressed Jack's hair.

"I'm fine now." It was easy enough to shake off once the music was no longer in her ears. "Sorry about that. That song is my emotional kryptonite. I have no defense against it."

"It's special to you. I get it." Dakota held her close and Jack rested her head against Dakota's chest. Because she could. Because Dakota was there and she was kind and understanding—and gorgeous.

"Speaking of emotional music," Dakota said after a while. "Do you know who my next-door neighbor is?"

"Please tell me it's Brandi Carlile and you're best friends and she will perform a private concert for us in your beautiful living room for our next date," Jack joked. She was ready for some light relief.

Dakota chuckled, making Jack's head bop against her chest. "Sorry, it's *only* Isabel Adler," she said.

"What?" Jack tore her head out of Dakota's gentle embrace. "You live next door to Isabel Adler?"

Dakota nodded. "And Gabrielle Mackenzie lives down the street. I did some work on her and her wife's house last year and we've been friends since."

Gabrielle Mackenzie was the hottest woman on Jack's TV. Along with Sadie Ireland, who used to play Leona King in *King & Prince*, the cop show Jack loved to hate-watch the most. A re-run of *King & Prince*, followed by the sports news delivered by Gabrielle Mackenzie was about as perfect as a night of television got for Jack.

"In fact," Dakota continued. "It was Mac's wife,

Jamie, who convinced me to change my Tinder preference to women. The three of us picked you to swipe right on."

"Are you kidding me?" Gabrielle Mackenzie picked her? Jack fixed her most piercing gaze on Dakota. "How do I know any of this is true?"

"You're the detective." Dakota leaned her elbow on the kitchen island. "And excuse me, but are you accusing me of lying?"

"You're just overwhelming me with all your massive name-dropping. Don't tell me you know Sadie Ireland as well." Jack wasn't sure she'd be able to handle that information, no matter how silly it all was.

Dakota shook her head. "Izzy probably knows her, though. For a self-proclaimed hermit, she knows a lot of famous people."

"Oh my god. Isabel Adler. That song she did with Lana Lynch." Jack pretended she had to shake something off. "Goose bumps every single time I listen to it."

"But wait, let's rewind a second." Dakota peered at Jack. "Are you telling me you have the hots for Sadie Ireland?"

"What? No! I've just been watching *King & Prince* forever and, well, I mean, objectively speaking, Sadie Ireland is not unattractive, I guess." Jack was at it again, fumbling her words because of Dakota.

"So by no, you mean yes." Dakota chuckled. "It's okay. Sadie Ireland is hot. She's shacked up with a woman now as well."

Jack took a moment to absorb all this information. "So you hang out with a bunch of lesbians all the time and then you decided it was high time to see what all the fuss was about?" Jack pouted her lips and nodded. "Welcome to the other side. I hope you like it here and stay a while."

"To be completely honest, that is kind of what happened. I was complaining to Jamie about another lackluster Tinder date one day and she suggested I look for women instead of men on the app. Now you're here. Drinking coffee in my house." Dakota waggled her eyebrows.

"Wow." Jack barely suppressed a giggle. "Please remind me to buy Jamie a toaster oven."

"Ha ha." Dakota must really hang out with the lesbians a lot if she got that joke. "We'll get her one together." She slanted her head. "I can have both Izzy and Mac, and their lovely wives, over here for drinks whenever you want, if you're into that. It would be the perfect opportunity to present them with their toaster oven."

What was Dakota suggesting? A dinner party with her famous neighbors? Earlier, before Jack's mini-breakdown, they had settled on uncomplicated sex. Now she wanted to introduce her to her friends?

"Sorry." Dakota chuckled. "I didn't mean to imply anything beyond our, um, arrangement."

"It's a hard thing to say no to," Jack admitted. Isabel Adler was one thing; Gabrielle Mackenzie—or Mac, apparently, as Dakota called her—was another thing entirely. "Out of curiosity, who would you introduce me as?"

"They all know about you, Jack."

"Right." Jack wasn't sure if she should be elated or worried about this. Either way, she felt a little giddy. "Maybe I should just say yes, then?"

"We usually hang out some time during the weekend." Dakota cleared her throat. "They don't know yet that I've gone on a second date with you, but they will be beside themselves once they find out."

Jack drew up her eyebrows. Did these successful, accomplished women have nothing better to do than get worked up over their neighbor's dating shenanigans? But Jack couldn't resist the exhilaration that came with Dakota's invitation. And just maybe, it was exactly what she needed to get out of her head and onto the next step of whatever this was.

CHAPTER 19

"Who are you and what have you done to my partner?" Nico grinned at Jack. "What happened to your usual no strings attached spiel?" He nodded as though he'd just gotten to the bottom of it. "All it took to change your mind was a model, huh? And you accuse me of being shallow sometimes."

The word model made Jack remember how Dakota looked yesterday, when Jack had left her fancy mansion in Cobble Hill. Before she'd opened the door, Dakota had pushed Jack against it, and kissed her in such a way that Jack wanted that door to remain closed forever, with Dakota pressed against her like that.

"You're the least shallow man I know," Jack said, trying to divert the conversation away from herself. But Nico's ego wasn't big enough for a trick like that to work on him.

"Gee, thanks, partner."

Jack stopped the car at a stoplight. They were on their way back from New Jersey and still had a long drive ahead. When trapped together in the confines of a car, it was hard not to share details about your personal life. Usually, Jack had nothing more to share than a quick low-down on how her date had been, if she'd had one over the weekend. Things were different this time.

"All of this is just as surprising to me as it is to you," Jack admitted. It was easier to confide in Nico than in Marley about Dakota, what with Marley and Curtis's outburst about the one percent of the one percent. Dakota was loaded, but that had nothing to do with why Jack had such a soft spot for her. The fact that she lived next door to Isabel Adler, and down the road from Gabrielle Macken-zie, did have an effect, however. She'd be a hypocrite to lie to herself about that.

Jack might be a dyed-in-the-wool cop, but just like most human beings alive in this day and age, she wasn't entirely immune to the allure of celebrity. She wished she was, that she could deem herself above it, but she'd been watching Gabrielle Mackenzie on TV for years, and she'd been listening to Isabel Adler's music for decades. There were plenty of celebrities Jack didn't give one iota about, but these two were different. And they just happened to live in Dakota's street. Jack wondered who else lived on that magical celebrity street in Cobble Hill.

"You had me thinking your principles were holy to you," Nico continued teasing her.

"I even told her about my dad dying in my teens."

Jack was back in traffic and kept her eyes firmly on the road, but she heard Nico huff out some air. He was having a great time needling her. But that's what partners did—otherwise, with the things they had to deal with on a daily basis, this job would be unbearable.

"And you've already set a next date! And you're meeting her friends!" From the corner of her eye, Jack saw

Nico shake his head. "Again. Who are you and where's the Jack Russo I know?"

"You can't be on my case about my preference for one-night stands and then also be on my case when I go on more than one date with a woman. You have to choose," Jack joked.

"I'm stunned. That's all."

"Anyway." Jack hadn't told Nico the juiciest details yet. "It will all make perfect sense once I tell you who Dakota's friends are."

"Who?" That shut him up—for a few seconds at least.

"Isabel Adler and Gabrielle Mackenzie."

Nico whistled through his teeth. Both Isabel and Gabrielle were so ubiquitous, even a middle-aged straight detective like Nico was impressed by them.

"What the hell happened when you swiped right on that Tinder model that day? Did you get beamed into an alternate universe?"

Jack briefly looked to the side to see Nico's face. He looked genuinely perplexed.

"Maybe I did," Jack said, only half-joking this time.

———

"She's so late." Dakota checked her watch again. Miraculously, both Izzy and Leila, and Mac and Jamie, had been free this Friday night—or maybe they'd rearranged their busy schedules just to meet Dakota's female lover.

"It's Friday night in Brooklyn. She's probably stuck in traffic," Jamie said.

Dakota sure hoped it was just Friday night traffic. It wasn't entirely inconceivable that Jack would bail on her.

That all of this was too much pressure way too soon in whatever they had going on between them.

They had exchanged dozens of texts and spoken on the phone once since they'd said goodbye last Sunday. But Jack had been at the forefront of Dakota's mind ever since. She'd told Corey all about their second date, although she'd left out the more spicy tidbits. He probably had read off her face how amazing it had been—some things didn't need to be spelled out. Dakota had also told her neighbors about Jack, and now here they sat. Waiting for her. Where was she? It was almost eight-fifteen and Dakota had invited everyone for half past seven, secretly hoping that Jack would arrive early so they could have a little private time for some much-needed kissing.

"You're nervous," Izzy said. "We get it, but stop pacing, please. Relax. I'm sure she'd let you know if something serious was up."

"She's a detective. She probably got held up at work. Does she work homicides?" Mac asked, her voice tensing up.

They hadn't talked much about Jack's work. *Argh.* Why couldn't she just text when she was running this late? How could Jack keep Isabel Adler *and* Gabrielle Mackenzie waiting? But Izzy was right. Dakota was edgy with nerves. She hadn't introduced a potential love interest—if Jack even qualified as that—to her friends in a long time, let alone a female one.

The bell rang. Dakota rushed to the door without checking the security camera. She pulled the door open wide, only to find Corey standing in front of her, a magnum bottle of Dom Pérignon in his hands.

He tilted his head and painted on his most sheepish smile. "Chase and the girls are at Grandma Van Ness and

I so didn't feel like going." He batted his ridiculously long lashes. "I would love to join you and the ladies tonight." He held out the bottle. "Obviously, feel free to tell me I'm grossly overstepping, which I know very well I am, but I had to try."

"I can't believe you're crashing my party." Dakota shook her head. Part of her was happy to see Corey. If it weren't for him, Jack wouldn't be on her way over tonight —if she was still coming. "Come in, but you owe me."

"I'll watch the girls any time you need." He lifted his eyebrows, as though implying Dakota would be needing Corey's child-minding services a lot more from now on.

"Deal." Dakota ushered him in. "Jack's not here yet."

"Ooh. She likes to make an entrance. I see." He grabbed Dakota gently by the shoulders. "Good for her." He gave her shoulders a little squeeze.

"Oh, it's just you," Leila said in an exaggeratedly disappointed tone, but greeted Corey with a warm hug to make up for it.

Maybe there were gay men who could stop themselves from fawning over Isabel Adler, but if there were, Dakota hadn't met any yet—and Corey most certainly wasn't one of them. He had gone out of his way to befriend Izzy, via Leila, when she'd moved in with her next door.

Before Leila, even though Dakota and Chase had lived in this house for years, they didn't even know the great Isabel Adler was their neighbor. After she'd lost her voice, she'd become invisible, even to the neighbors.

The bell rang again. Dakota nearly jumped out of her skin. This time, it had to be Jack. Dakota did check the camera feed now. Just to rule out any more surprises. There she was, in sharp focus. Jack Russo.

Dakota hurried to the front door. She took a deep breath, then opened the door.

At the sight of Jack, who looked a bit haggard, her nerves melted away miraculously.

"I'm so sorry," Jack started rambling. "We're working a major case and we were chasing a lead and then my phone just died, even though I'd charged it, and then the taxi driver took the wrong way, despite me telling him not to go that——"

Dakota held out her hand. "Come here," she said. She pulled Jack inside the house, then into her arms. "I'm so happy you're here." She took Jack's phone out of her hand. "I'll plug this in to charge for you."

"Thank you." Dakota felt Jack relax just a little. "I'm already so worked up and now I have to go in there and meet my idols." Jack's chin bopped against Dakota's chest as she shook her head. "I didn't even have time to change."

"It's going to be just fine." Dakota wrapped her arms around Jack a little tighter. She felt so protective of her. "You won't meet a superstar more down-to-earth than Isabel Adler. And Mac's just Mac." She caressed Jack's back. "Corey showed up, just so you know."

"I catch killers for a living," Jack said on a sigh. "I suppose I can pull it together for your fancy friends."

"At least you're not meeting my kids," Dakota blurted. "I'm sorry. I shouldn't have said that." Dakota didn't know why she did. It was too soon to even consider it. If she was totally honest, she had a hard time imagining it. As though something about it wouldn't click yet in her mind when it came to all of this. Probably because neither one of them knew what it currently was.

"It's okay. We're both nervous." Jack inhaled deeply. "I

don't do this—the meeting-the-friends-thing—like, at all." Jack waved at the door to the living room. "Ever."

"I must be very special, then." Dakota grinned.

"You damn well are." Jack sounded as though that was a bad thing instead of a good one.

CHAPTER 20

Jack entered the living room hot on Dakota's heels. She tried to shake off the day's stress, to free up some emotional bandwidth for this extraordinary moment.

"Everyone, this is Jack," Dakota said, while holding her hand. "Jack." She gave Jack's hand a little squeeze. "A very select group of my neighbors-slash-friends. And Corey." Dakota shot Corey a grin, then swiftly plugged in Jack's dead phone and put it on the sideboard.

Jack had seen pictures of Corey on the internet, but they didn't do justice to how effortlessly handsome he was in real life. Broad shoulders. Salt-and-pepper hair that was styled just right. Soulful brown eyes. A smile so wide and warm, it seemed to cut right through her ultra-tough police detective veneer. Or maybe it was just easier to focus on him instead of the celebrities dotted around Dakota's couch.

Corey stood to greet her and the others followed suit, as though Jack was royalty who needed to be curtsied to. But she was just Jack, in her wrinkled suit, exhausted from a long day, feeling extremely unglamorous next to all these beautiful, wealthy people.

Still, Isabel Adler offered her the biggest smile. Her wife, Leila, even hugged her. And then there was Gabrielle Mackenzie, who looked so strangely familiar, because Jack saw her on TV all the time. Television could give you the wrong impression that you kind of knew someone without ever having met them. Jack supposed that was the secret ingredient that kept newscasters on the air for decades. The familiarity of their faces; the comfort emanating from the same old inflections in their voice; that they were always just there, day after day, keeping people up-to-date on what was going on in the world. Because of Gabrielle Mackenzie, Jack knew so much more about sports than she otherwise would. Most nights, she turned on the news, just to see if Gabrielle was presenting, and she was always strangely happy—ridiculously so, really—when she was. Now, she wasn't just shaking her hand; Gabrielle was very personable and drew Jack toward her, planting a kiss on her cheek. Like Jack had suddenly landed in the middle of a dream where she was being pulled into her television.

"Wow," Jack mumbled. "I'm trying my best to be cool about this, but it's a challenge."

"That's perfectly normal," Corey offered. "Don't worry. It'll blow over in five to ten minutes."

"Like it took you only ten minutes to be yourself again after meeting Izzy," Leila said, sending Jack a wink.

"There are always exceptions, obviously," Corey said. "I grew up with Izzy's voice in my ears. That's a whole other level of adoration. So, yes, it took me a little longer to come to terms with the fact that we were neighbors, and later became *the* best of friends." He fixed his gaze on

Jack. "It's a gay thing. I'm sure you lesbians are far more down-to-earth about these things."

"Jack was hoping Brandi Carlile was my neighbor," Dakota said, curling an arm around Jack's waist, pulling her close.

"I'll happily take Isabel Adler and Gabrielle Mackenzie." Jack leaned into Dakota, and not just for comfort. She had missed her. Every free moment, her mind had drifted to the time they'd spent together—and how she was going to stop herself from falling head over heels in love with her. Because she might be in a room with Isabel Adler and Gabrielle Mackenzie, and their gorgeous wives, but now the introductions were over, Jack only had eyes for Dakota. She looked impossibly glossy again, easily outshining the celebrities in her living room, like she had a secret makeup department at her disposal in the next room—maybe she had. For all her experience dealing with people, Jack had no clue how the ultra-wealthy lived.

"It's a real pleasure to meet you," Jamie, Gabrielle Mackenzie's wife, said.

"Jamie's most responsible for you being here," Dakota said.

They all took a seat and Corey poured Jack a glass of champagne without asking if she wanted it—although she did. He shot her a quick wink as he gave it to her. This whole situation was so odd, so far removed from Jack's regular life.

"I'm very proud of my work," Jamie said.

"You make it sound as though this is all your doing," Gabrielle replied. "As though you waved some magic wand and made this happen."

"I planted the seed," Jamie said matter-of-factly. "There's no fruit without a seed."

"Too much talk of seed," Leila butted in.

"Even for me." Corey blew Leila a kiss. Jack didn't really know what to make of him. He wasn't camp, yet he was blowing kisses and winking at everyone. She also hadn't expected him to be here.

"As ecstatic as we all are that you're here, Jack," Leila said, "it's a bit of a surprise."

"It's mostly a surprise to me that *you* all are here," Dakota quickly responded—possibly to take the heat off Jack, which made her melt even more.

While Jack had been excited to meet Dakota's famous friends, she'd still prefer it were just the two of them. Because all throughout this week, even though her squad was working a hell of a case that took most of her energy, Jack's head had been filled to the brim with all things Dakota. She couldn't explain it. She had no defense against it. She had agreed to a friends with benefits arrangement she didn't believe in. She had said yes to booty calls. But, most of all, she had, somehow, allowed herself to develop feelings for this woman who she had no business falling for. And instead of doing the sane, logical thing, instead of staying far away from Dakota, here she was, in her living room, meeting her friends.

"I truly thought you'd be too busy on a Friday night to accept my impromptu invitation." Dakota rested her gaze on Corey. "Especially when you weren't invited."

Clearly, they were all close enough to make these kinds of jokes with each other. Jack didn't have a tight group of friends like that. She had Marley and Curtis—who might come around a little on her still seeing Dakota when she told them about her celebrity neighbors—and she had Nico and a few people at the precinct she sometimes had a beer with. This situation she found herself in, this group of women with the additional gay man, was not one Jack was overly familiar with.

"Guilty as charged." Corey held up his hands. "Please, officer, don't arrest me for being here. Curiosity isn't a crime, is it?"

"I did let him in," Dakota admitted.

"I was the one who made you text Jack last weekend." Corey batted his lashes. "Maybe I deserve to be here."

"You're really keeping this from Chase?" Izzy asked Corey.

"It's not my place to tell him." Corey scratched his perfect head of hair.

"There's really not that much to tell." Dakota wriggled in her seat. "Jack and I, we're not, um…" She didn't finish her sentence.

"I was just really curious to meet you. That's all," Jack said. "It's a real honor that you're here for, um, me." Jack chuckled. She didn't have any experience getting to know a date's friends—why would she? The only reason she had agreed to this was so she could meet Gabrielle Mackenzie.

"We know you're not into the whole dating thing," Jamie, the most forward of them all, said. "But neither is Dakota, really." She peered at her neighbor. "You're on Tinder all the time, yet you've never introduced us to anyone until now."

"But here we all are," Corey said.

Jack didn't know what to say to that. This wasn't a conversation she wanted to have with Dakota's friends. This was between her and Dakota—and they'd discussed it plenty already. Unless this was some sort of trap to lure her into making a promise she shouldn't make. Although Jack didn't get that vibe. Nor did Dakota look comfortable with the direction the conversation had taken.

"What kind of detective are you?" Gabrielle Mackenzie asked, her TV smile turned on to full wattage. Jack felt a pang of gratitude at Gabrielle coming to her rescue.

"Homicide," Jack said—that shut them up for a few moments.

Jamie swallowed hard. "Is seeing a dead body just another day at work for you?"

Jack shook her head. "You never get used to that." Truth be told, Jack had gotten more used to it over the years. She'd had no choice. But that was not something you shared with civilians.

"You put away murderers." Corey huffed out some air. "I can't really wrap my head around that."

"What do you do?" Jack asked.

"I work for the family business. I'm a lawyer at Van Ness Holdings."

"Is that how you met Chase?" Jack asked.

"No." A grin appeared on Corey's lips. "I was opposing counsel for a company that was naive enough to sue VNH. Chase was a witness. I cross-examined him *real* good."

Even though Jack didn't know where this was going, and she and Dakota weren't even really friends with benefits, she was getting increasingly curious to meet Chase Van Ness.

Then Jack's phone started ringing. She couldn't afford to put it on silent—especially when they were this close to bringing in their perp.

"I'm so sorry. I really have to take this." She shot up, picked up her phone from the sideboard, and took the call in the kitchen. "Yes, Nico."

"I hate to crash your hot date, partner," he said. "We got him." Nico gave her an address.

"I'll be there in twenty."

They hung up. Jack sighed. This was another big reason why intimate relationships were difficult. Even when she wasn't on call, this could happen. Life with a cop was full of interrupted dinners and conversations that had to be picked up later.

Dakota had followed her into the kitchen.

"I'm so sorry, but I have to go."

"Now?" Dakota's eyes grew wide.

"I can't go into detail about this case, but, yeah. It can't be helped."

"Are you serious?" Dakota furrowed her brow.

"Deadly." Bad joke, but still.

"I thought you were staying the night." Dakota sidled up to her. "I got us something. A present. For later." She kissed the side of Jack's neck.

"I'm really sorry. This is how it is." Jack never made excuses when it came to her work.

"Can you come back later?" Dakota whispered in her ear.

"It might be very late and I might not make it back." Jack knew better than to make a promise she wasn't sure she could keep.

"Will you call me? No matter how late?" Dakota wrapped her arms around her, making Jack very reluctant to leave. "We need to set up our next date."

"Booty call, you mean." Jack snickered, despite herself. "I'm sorry, but I really have to go."

"Pfff," Dakota groaned. "Please, please, please, come back later."

Jack's knees went a little weak. "I'll do my best." She

tried to wriggle free from Dakota's embrace, but she held on tight. "If not tonight, then tomorrow," Jack said.

"I have a fundraiser at the girls' school tomorrow," Dakota said. "Sunday?"

"I have dinner at my mother's in the evening, but I'm free during the day."

Dakota shook her head. "I'm taking the girls to—" Jack's phone started ringing again. She hoped it was Nico telling her they didn't need her anymore, but it was Marley. Jack let it go to voicemail.

"I'm sorry. I really have to go now. I'll call you when I can." Welcome to a cop's life, she thought, as she kissed Dakota goodbye.

Jack stuck her head into the living room to announce she'd been called away—and offer more apologies—then went on her way.

CHAPTER 21

"Refill, please." Dakota held out her empty glass to Corey.

"Justice waits for no one," Leila said meekly. Everyone looked deflated after Jack's sudden departure. She'd barely been there for half an hour, and that was after making them wait for forty-five minutes.

"I'm so bummed." Dakota knocked back her freshly poured glass in a few large gulps.

Corey stared at her, his head tilted. "Booze is not the answer." He reached for the bottle for another refill, though.

Dakota thought about the toy she'd bought—the surprise she had in store for when Jack stayed the night.

"I thought *I* had a busy work life," Mac said.

"She didn't even have time to moon over you." Jamie shot her wife a grin.

"Jack was way too busy making eyes at Dakota to be impressed by any of us," Izzy said. "For what it's worth, I think she's *really* into you." Izzy sent Dakota a warm smile.

"Which begs the question," Leila said. "How into the hot cop are you? Considering, you know, *things*."

"We can call a spade a spade," Corey said. "I'm married to her ex-husband. We can all speak our truth here."

"Judging by how annoyed I am that she got called away, I'd say I'm fairly into her," Dakota said.

"Even though she's a woman?" Mac asked.

Dakota just nodded. In this moment, it didn't matter that Jack was a woman—the only thing that mattered was that she wasn't there.

"But," she continued. "Jack's been very honest with me from the start. She doesn't date, or do relationships, precisely because of the life she leads. She's married to her job. At least now I know exactly what she means." Dakota straightened her spine. She'd already had enough of feeling sorry for herself. The evening was a dud, but her friends were still here.

"Regardless of her job and what she wants," Jamie said. "Do you think you could actually fall in love with her?"

In a heartbeat, Dakota thought—knew for certain, in fact—but didn't want to admit to her friends. She tried to shrug off the question, but she found she couldn't. "I don't know but, either way, it's too complicated. She has her job. I have the girls." *And I thought I was straight.* "We want different things. I should probably put some distance between us before it becomes too difficult." What a ridiculous thing to say while all Dakota wanted was for her phone to ring so Jack could tell her she was on her way back. Or maybe they should just have one final, epic night together, before going their separate ways. Dakota truly didn't know. All she knew right now was that it sucked that Jack was a cop.

"I'm no expert," Izzy said, "but as far as I can tell, it's pretty obvious."

"They've just got the hots for each other, babe," Leila said.

"They're in lust," Corey added. "Sometimes, it becomes more. Mostly, it doesn't." He leaned over and put his hand on Dakota's shoulder. "That doesn't mean you shouldn't give it a chance."

"Oh god, this whole thing," Dakota said on a sigh. "I've spent so much more time thinking and talking about Jack than actually being with her." She took a breath. "What did you make of her?" She cast her gaze over her friends one by one while she awaited their verdict.

"A little frazzled at first," Mac said. "But only momentarily fazed by Izzy and me."

"She did have some hot cop swagger about her," Izzy said, nodding.

Leila gave her a look. "I didn't know you were into that."

"What do you mean, babe? I'm just answering Dakota's question." Izzy innocently grinned at her wife.

"She looked like she's not easily impressed, which is probably a result of her job," Jamie mused, ignoring Leila and Izzy's banter.

"First impression: wonderful," Corey said, "although you should take her shopping." He winked at her. "Give her a Van Ness makeover."

Dakota rolled her eyes. "Over my dead body."

"You might get to see her then." He pursed his lips. "Although you would be dead."

The evening went by, without Jack. Dakota waited up

in vain until past midnight for Jack's call. She'd just slipped between the sheets, exhausted but wired at the same time, when her phone rang.

"Is it too late?" Jack asked.

"Never," Dakota replied, her spine tingling with delight—and lust—already.

CHAPTER 22

"If I didn't know any better, I'd say you wanted to get out of spending time with my friends." Dakota sat on the edge of the bed with a box in her hands. Jack had insisted on a hot shower before she touched Dakota. It was the only means to put the day, and all the gruesomeness it entailed, behind her. Sometimes, it did the trick. Other times, it didn't. Tonight, with Dakota barely dressed and waiting for her, her smooth skin shimmering in the bedroom's low light, the present she got for them waiting in her hands—Jack would be a very bad detective if she didn't know what it was—it was easy enough.

"Every fiber of my being hated having to leave Gabrielle Mackenzie and Isabel Adler in the lurch like that." Jack wasn't in the habit of apologizing for her job. She protected the public. They'd caught a particularly nasty killer today after weeks of running down leads that went nowhere. For once, Jack had experienced the kind of job satisfaction TV shows loved to make viewers believe was commonplace—although satisfaction wasn't the right word for it. When it came to catching killers, there was no such thing as total satisfaction, because someone had died. Jack had done her job so that justice could be served. How could she apologize for that? But she understood it was irritating for Dakota, especially because she'd set it all up so Jack could meet 'Izzy' and 'Mac', as she called them. "But the city's a safer place for it."

"Thank you for your service, officer. Here's my thank-you gift." Dakota held up the box.

"What on earth could that possibly be?" Jack made a spectacle of shaking the box and examining it from all sides.

As soon as she started opening her present, the mood in the room shifted from banter to something else entirely. To something heavier, something that needed to be dealt with instantly.

The strap-on Jack unearthed from the box was decidedly not small, but if its size was intimidating, that was undone by all the colors of the rainbow it came in. Still, its whimsical appearance didn't so much as elicit a chuckle from Jack. Something had come over her. A desire so piercing, so forceful, it terrified her. One thing she knew for certain; Dakota wouldn't be the one strapping it on tonight.

———

Exhausted though she had been, Jack had barely slept. She couldn't after the twenty-four hours she'd had. It was too much for her brain to process, which is why Jack preferred a simple life. Work was complex enough. She had a couple of good friends, and her family. That was it and life was good like that.

Now, she had to deal with meeting celebrities and a woman she barely knew but for whom her lust ran absolute riot, a woman who had a billionaire gay ex-husband and teenage children. There was nothing simple about that. Yet, after she'd finished work last night, even though it had been almost one in the morning, Jack hadn't had a single smidgen of a doubt in her mind. She had come to see Dakota—and come they had.

Thank goodness it was Saturday. Jack turned on her side and pressed her belly against Dakota's back. She curled an arm around her and pulled her close. How was it possible to feel this way about someone she'd only seen a few times? Was this what love at first sight felt like? Or was it just an extreme case of delirious lust? And how was Jack ever going to put a stop to it? Maybe it would just fizzle out on its own—

"Mom!" The bedroom door flew open. "Mom, you know I have—"

Dakota shot up. So did Jack. She looked into the face of a blond teenage girl.

The girl's mouth was agape. Her eyes wide. Everything about her body language was stunned. Jack understood how she felt.

"Sweetheart, um…" Dakota scrambled for the sheet. She didn't look at Jack. Maybe she hoped she could wish her away by pretending she wasn't there. Jack, on the other hand, hoped they'd left the toy in the en suite bathroom last night and it wasn't lying in the bedroom somewhere. "Give me a second." With the swiftness perhaps only mothers can muster, Dakota jumped out of bed, somehow covering herself up, and ushered the girl out of the room.

Jack fell back onto the mattress. Oh, fuck. Maybe this

would set her straight. Maybe this was exactly what she needed to shake herself free from this madness that had taken hold of her heart—and a few other body parts.

CHAPTER 23

"Sweetheart, I'm sorry." Dakota pulled the hastily snatched bedsheet tightly around her. What was Aubrey doing here? Where was Corey? What the hell was going on? "Are you okay?"

"Who was that?" Aubrey's voice was eerily calm.

"Just, um, a friend," Dakota said.

"Naked? In your bed?" Aubrey narrowed her eyes. "I'm not blind and I'm not stupid."

Someone knocked on the door that led to the communal staircase connecting Dakota and Chase's living quarters.

"It's me," Corey shouted. "Can I come in?"

"No!" Aubrey shouted.

"Yes," Dakota said.

Corey barged in. "I'm sorry. Big misunderstanding." He looked from Aubrey to Dakota, taking in the situation, quickly processing it, and drawing obvious conclusions.

He gave Dakota a quick nod, then put his arm around Aubrey, who allowed herself to be comforted for only a moment before shaking him off.

"Why don't we give your mom some privacy?" Corey said. "And a few minutes to get her bearings. We can all talk later. Okay, Aubs?"

"What the hell, Mom?" Aubrey's voice broke. Poor thing. She was only thirteen. She couldn't deal with walking in on her mother like that. She shouldn't have to. Had Dakota stupidly forgotten to lock the door?

"Darling, we'll talk in a minute. Okay? I'll come upstairs." Knowing Aubrey, the first thing she would do was tell her sister, then, most likely, her dad.

"I have ballet. I couldn't find my shoes." Aubrey suddenly sounded dejected.

"Why don't you skip ballet today?" Corey said.

"What? No," Aubrey said. "I just want to get out of here." With that, she turned on her heels, and stormed out of the room.

"I'm sorry," Corey said. "I take it Jack's here?"

Dakota nodded, but her mind was far more focused on her daughter. "I'll get Aubrey's shoes."

Aubrey was the kind of kid who would forget her own head if it wasn't part of her body. As a solution—and probably shoddy parenting—they got her doubles and triples of most items she left lying around, but ballet shoes had to be worn and trimmed to feel right and were therefore unique. Dakota's mind had been too preoccupied last night to think about her daughter's shoes. She was pretty sure she'd locked the door, though. But the girls were plenty old enough to put a key in a lock.

Dakota found the shoes in Aubrey's room and hurried back into the living room, still only dressed in a bedsheet.

"Here." Dakota gave Corey the shoes—at least it wasn't Chase who had come down. "If there's any way you can keep her from spilling the beans just yet, that would be good." What a roller coaster of emotions. Dakota was right back to that feeling of deflation she'd had last night when Jack got called away. But then she'd come back, and the time they'd shared had been mind-blowing again—until now. "We'll talk when she's back from ballet."

"We should tell Chase something. Do you want me to do it?"

Dakota sighed. She didn't owe Chase an explanation because he was her ex-husband, but because he was the father of her kids, one of which had just walked in on her and Jack, spooning naked in bed. Thank goodness they weren't doing anything else.

"Yes, please." It was a cowardly way to go about it, but if anyone could make that particular conversation easier, it was Corey. Dakota was glad to have him be a part of this.

"On it." Corey made for the door. "I'd better run." Before he walked out, he turned around. "Say hi to Jack from me."

Pulling the sheet tightly around her, Dakota sank into a chair. She closed her eyes and took a few deep breaths. Poor Aubrey, but also poor Jack. What a mess.

"Hey." Jack appeared in the living room fully dressed. Her suit looked cheap and worn, yet she somehow managed to look good in it. That baby-blue blouse did wonders for her complexion and—*Jesus*. What was wrong with Dakota? Her brain had been taken over by some-thing she wasn't used to anymore—and it was having a serious effect on its function. "I guess I met your daugh-ter," she joked.

Dakota laughed, because what else was she going to do?

"Oh, fuck. I'm so sorry, Jack. They're so used to

coming and going between floors."

"Do they always barge into your bedroom like that?"

Dakota shook her head, but contradicted herself by saying, "I'm their mother." To her, it explained everything, but it might not to Jack.

"Is there anything I can do?" Jack crouched beside her. "To make this better?"

It was such a sweet thing to ask. "I wouldn't know what."

"Next time, we'll go to my place."

Next time? After the past twelve hours, Dakota wasn't sure there should be a next time. Despite that line of thinking, she nodded.

"Do you want me to stay or go?" Jack put a hand on Dakota's knee. Regardless of the high thread count of the sheet she was wrapped in, the warmth of Jack's touch shot through her as though there wasn't any fabric between them. Because in between Jack being called away and Aubrey bringing an abrupt end to their time together, they'd had a hell of a night. Dakota's new purchase had not been in vain. Jack knew how to deploy it extremely well.

What had Corey called it last night? Being in lust. Dakota was deeply in lust with Jack, with a woman. Corey had said something else as well: sometimes, it turns into something. Mostly, it doesn't. The odds of her lust for Jack turning into something were stacked firmly against them. Because for something to actually blossom between them, they'd have to give it a proper chance, and Dakota wasn't sure Jack wanted that. In fact, even though she hadn't acted that way—especially not last night after she'd returned—Jack had clearly spelled that out for her, and more than once already. Was it even worth all this grief?

Was it worth upsetting her daughters over? Aubrey was already upset—she'd seen something a girl her age shouldn't have to see—so it was too late to prevent that.

"I don't really know," Dakota said, because she had no clue what she wanted. Take tonight, when she'd be going to a fancy fundraiser for the girls' school. Could she imagine ever taking Jack as her date to an event like that? Jack probably wouldn't want to go.

"I'll give you some space." Jack pushed herself up. "You look like you need it." She leaned toward Dakota and planted the softest of kisses on her temple. "Call me if you want to talk or, um, something else."

As she watched Jack walk out of the room, something twitched in Dakota's belly. Something caved inside of her, giving the simple act of Jack walking out of the door an air of finality. Maybe it was time for Dakota to come back to her senses. After all, this thing with Jack, whatever it was, had just been an experiment. It was never meant to be anything serious. Dakota could hardly call herself straight any longer, but then she was *fluid*. Wasn't that what the kids called it these days? She could hardly ask her own.

She huffed out some air. She had an awkward conversation ahead of her.

———

"Are you gay now as well?" Peyton asked. She didn't look particularly fazed by this—but she hadn't seen her mother in bed with another woman. She hadn't been as shocked as Aubrey had. Aubrey was still at ballet. Peyton hated ballet with a vengeance, and it was the first non-joint hobby one of the girls practiced.

"No. I mean, I don't know." Bisexual, Dakota assumed. "I'm sorry this happened, darling. It shouldn't have. What did Aubrey tell you?"

"That she walked into your room and you were in bed with a woman. Naked."

"Okay. Well, yes, that's true. But this woman—her name is Jack—and I, we're just friends, really." Friends-with-not-so-many-benefits right now, Dakota thought. "I know it's confusing, but…" How did Chase have this conversation with the girls when he introduced Corey? Dakota wasn't there, but the girls had told her all about it. She'd probably still been too hurt to remember. Anyway, this wasn't like introducing a serious partner—which Corey already was to Chase at the time. Mostly, Dakota felt like a really bad mother. How was she supposed to explain this to her daughters when she couldn't even explain it to herself? She needed help. She didn't want to do this alone. "I'm here if you have questions, but why don't we continue this conversation when your sister's home? All five of us can sit together and, um, talk about it." The horror, but still, it was better than this. Chase was gay, for crying out loud. He'd been married to a man for years. He was the girls' father, and he could help Dakota with this, because she didn't have a clue what to say.

"Knock, knock." Chase walked into the kitchen. "Everything okay here?"

"Fine." Peyton slid off the barstool she'd been perched on.

"Hey." Dakota reached for her daughter's hand. "Come here, baby." She pulled her close. They were at an age where an impromptu hug wasn't always welcome any longer, but Peyton accepted it today. She even, very briefly, put her head on Dakota's shoulder. "It's all good. Okay?"

Peyton nodded, then exited Dakota's embrace, and the kitchen.

"So." Chase leaned on the counter with his elbows. "Do you have something you want to share with me, Mama?"

Still, after all that had happened, after he had hurt her in the worst possible way, looking into Chase's handsome face was comforting to Dakota.

"What happened with Aubrey earlier shouldn't have happened. I'm sorry about that."

"She'll get over it," Chase said. "We'll talk to her. Explain things… if there is anything to explain." He shot Dakota the warmest smile. "What's going on, Dax?" Chase was the only one who'd ever been able to make that nickname stick. She'd let him use it because it was something of the two of them. To him, she was Dax. But only to him.

"Oh, fuck, Chase. I don't even know. What did Corey tell you?"

"Just that you had company, and not of the gender that I might be expecting." A small smile played on his lips.

"It was just meant to be an experiment." If she was honest, it had stopped feeling like one about midway through their first night together. "As far as experiments go, it's been rather successful, but… I think I like her, but I don't know her that well. And she made it perfectly clear from the start that she doesn't want anything serious. Like, absolutely totally clear, with no room for misinterpretation. Which, I guess, made it easier in a way to go along with the whole thing, but now… I think neither of us know what we want right now."

"Hey." Chase slid his hands across the counter. "It's

okay to not know. To be confused. Because this is confusing. Nobody's expecting anything from you. You don't need to have all the answers right now."

Dakota wrapped her hands around her ex-husband's. This man. No wonder she couldn't stop looking for an almost exact replica of him—minus the queer parts. He always knew what to say to make Dakota feel better. To take the pressure off a tense situation.

"I don't really know her. She's a cop. Well, a homicide detective, and quite an unavailable one at that." Time-wise as well as emotionally, Dakota thought.

"She's a cop?" Chase's hands tensed up underneath her own. "She's not deep undercover, running a secret investigation into VNH, is she?" He chuckled, because surely Chase knew how utterly ridiculous that sounded.

"That would be extreme deep cover." Dakota peered into Chase's bright blue eyes. "And what are you saying? Is there anything to investigate?"

"No." Chase's tone was resolute. "Back to you and your cop."

"I don't even know what to tell the girls. There isn't really anything to tell, but I have to say something, because Aubrey saw me in bed with her." Dakota blew out some air. This was not supposed to be part of the experiment.

"Just be honest. Explain to them that you're exploring and that's a good thing."

"We're going to have to work out better home logistics, by the way."

"So Hot Cop is coming back?"

Dakota shrugged. "She might. We left things kind of open-ended." Her kids roaming freely around all floors of the house was the main, but not the only reason Dakota preferred not to bring dates back to her house. Jack was an exception—to so many things. Dakota wasn't in the habit of sharing, on a first date, who the father of her children was. Not bringing strangers into her house was a big part of that—not until she got to know them better.

"I'm here for you. So is Corey," Chase said.

"Sorry I made him keep it from you. I didn't want to make a big song and dance about it because… it was meant to be nothing. Just some fun. And it was fun. A lot of fun." A spontaneous smile broke on her face. "But I'm not sure we should continue seeing each other. Either way, I don't really want to think about that right now. I need to deal with the girls first."

"Hey…" Chase squeezed her hands. "Whatever you need, okay? If that means bailing on tonight, I'll go to the fundraiser with Corey."

"Your mother's going to love that."

"That's the big advantage of not being married to a Van Ness anymore. You don't have to worry for one split second what Grandma Van Ness thinks about anything you do."

Dakota burst into a full-on laugh. "Imagine telling her that I'm with a woman."

Chase shook his head. "Despite her excellent health, she may have a heart attack."

Initially, Chase's coming out had not gone down well in the conservative Van Ness clan. He was their golden boy. Handsome. Smart. Responsible. Polite to a fault. The perfect person to take over the Van Ness empire when he came of age. No wonder he had caved under that immense pressure—under all those family expectations—and hidden who he really was.

Although it was impossible for Dakota to not hold that

against him—because she'd believed him when he'd said he loved her. She'd been over the moon when he'd said 'I do' at the Van Ness Martha's Vineyard estate. It was a wedding fit for the most romantic of fairy tales, followed by, several years later, a marriage straight out of some sort of horror comedy crossover.

But family was family, and what were the Van Nesses going to do? Excommunicate their golden boy just because he was gay? By the time he came out, Chase had already risen through the ranks at lightning speed. He was good for the company and whatever was good for the company, was, ultimately, good for the family.

The Van Nesses wouldn't be hoisting a rainbow flag at their company headquarters any time soon, but they had accepted Chase for who he was. Then Corey had arrived and he had the kind of personality that won over Chase's mother in the span of an afternoon. It helped that he was a good-looking hotshot lawyer. Not long after his and Chase's engagement, he was made chief counsel of VNH's legal department.

These days, Chase and Corey were the Van Nesses golden dream couple. Two preposterously handsome gay men, father and stepfather to two beautiful twin girls. The Van Nesses could even play the diversity card now, although that was not Chase's style. All the while, Dakota had been reduced to some hanger-on, at least that's what it felt like sometimes. Through her daughters, she'd always be connected to the Van Nesses, but she didn't feel like a part of the family anymore. And Chase was right; she wasn't.

Noises in the hallway alerted them to Aubrey's arrival home. The fun times were about to begin.

CHAPTER 24

Jack needed to talk to someone. She called Marley.

"Congrats on your big collar last night," Marley said as soon as she picked up the phone.

With everything that had happened after, Jack had almost forgotten about their case breaking open.

"Thanks. Can I buy you lunch to celebrate?"

"Um, sure," Marley said. "Girls only? Usual place?" Marley might have a desk job these days, but she was still very good at detecting, especially when her best friend needed to talk.

An hour later, they were sitting opposite each other at their favorite diner in Queens, steaming mugs of coffee in between them.

"Did that perp keep you up all night confessing?" Marley peered at Jack's face. "You should be in bed instead of here with me."

Jack waved her off. "I'm going to tell you something and I need you not to judge."

Marley raised her eyebrows. "Way to passive-aggressively shut me up beforehand."

"I know, and I'm sorry, but I need to process something, and I can't do that if I know you're judging me."

"Why would I judge you?" She narrowed her eyes. "Oh. I see. It's that Van Ness woman, isn't it?"

"Very much so."

"M-hm." Marley sounded more judgmental than ever. "Talk to me."

Jack recounted the events from last night, leaving out the spicy bits, and ended with one of Dakota's daughters walking in on them.

"Let me get this straight," Marley said. "The Van Ness kids were in the house when you went over for a booty call?"

"Technically, yes. But they weren't supposed to be in that part of the house." Jack wasn't up to speed with all the details of the living and co-parenting arrangement Dakota had with her ex-husband.

Marley shook her head. "Whatever happened to living in separate houses after a divorce? I did some Van Ness googling after you told me about your rich chick. Her ex-husband is remarried. Why does she keep living in his house?"

So much for Marley not judging. Jack knew it would be impossible when she asked.

"For the kids, so they can go from their dad's place to hers without friction, I guess." But what did Jack know?

"Let's address issue number one first." Marley tapped a fingernail against the linoleum table top. "You're still seeing her?" Marley shook her head. "I don't get it."

"You're the one who told me to give her another chance." Jack knew full well how ridiculous that sounded.

"I need to do some processing as well. What the hell?" Marley sipped from her coffee, glaring at Jack over the rim of her cup. "Whatever happened to your sacrosanct motto of one-night stands only?"

"I have no clue. I don't know what this is supposed to feel like. I never let myself get this far. You know that. But now… she's gotten under my skin and part of me wants to keep seeing her so badly, even though I know it's such a bad idea." Jack took a beat to mull things over. "Although, you and Curtis did fly off the handle too much after I told you she was a Van Ness, because it's not really about that. But after this morning, I don't think I want to get involved in a complicated family situation like that." Jack shook her head. It was the very last thing she wanted.

"Then don't. Do what you always do. What you're so good at." Marley put her cup down with a loud thud. "Walk away, Jack. Simply walk away."

Jack swallowed hard. Her stomach shrank into a tiny ball. "I'm not sure I can."

"Of course you can't when you keep on taking her booty calls. That's the first step. Break off all contact. Block her on your phone. It's easy these days, you know?"

"I don't think I want to do that."

"So, you want two opposite things at the same time. You want to get to know her but you also don't." Marley pouted. "If it's fifty-fifty, choose the easy way out."

"Can you also give me the advice you'd give if you didn't know Dakota used to be married to Chase Van Ness?"

"No, because this is not a hypothetical situation. She is who she is. You are who you are. You know, deep down, that it can't work. That it's unlike you to get involved with a woman like that." She held up her finger. "Which doesn't mean you shouldn't get involved with any other woman ever. That's not what I'm saying here. All I'm saying is that, to me, it's crystal clear that Dakota Van Ness is not the woman for you to ditch all your precious rules for. If she was, you wouldn't be sitting here with me right now."

Hearing Marley talk was like the old flip-the-coin trick. If you can't make up your mind about something, flip a coin. If the result of the toss-up makes your heart drop all the way into your shoes, you know that you have to do the opposite. Hearing Marley say that Jack should walk away —that she should take 'the easy way out'—made the opposite crystal clear to Jack. She couldn't walk away. If she could, she would have done so already. Then that would have been the easy way out. Jack was choosing the hard way in. She wasn't sure—at all—that was what Dakota wanted, however.

"You're wrong." Jack smiled at her best friend. "But thank you so much for clearing that up for me."

"What? Oh-no. Don't tell me my reverse psychology worked on you now when it really wasn't supposed to." Marley scrunched up her lips.

"Dakota is not the devil, Mar. She's really not." Quite the contrary. Jack didn't believe in heaven or angels or anything like that, but if she had to imagine an angel descending from the heavens, she could only imagine Dakota. "She's…" Oh damn. Jack's eyes grew a touch moist. She quickly regrouped. Marley wouldn't be having any of that. "How about you meet her instead of dismissing her?"

Marley chuckled. "You're going to organize a dinner party for me and Dakota Van Ness?"

"And your lovely husband, of course."

"Oh, I'll be there, sister. With frigging bells on." Marley scoffed. "I can't believe this. You're going to introduce us to a woman? An actual love interest?" She looked around theatrically. "Are pigs flying now?"

"Cut the drama, please." Marley was nothing like Dakota's poised, famous friends. She was loud and in-your-face and never kept an opinion to herself that she could share instead.

"What drama? This is my personality you're criticizing. Now who's being judgmental?"

Jack grinned at Marley while she shook her head. "Who even needs a girlfriend with a best friend like you," she joked.

"A best friend doesn't come with the same benefits. As long as we're also clear on that." Marley batted her lashes.

"So you're agreeing to meet Dakota?" Marley was right to make a drama about that. Jack had introduced a love interest to her best friend exactly zero times.

"If she deigns herself worthy of meeting a lowly police captain and her firefighter husband."

"Oh, come on." Jack leaned over the table. "She's sleeping with me, and I haven't even taken the sergeant's exam."

"Good point. I outrank you in every way, detective. Yet you simply ignore my best advice." Marley sighed. "I hope that doesn't come back to bite you in the ass."

"You and me both," Jack said. She wasn't even sure she and Dakota were still on. Either way, they probably wouldn't see each other again this weekend, but she'd text her later, on her way home.

CHAPTER 25

"How do you feel?" Dakota asked Aubrey.

Ballet class had calmed her down. She just shrugged.

"I want to apologize for what you saw. That shouldn't have happened," Dakota said. She didn't want to make too big a deal out of it, but still.

"We always knock before we come into your rooms," Chase said. "I think it's about time you extend us the same courtesy."

"They do always knock before they come into *our* room," Corey added.

"Because you and dad are..." Peyton said, then paused. "You're a couple."

"I will *always* knock from now on," Aubrey said. "I promise."

"Thank you." Dakota looked at Peyton.

"Me too," Peyton said.

Dakota cleared her throat. "Um, about that woman you saw. Her name is Jack. We had a little get-together with the neighbors last night and she, um, stayed the night. We're kind of seeing each other. But it's not very serious. You were never meant to meet her. It's not like your dad and Corey." It didn't even come close— and yet.

"Are you into women now?" Aubrey asked, echoing her sister's question from earlier.

"I might be. I don't know yet. I'm… experimenting." Christ. That word. It was starting to sound utterly absurd.

"It's okay if you're gay, Mom," Aubrey said.

"Or bi," Peyton corrected her sister. The girls were only thirteen, yet they already knew so much.

"I know it's okay. It's just a little confusing right now, but it's nothing for you girls to worry about. Okay? I'll figure it out."

"Is she nice?" Aubrey asked. "The lady in your bed."

"Hm." Dakota didn't want to answer that. She didn't want to put any more ideas in her children's heads. "Yeah, but…" She took a breath. "As I said, it's nothing serious. We only just met. If anything changes, I will tell you. You'll be the first to know." She couldn't just erase Jack from their memories—especially not Aubrey's. Not that she wanted to.

"I met her and she's very nice," Corey said.

Dakota rolled her eyes. She wished he would stay out of it for once, but Corey could get away with everything now. It had most certainly not always been the case. Peyton, in particular, hated Corey when he and Chase first got together. Dakota knew, because Peyton had told her over and over again, while crying in her arms.

"I don't understand why Daddy is with that man and not with you," Peyton used to say. "It's not how I want it to be." At the time, Dakota could only agree, although for everyone's sake, she wasn't allowed to say that out loud.

But here they were, so many years later, with Corey fully integrated into their not-so-traditional family.

"She is?" Aubrey asked. Even though they were growing up fast, the girls were really still kids, displaying such sudden wonder, such utter surprise, at something being said.

"She's a cop," Corey said.

Aubrey's eyes went wide. "That's so cool."

The bell rang. While Chase checked who it was, Dakota tried to shoot Corey a look to stop him from talking about Jack.

"Girls, get ready," Chase said. "Jamie's here to pick you up."

"I hope she brought some of that bread your dads don't eat," Dakota joked. "All the more for us."

"Carbs are not the enemy!" the girls shouted in unison, just like Jamie had taught them. Before they scurried off to get their things, Dakota grabbed hold of them, and pulled them close.

"My darlings," she whispered into their divine-smelling hair. "I love you so much."

"Love you too, Mom," they said. Luckily, they weren't too old to say it back yet.

"What's up, Van Nesses?" No matter how many times Chase and Corey had begged her, Jamie couldn't help herself. She always, invariably, arrived with a bag full of bread and other baked goods. "I come bearing gifts in exchange for twenty-four hours with your delightful children."

As far as neighbors went, Jamie and Mac really were the gift that kept on giving. Not only did Jamie always bring fresh sourdough, but she and Mac adored spending time with the kids—they didn't have any of their own.

They loved spoiling the girls—as if they needed more of that.

After Aubrey and Peyton left with Jamie, Dakota sat with Chase and Corey in their kitchen.

"What are we going to do with all this bread?" Corey looked at it as if it were poison instead of the most delicious sourdough you could find in all of New York.

"Maybe I'll take some to Jack," Dakota said, because she could say that now. And they needed to have a conversation, preferably sooner rather than later.

"Does that mean I'll have to be the Van Ness arm candy tonight?" Corey batted his lashes.

Tonight's fundraiser at the girls' school was just another example of how Dakota's life was still so intertwined with Chase and his family. The Van Nesses had organized the fundraiser for decades—since long before Chase had attended the school himself—and it was one of those events Dakota still felt obliged to attend, especially because it was at the girls' school, although her daughters wouldn't even be there.

"I think you'll be able to cope with the pressure," Dakota joked.

"When will I be meeting this Jack?" Chase asked. "Both Corey and Aubrey have met her. I'm feeling a little left out here."

"That's the kind of pressure I can't cope with." Dakota shot her ex a look, even though she knew he was joking. Although he must be curious. Just as Dakota had been both dreading and dying to meet Corey back in the day. Although, in Chase's case, no dread would be involved. He was just curious. But he would have to wait —possibly forever. Or not. Dakota was keen to find out.

CHAPTER 26

To her mother's great despair, Jack wasn't much of a cook. She didn't have time to let a pot of sauce simmer on the stove for hours to attain the particular flavor she was after. Besides, her mother always made enough of any dish to feed two large families. Because her mom didn't have room in her apartment for an extra freezer, Jack and her brother always ended up with the most delicious homemade Italian food—which came in very handy tonight.

Jack heated up the osso buco and risotto in her tiny kitchen while Dakota leaned against the door frame, a glass of Vernaccia in her hand. Jack had prepared for a relaxing night on the couch, eating dinner in front of the TV, before catching up on some much-needed sleep. Until Dakota had called her, asking if, by any chance, she wanted some of Jamie's bread. It turned out to be just that, and not some sort of euphemism. Who was Jack to say no to Sully's Sourdough? She'd take some to her mother's for dinner tomorrow, who would definitely have an opinion about it that would make Jack laugh.

"So they look after your kids and pay you for the privilege in bread?" Jack had asked when Dakota showed up at her door. "I really can't wrap my head around the lives of the rich and famous. You might as well be aliens to me."

Dakota had only kissed Jack chastely on the cheek before handing her a tote bag with a huge loaf of bread and two hefty portions of carrot cake—a totally different kind of present to the one Dakota had got Jack the night before.

Jack didn't want to burn the food she was heating, but it took a lot of energy to keep her eyes off Dakota. She was just wearing jeans and the simplest white shirt you could imagine—although it probably cost half of Jack's paycheck—yet she appeared ready for a glamorous photoshoot.

Jack had slept with Dakota a few times now, but she hadn't been able to unearth the secret of how she always managed to look so fantastic.

"How's Aubrey?" she asked, hoping she'd got the name of the child who had walked in on them right.

"She'll live." There was something slightly different about Dakota tonight. Jack didn't quite know what to make of her energy. She was more distant than last night, but still; she was here. "Chase and I talked to her. Explained the situation."

Always Chase. Jack had better not get a secret drinking game going for every time Dakota mentioned her ex-husband's name. She'd be wasted most of the time.

Jack tasted the food. It needed a few more minutes on the stove. She'd laid the table before Dakota had arrived, wondering when Dakota would have last dined in such humble surroundings—until she'd shut down that train of thought before it drove her nuts. Although it was another point of contention between them, added on to all the other ones already identified and clearly stated. But the realization she'd had following her last conversation with Marley burned brightly within her.

She didn't want to walk away. She'd been pretty much beside herself when Dakota had called not long after, asking to meet—her calendar having magically freed up. Although that hardly meant they were on the same page, especially after what happened with Aubrey this morning. Dakota was the sort of woman who still shared a house with her ex-husband for the sake of her kids, which said everything Jack needed to know about her priorities in life. Her kids came first, which Jack understood perfectly. Whether Dakota put herself or her ex-husband second wasn't very clear.

"I'm glad you're here," Jack said.

"Me too." When Dakota smiled, all doubts in Jack's mind evaporated. "Can I help?"

Jack shook her head. "Just standing there, looking absolutely gorgeous will do." An arrow of pure lust burrowed its way through her flesh.

Dakota chuckled. "Any particular position I should adopt?" She undid a button on her blouse. "Like this?" She tilted her body a fraction.

"Stop right there, please." Jack couldn't look away now if she tried. "Don't move an inch while I'm still cooking." Jack turned off the stove. "Actually, maybe it's safer if you go into the living room." Silly though it sounded, it was also true.

———

"Oh my god." Dakota looked at Jack the way she'd done in bed a few times. "What's in this sauce? It's so good." She narrowed her eyes. "I didn't know you could cook like this."

"There's so much you don't about me." Jack grinned.

"True. But seriously, this sauce is out of this world. Did you add lemon? I wasn't expecting it be so zingy." Dakota sounded so impressed, Jack didn't want to keep the charade going any longer.

"You'll have to ask my mother." She shot Dakota a wide smile to make up for her lack of cooking skills. "She prepared it."

"Ah. But still, you heated up that meat like a pro, and the risotto is cooked perfectly." Dakota winked at her, and Jack nearly melted into her chair.

"I don't have much time for cooking. But I'll pass your compliments on to my mother." *Yeah right.* Jack was close to her mother, but she wasn't in the habit of telling tales about her one-night stands. Her mother had given up long ago trying to set her up with suitable bachelorettes, hoping that Jack would choose a family life over the single existence she preferred—her mother knew better than anyone why Jack was how she was, and that it was futile to insist she change.

Even though they'd spent three incredible nights together, and having dinner was a perfectly logical next step, the evening felt a little weird to Jack. Despite their flirty banter, something else hung in the air. Jack supposed that was also only logical after what had happened this morning. She was just meant to be an experiment for Dakota, not someone her daughter walked in on during a naked embrace.

"Please do," Dakota said. A drop of sauce clung to her bottom lip and all Jack wanted to do was lick it off.

"So…" Even though not specifically stated, Jack sensed this wasn't just a booty call. So much was left unspoken between them—mostly because Jack truly believed there was no need to say anything. But clearly stating their intentions obviously didn't cut it anymore. Something had shifted already. Things were getting complicated. And still Jack wanted more. She didn't really know how to say that out loud, though. First, she needed to gauge what Dakota wanted. "How are you feeling about the past twenty-four hours?"

Dakota chuckled, probably at the vagueness of Jack's question. "It's been a bit of a whirlwind, to say the least."

"Yeah." Jack put her fork down. As delicious as her mother's food was, her stomach was too tense to ingest any more.

"To be honest." Dakota speared another piece of meat onto her fork. "I don't really know how I feel about it." She took a breath, then put the fork, with food, down. "This morning, I was leaning toward putting an end to…" She waved her hands about. "Whatever this is. But then, when my evening freed up, all I wanted was to spend it with you."

Butterflies danced in Jack's stomach. "I talked to my friend Marley about what happened. About us." Even though Jack didn't do feelings, she nonetheless found she had a vocabulary she never used at the ready. "If that conversation made one thing clear to me, it's that, for you I'm willing to bend all my rules." Toss them out of the window, more like, with all the carelessness in the world. "I, um, I'd like to keep seeing you. Find out where it goes." So much for gauging what Dakota wanted. "That's how I feel."

"Is that wise?" Dakota sucked her bottom lip between her teeth.

"It's the most unwise decision of my life, but I can't help myself." Jack knew this was ninety-five percent physical attraction, an irresistible chemistry between them that drove her to this madness—that didn't let her walk away.

"Let me get this straight."

Jack raised her eyebrows at the use of the word.

In response, Dakota just grinned, then said, "You want to date me. Properly. Without all the coyness and conditions and rules you live by?" She arched her perfectly sculpted eyebrows all the way up now. "Color me a little surprised, Officer Russo."

"Detective," Jack said.

"Are you detecting some feelings, perhaps?" Dakota narrowed her eyes.

"Some," Jack said, being coy again. But it was time for Dakota to respond with a little more than what she was giving.

"My life is terribly complicated and…" Dakota painted on a small smile. "I'm not even gay."

"You're plenty gay when you're in bed with me." Jack caught herself. If she wanted honest answers from Dakota, she had to tone down her own flippant responses.

"It's easy enough to sleep with you, Jack. I'm very attracted to you, but… I've never fallen in love with a woman before."

"Neither have I. Well, not for the past ten years, anyway."

"Seriously?"

"I've never let myself."

"It's hardly the same." Was that pity in Dakota's voice? Jack didn't need pity about her non-existent love life from a woman still so hung up on her ex-husband.

"We're not really talking about falling in love here." Having this kind of conversation was hard. So hard, in fact, Jack felt vindicated for not having them in her life. Who needed all this difficult drama?

"What are we talking about then?" Dakota was being the coy one now.

"Just getting to know each other without the preconceived notions we clung to before."

"Okay." Finally, Dakota smiled. "I think I'm down for that."

"It would basically just be the booty calls we agreed on last week with a few dinners thrown in here and there." Old habits died hard in Jack's case. When you'd protected your heart since the tender age of seventeen, it was no mean feat to just let it beat freely all of a sudden—it was near impossible.

"If those dinners taste anything like this one, I'm definitely game."

"Actually, um, speaking of dinner. Marley and her husband, Curtis, are dying to meet you."

"So is Chase. He's feeling a little left out, seeing as Corey has met you."

Jack tried not to get worked up at another mention of Chase. How common was it to introduce someone you were casually dating to your ex-husband? Jack didn't have a clue, yet she was an excellent detective, and this didn't sit entirely right with her.

"Do you want to do a big dinner where everyone can mingle?" Dakota asked.

Jack huffed out some air. Marley and Curtis having

dinner with Chase Van Ness? Talk about a recipe for disaster. She shook her head. "Let's keep it small."

"Sure." Dakota offered her upturned palm.

Jack put her hand in Dakota's. "Let's take it day by day. There's no need to rush."

"I am of half a mind to rush you into the bedroom." Dakota fixed her gaze on Jack and she might as well be kissing her already. It was so physical, it scared Jack a little —but it was a good kind of fear. It was thrilling instead of paralyzing. It was the kind of fear she no longer walked away from.

CHAPTER 27

"When did you know you were gay?" Dakota asked Jack. They were lounging in bed on Sunday morning. Her kids were well taken care of by Mac and Jamie and Dakota relished this lazy time she could spend in Jack's arms.

"It's hard to remember a time when I didn't know," Jack said. Dakota found it difficult to work out when Jack was being serious or just saying something for the sake of it. Sometimes, it was blindingly obvious that Jack was very skilled at first dates, but not so much at what came after. She excelled in quick wit and clever repartees, but a conversation that went a little deeper didn't come easy.

"Did you date boys?"

"Sure, but my heart was never really in it," Jack said. She lay in the crook of Dakota's arm, her hair tickling Dakota's skin.

"When did you first go on a date with a girl?" Dakota kept pushing, otherwise getting a straight answer out of Jack when it came to something personal wasn't likely.

"In my senior year at high school, but I wouldn't call it

dating. It was all very much on the down-low." Jack was drawing circles around Dakota's belly button and Dakota was about to lose her resolve. Maybe she didn't have to worry about what a possible future with Jack might bring, because Jack was clearly the kind of person no one could have a future with.

"When did you first kiss a girl?" Dakota continued.

Jack didn't immediately reply. Maybe she had to think about it. Dakota couldn't see her face. She dragged a fingertip along Jack's spine.

"About two weeks before my dad died," Jack whispered after a few more moments of silence.

"I'm so sorry." Dakota curled her arm around Jack's waist.

Jack slipped out of her embrace and lay on her side. "My turn," she said, "to ask you some questions."

Dakota flipped onto her side so she could face Jack. "Consider me an open book." She looked into Jack's dazzling dark eyes.

"What was it like when Chase told you he was gay?"

Dakota scoffed. That was Jack's question? Was it some sort of payback because she felt Dakota had pried too hard into her emotions, even though, according to her own standards, she had done no such thing? Dakota had merely asked when Jack knew she was gay. Under the circumstances, it was a perfectly acceptable question.

"It was awful," Dakota said, truthfully. Because, maybe the only way to get Jack to open up to her was to lead by example. "Like the ground opened up beneath my feet and my life as I knew it disappeared into that gaping black hole forever."

"I'm sorry you had to go through that."

Dakota shrugged. She'd had ample time to process her

fury and shame—she'd had no choice, because she and Chase shared two beautiful daughters—but she suspected she'd never fully get over the shock of that moment.

"What I don't get is, if he hurt you so much, why you're still so close to him," Jack said.

"Because of the girls," Dakota said. "I didn't want them to grow up surrounded by animosity, with parents who despised each other."

"Sure, but there are other ways to co-parent than living in the same house and... I don't know, being up in each other's business all the time."

"That's not how it was at first, I can assure you. I detested him for lying to me. For pretending. For making me love him the way I did. For having kids with me. For the sham he forced me into. For using me. And for making such a fool out of me for not seeing through it all."

Jack softly caressed her arm. "Yet you forgave him for it all."

Dakota nodded. "I did."

"That's really beautiful. It says so much about who you are as a person."

Dakota blew some air through her nostrils. "What infuriated me the most was that I truly believed I knew him so well. That I had my husband all figured out. That I walked around feeling very pleased with myself for marrying such a thoroughly good guy. A dream guy, really." Dakota paused. "But dreams are never real. I found that out the hard way."

"But you have two great kids now. And they have a father they can rely on."

"And a nosy stepdad," Dakota said.

"Corey seems nice," Jack said.

"He is. And Chase is also, still, just a really good guy.

He's such a great dad. He's so present with the girls and is always there for them. Always. He's the opposite of an absent father. His kids truly are the most important people in the world to him, which is one of the reasons it took him so long to come out. I was only twenty-three when I got pregnant. It was hardly planned. We'd just graduated from Yale. We had big plans for our future. We weren't even married yet."

"But surely he knew he was gay by then?" Jack was teetering a bit too much on the edge of detective mode for Dakota's liking, but it was no longer painful for her to talk about this. She was sharing something fundamental about her life with Jack, increasing the intimacy between them.

"He did, but he hadn't gotten over his self-loathing about it yet. Being born a Van Ness isn't always a walk in the park. Instead of coming out the closet, he asked me to marry him. I said yes. The rest is history."

Jack shook her head. "I thought my life was complicated."

"We're all messed up in our very own unique way."

"Tell me about it." Jack scooted closer. "I see the results of that every single day on the job."

"Which brings us back to you…" Dakota found Jack's hand and laced her fingers through hers. "Tell me about the last time you fell in love."

"The last time, huh?"

"And no cop outs this time." Dakota looked deeply into her eyes again. God, those eyes. She could drown in them. They were so dark and bottomless and soulful.

"I think it was about two weeks ago when I was scrolling through Tinder." Jack's lips widened into the biggest grin.

"Oh, really?" Dakota's stomach did a silly little flip-flop. "In love?"

"Well, in lust, I guess. But who knows where it will end?"

Dakota had no choice but to end the conversation and kiss Jack with all the overwhelming tenderness that tumbled through her.

CHAPTER 28

For the last couple of weeks, the booty calls had blissfully continued, interspersed with sharing the odd meal together, but they had held off on the introduction to friends. Although Jack was curious, she wasn't exactly jumping out of her skin with excitement to meet Chase Van Ness. Nor was she on tenterhooks to organize that dinner she'd promised Marley. She just wanted to keep Dakota to herself for a while longer. She wanted to get to know her without any outside pressure.

In fact, the way things were going now—seeing each other for a longer stretch of time during the weekend and, if she was lucky and the job not too demanding, a quickie on a weeknight—was pretty perfect for Jack.

She'd even stopped tidying up compulsively before Dakota arrived. Since the daughter-walking-in-on-them incident a few weeks ago, they always met at Jack's, and Jack didn't have time to make her kitchen look squeaky clean all the time—it's not as if she used it for anything else than warming up food.

The bell rang and she buzzed Dakota in. The elevator

in Jack's building was slow, giving the butterflies in her stomach ample time to become frantic by the time Dakota arrived at her front door. Tonight was no different. As soon as Jack opened the door to Dakota, the corners of her mouth shifted upward and, invariably, her clit started throbbing with anticipation.

She ushered her inside, taking the bags Dakota was carrying from her hands, so they were free for other, more pressing things.

"I've missed you too," Dakota said after they broke from their passionate kiss hello. "But, um, can we take things a little easy tonight?"

"If by easy you mean have dinner before I drag you into the bedroom, sure. Let's eat quickly, though." Most of the time, Jack felt like a horny teenager around Dakota—another reason why she didn't want to introduce her to anyone yet. She couldn't keep her hands off her. The whole thing was still so physical, so subject to Dakota's out-of-this-world hotness, that it made Jack question her own sanity sometimes.

Dakota kept her at arm's length. Now that Jack paused to properly take in her face, she did look a little pale.

"How about we keep the bedroom just for sleeping tonight?" Dakota said.

"Are you okay?" Jack stepped closer.

"Just a bad case of woman times for which all the Tylenol in the world is no match."

"Oh, poor baby. Come here." Jack hugged Dakota as though she was the most delicate creature on earth. But that was one of the big advantages of dating—because that was what they were kind of doing now—another woman. Jack didn't need one word more of explanation —she already completely understood. "Make yourself comfortable on the couch. I'll get a heating pad for your belly." She shot Dakota a smile. "We can even eat in front of the TV, if you like." This all suddenly felt very homely —and quite different from the booty calls they excelled at.

"You're so sweet." Dakota grinned at Jack. "You're exactly what I need on a day like this." She pulled her close and Jack was delighted to find that kissing was still very much on the menu. That, and the food Dakota insisted on bringing because they couldn't always have Jack's mother's leftovers.

"Which takeout did you get?" Jack asked as Dakota settled on the couch.

"Milena's homemade pierogis," Dakota said.

"Is that in Cobble Hill?" Jack asked from the kitchen. She'd never heard of the place.

"Very much so. Milena's our housekeeper."

"Oh. Right." Dakota must have mentioned Milena, just as she'd mentioned Inez, the girls' nanny, and Johnny, Chase's driver who Dakota sometimes used as well.

"Just put them in the microwave for two minutes." Dakota pulled Jack's favorite blanket over her legs. She still looked out of place in Jack's apartment. Even when she wasn't feeling her best, Dakota still looked like a million bucks. Maybe that's how it was when you had a couple of million bucks—Jack really had no idea—in your bank account.

She warmed up the pad so Dakota could drape it over the spot where it hurt the most, then went to work on the pierogis.

"Do you want to talk or watch TV?" Jack asked when she'd settled next to Dakota, both of them with a plate of food in their laps.

"I'm sorry about tonight. I'm sure you had other plans for me." Dakota cut a pierogi in half.

"You never have to apologize for being a woman," Jack said. "You're here. You made the effort to come here despite not feeling well. I appreciate that so much." Jack tried some food. "Oh my god. Where have you been hiding Milena?"

"She mostly works for Chase," Dakota said matter-of-factly. "Hey, I was wondering…" A sparkle that hadn't previously been there appeared in her eyes. "Do you want to go away for a weekend some time? Just the two of us?"

More escalation of their dating situation, Jack thought, although she was hardly opposed to the idea of having Dakota's undivided attention for a full forty-eight hours.

"I would love that."

"We can either go to Martha's Vineyard, Napa, or Aspen if you're into that. Or just the Hamptons."

Just the Hamptons. "I take it we won't go camping upstate, then." Jack assumed that the towns Dakota had just mentioned were places where the Van Nesses had vacation homes.

"If you want to go upstate, I can ask Izzy if we can stay at her house. It's so beautiful up there."

"Your ex-family-in-law doesn't have a house there?" Jack sometimes wondered at the ex-part of the Van Nesses in Dakota's life.

"No." Dakota put down her fork. "Was I just being an entitled rich bitch?"

"I would never dream of calling you a bitch." Jack couldn't help but smile whenever she looked at Dakota. "What was your life like before you met Chase?"

"Perfectly ordinary," Dakota said. "My parents could just about afford to put me through college without me having to get any hefty student loans, if that's what you're asking."

Dakota mentioned the Van Nesses more than she did her own family—the Gallaghers. She'd even kept the Van Ness name.

"Are you close to them?" Jack asked.

"My parents live in Oregon so we don't see each other that much, but we talk on the phone regularly."

"Don't they want to spend time with their grandkids?" Jack's mother would go crazy if she didn't see her brother's kids at least once a week, although she saw them much more than that.

"They're not really into the whole billionaire scene. They don't let me pay for anything, not even flights up here," Dakota said. "They're funny about money like that."

Jack tried to imagine her own mother on the 'billionaire scene' as Dakota had called it. She'd be firmly in the Gallaghers' camp when it came to that—and so would Jack. It was yet another reason why she wasn't pushing to meet Chase. That and the prospect of having to live up to this dream of a man who'd broken Dakota's heart in so many pieces, yet still carried a part of it in his back pocket.

"So? Where would you like to go for our weekend away?" Dakota changed the conversation.

"If Izzy's house is an option, I won't say no to that." Going to Isabel Adler's house was a win-win, because Jack would get to stay at a music icon's vacation home, and she wouldn't feel as though she owed the Van Nesses anything. "Isn't she notoriously private, though? Does she let other people stay in her house?"

"I'm not just other people. Izzy loves my work and I

designed the guest house for her upstate property." Dakota smiled. "Hence, I'm always welcome there."

"Oh, really? I didn't know that was one of the perks of being an architect."

"Obviously, Izzy's also my friend. I don't get to stay at everyone's house I drew up the plans for."

"How long have you known her?"

"After Corey moved in with Chase, he befriended Leila. That was almost five years ago. Things snowballed from there."

Yet here Dakota sat, on Jack's old couch, a worn blanket covering her legs.

"If you have any grand design ideas for my apartment, do let me know," Jack joked. "Although I probably won't be able to afford your fee."

"You can always pay me in kind. You're *very* good at that."

Heat rolled through her flesh. Jack hadn't seen Dakota since Tuesday. She'd have to wait a little longer, although she was perfectly happy with kisses and cuddles. This evening was turning out very differently than she had expected, and while not necessarily a bad thing—let alone a disappointment, which wasn't possible in Dakota's company—Jack did, once again, conclude that they were very different people, indeed.

CHAPTER 29

Rain lashed against the windowpane. Jack, dressed in only panties and a barely-there tank top gazed wistfully outside. "I guess we'd better stream some *King & Prince*," she said.

They were at Izzy's house upstate and it had been raining non-stop since they'd arrived, which wasn't a huge problem, because they had other things to do than go for long walks and inhale the fresh country air. But they'd already spent the better part of the day in bed and Dakota could sense Jack was getting antsy. She was probably not used to so much time indoors.

"I thought you hated that show."

"I don't *hate*-hate it." Jack leaned against the windowsill. Sometimes, Dakota had to blink a few times when she looked at Jack, to make sure this was her real life, and she was spending all this time with another woman. "I *love*-hate it," she admitted.

Jack was funny, infinitely sexy, and a little unpredictable. They'd been dating for almost two months now and Dakota guessed it was time she started asking herself some hard questions. Because two months was not very long, but it was also not nothing. The first month, they'd pretty much spent in bed—every second of it glorious, albeit, for Dakota, also plenty confusing. Then, they'd started talking more. Asking more probing questions. Delving into each other's past. Getting to know each other beyond the booty calls. Now here they were, on their first getaway together.

"There's no other show I enjoy hate-watching more." Jack walked over to her.

"Oh yes, because you have a crush on Sadie Ireland." Sadie Ireland's character in *King & Prince* was a dark-haired, working-class, tough as nails police detective—about as opposite to Dakota a woman could be.

"I do not." Jack wrapped her arms around Dakota and nestled her head against her chest, Dakota towering over her. "I have a crush on you, in case you hadn't noticed."

"It's kind of hard to miss." Dakota curved her arms around Jack in response. "You spend so much time with me, I worry about the city's crime rate."

Jack's body shook against hers as she chuckled. "My partner's very happy these days that I don't always make him work overtime. Not to mention his wife. I think she may have a crush on you as well for this very reason."

"All these lady crushes on me," Dakota joked. "I'd better not let it go to my head." Surely Jack knew Dakota had a massive crush on her as well. She held her close, inhaled the intoxicating scent of her hair.

"You're fairly levelheaded for a rich blond knockout on whom so many have a crush."

"Fairly?" Dakota pinched Jack lightly in the side.

Jack pulled away from her. "In my humble opinion."

Maybe, instead of asking herself the harder questions, Dakota should engage some more in the very reason she had to ask those questions in the first place. She didn't want to watch *King & Prince*. Why would she watch TV cops when she had a real-life hot cop sequestered with her in this gorgeous house in the countryside?

"You know what?" Dakota pulled Jack close again. "I'm going to be the bigger person here." She made a point of stretching her neck, emphasizing the height difference between them. "I'm going to take this lying down, with you on top of me." Jack brought out her silly, zany side. Dakota never made silly jokes like that with Chase—not that she remembered, anyway. But Jack made her feel safe and special and, most of the time, like she was the most exquisite person on the planet. Jack made her feel as though she could tell the lamest joke in the world, and she'd laugh at it as though it was the best, just because it was Dakota who told it.

"I can only applaud such selfless bigheartedness." Jack took Dakota's hand and dragged her up the stairs.

———

They most certainly didn't always use a strap-on, but when they did—like now—it was always after a silent, but oddly clear agreement as to who would be strapping it on. Dakota's breath hitched in her throat at the sight of Jack with the dildo jutting out from her hips. Another thing she didn't understand about herself was why this turned her on so much—and not just her. But she was too aroused to consider this particular thought right now. She was ready to spread her legs for Jack. To let her in.

"You're so gorgeous," Jack whispered. "You got me all hard again."

Dakota wasn't sure if that was meant as a joke or not. Either way, she was too excited to laugh.

Jack guided Dakota's hand to the toy between her legs. Dakota's fingers slid through the slippery lube. The toy was hefty against her palm. Heavy and big. Jack squirted some more lube into her hand and transferred it to Dakota's sex.

The past few months, Dakota'd had to revise her views on what sex was. She'd discovered that there were things that drove her nuts that she had previously barely been aware of—like this moment. This anticipation. Jack's fingers edged along her clit and if she kept at it, Dakota would come in no time, but there was something else on the menu first—something extra delightful.

"You're so hard," Dakota played along.

"You're so wet," Jack replied. "Ready?" Jack looked into her eyes and Dakota melted, again, at the intimacy of what they had between them. That, along with the surprise of it, was already undoing her. Two months into whatever this was, Dakota couldn't stay away from Jack if she tried.

She nodded. In response, Jack kissed her gently, then guided the tip of the toy to her entrance. Slowly, she slid inside Dakota, with a tenderness that floored Dakota every single time.

The toy filled her in the most exquisite way but what was most magnificent about it, was Jack's gorgeous face hovering close to her, Jack's soft lips almost touching hers, Jack's hot breath on her cheeks.

Before her mind went blank with pleasure, Dakota wondered if she could actually fall in love with Jack—in addition to being deeply in lust with her, and how crafty she was with sex toys.

Jack kissed her neck as she drove the toy inside Dakota, as she took her to higher heights. Dakota had learned the past few weeks that Jack could climax in this position, while she needed a different kind of stimulation. But Jack liked to take her time, liked to drive Dakota plenty crazy, before flipping onto her back, enabling Dakota to ride herself to a sweltering climax on top of her —with Jack's thumb expertly manipulating her clit. It was a pleasure so out of this world, Dakota always needed ample time to get off the cloud she'd been catapulted on. Today would be no different, she could feel it all the way in her bones.

It started with a subtle vibration deep in her muscles, working its way up to her skin, as if all the tension she'd saved over the entire course of her life was being released from her body. Dakota knew it didn't make sense, because it happened over and over again—countless times since her first night with Jack—but still, that's what she compared it to. That's what it felt like. As though Jack had a secret key to the innermost parts of her body, and knew exactly how to turn it, no matter how complicated the lock. Because with Jack, Dakota felt somehow unlocked. Even though emotions between them were so complex, in bed, it was all thoroughly uncomplicated. The layers of complexity easily unfolded, painting their affair in the simple, bright light of their pure attraction to each other. Reduced to only their bodies, they made perfect sense together—they made all the sense they didn't allow themselves to make outside of the bedroom, where life was convoluted and feelings much harder to deal with.

But now, with Jack's toy inside her, and Jack's body soft

against hers, her tongue traveling along the sensitive skin of Dakota's neck, everything made perfect sense. Jack and Dakota together made perfect sense.

Ever so slowly, Jack pulled out of her, leaving Dakota momentarily empty and wanting so much more. Jack lay on her back and reached for the lube, but Dakota didn't need more lubrication. She was plenty wet. She lowered herself on Jack's rainbow-colored dildo, reveling in the sensation of being deeply penetrated. As expected, Jack touched her thumb against Dakota's clit, and then the colors of the rainbow were transported to the back of Dakota's eyelids, where technicolor fireworks exploded— echoing the fireworks going on inside her flesh.

"Fuck," Dakota groaned, as she came long and hard, her muscles emptying of all tightness, her body surrendering to Jack once more. I must be falling in love, she thought, but didn't dare say out loud, because what else could this possibly be?

CHAPTER 30

Jack gazed at Dakota. The bed in Izzy's vacation home was so big, at least two other people could fit comfortably between them, but there was no room for anything or anyone else in this giant bed. Only the two of them. And yes, it was strange that Jack was lying in this particular bed in Isabel Adler's gorgeous house, but that wasn't the strangest of all. The prize for biggest oddity in her life right now went to Jack falling in love.

Because Jack Russo didn't fall in love—nor did she usually spend her weekends in a music icon's second home. None of this was like her—and it was all Dakota's fault. She was supposed to be straight. Although Jack could hardly blame Dakota for not putting a stop to this before more feelings became involved. That was all on her. Still, she felt she had the right to ask the question.

"So…" She ran a fingertip over the graceful slope of Dakota's cheekbone. "How's that experiment working out for you? Do you have plans to draw a definite conclusion any time soon?"

"Hm." Dakota's eyes still looked a little glazed over

from the orgasm she'd just had. "I can definitely conclude that sex with a woman is never disappointing."

Warmth bloomed in Jack's chest. "Sex with *this* woman, you mean." As an expert in one-night stands, Jack knew very well that sex with a woman could be plenty disappointing. That the chemistry she thought was there upon first meeting didn't always transfer between the sheets. That her decision-making process had let her down often in the past, and still sometimes did now, after years of honing it. That any two women in bed together didn't automatically equal orgasmic fireworks, but that it was all in the combination of their personalities and any number of other factors, big and small, like the day they'd had or the last phone call they'd taken. Mostly though, Jack had learned, it came down to how much stress they held in their bodies, and how it affected their thoughts. How quickly they could let go or how desperately they clung to it. But none of that mattered when it came down to her and Dakota. None of the usual rules applied.

"You sure know how to wield a strap-on," Dakota said, a flush appearing on her alabaster cheeks.

"It took you all of a minute to get the hang of it yourself." Maybe it was because their very first night together had been so spectacular that it had grown into something much larger deep inside of them. It was a night that simply couldn't be ignored.

"Isn't it terribly heteronormative to use a strap-on?" Dakota asked, her facial expression surprisingly serious.

"It's the exact opposite," Jack said.

"How so?" Dakota trapped Jack's hand against her cheek and held it there.

"A toy is not a penis and a strap-on doesn't turn a woman into a man. It's just a pleasure device." Ah, pleasure. That was how this whole thing had started. Jack and Dakota, both in their own ways, looking for a simple night of pleasure. "Not being attracted to men doesn't equal not enjoying penetrative sex."

"But I *am* attracted to men," Dakota said matter-of-factly.

"But also to women," Jack countered.

"To *you*," Dakota replied.

Flattered though she was, Jack didn't really know what to do with that statement because it was such a red flag.

"You've gone awfully quiet," Dakota said after Jack hadn't responded for a while.

"Only because I don't really know what to say to that."

"Because you have a crush on me?" Dakota asked.

Jack nodded. "I guess." This was no longer just a case of protecting someone else from getting involved with her and potentially getting hurt, this was quickly turning into Jack opening her heart in a way she hadn't in a very long time—a way she didn't really know either.

"I'm not only attracted to you," Dakota said. "I like you. A lot. I have a crush on you too. I have feelings, too."

"Oh, fuck." Jack threw in a sigh.

"Would you rather I didn't have feelings for you?" Dakota arched up her eyebrows.

"No." She shuffled closer to Dakota and kissed her on the lips. Then she looked behind her, out of the window, to see if the rain had let up and they could go outside. It was still pouring down, but maybe that didn't matter. They were not made of sugar. People walked outside in the rain all the time—and Jack was in desperate need of some air.

"It's really hard for you to talk about this stuff, isn't it?" Dakota interlaced her fingers with Jack's.

"I usually don't have to."

"I understand it's confusing. It's confusing for me too." Dakota shot her a reassuring smile. "Life can be confusing like that. I think we both know that." She gave Jack's fingers a squeeze. "I've had a few weeks to mull this over now and, just for the record, I no longer see you as an experiment. That would be totally disrespectful. But I can only take this day-by-day. I can't make any grand statements, let alone promises. What I can do is tell you that I think about you all the time and that I want to spend as much of that time with you as possible."

"That sounds fair enough." Jack didn't want promises, nor grand statements. Maybe the real question she had to ask herself was whether she wanted to fall in love or not—and if she still had a choice in the matter. Probably not. And was that really so bad?

CHAPTER 31

"Mom! *Mooooom!*" Aubrey yelled. "You're not listening."

"What is it, sweetheart?" Dakota was distracted, that much was true.

Aubrey rolled her eyes, probably because Dakota had called her sweetheart, and that was no longer allowed according to the ever-changing rules of being a teenager.

"I don't want to stay at Granny's tonight. Why can't we just stay home?"

"You used to love sleepovers at your granny's." Chase being Eleanor Van Ness's only child, and Aubrey and Peyton her only grandkids, brought out Dakota's ex-mother-in-law's softer side. In her own way, she spoiled the kids rotten whenever they came to her house, instructing her staff to make it into the kind of event that would delight any child.

Dakota and Eleanor were of different generations and had their differences of opinion on how to raise kids and on how to live life in general, but they'd always been friendly and warm with each other—until Chase had come out of the closet.

Eleanor had summoned Dakota to her penthouse on Park Avenue and had asked Dakota, her face never more serious and stern, why she hadn't been able to stop Chase from wanting to give in to his homosexual proclivities, because wasn't that her biggest job as his wife?

Dakota had never told Chase about what his mother had said to her that day, not wanting to make everything worse than it already was. But Eleanor had never apologized to Dakota for speaking to her like that, not even after Chase married Corey, and the Van Nesses resumed their lives as if nothing ever happened. Dakota had never forgiven Eleanor for kicking her when she was down, no matter how much or little she understood the hurt her son was causing. Dakota was the biggest recipient of it, and anything but the cause.

"Is your girlfriend coming over?" Peyton asked matter-of-factly. "Is that why we can't be here?"

Aubrey rolled her eyes again. "We promise to stay upstairs at Dad's. Okay?" she said it as though it was a done deal already, and Dakota hadn't even confirmed yet that Jack was coming over. "I don't see why we need to be punished for you having a girlfriend."

"Since when is staying at Granny's a punishment? She loves to spend time with you."

"She takes away our phones as soon as we arrive," Peyton said. "It's just not fair."

"And we're not even allowed to watch TV. Last time, we had to bake cookies!"

"Oh, wow," Dakota said. "The horror."

"We're too old for that s—" Peyton just caught herself. "Mom, come on," she continued unperturbed. "We just want to sleep in our own beds, in our own house. Is that really too much to ask?"

"If you're going to stay at your dad's, you have to discuss this with him." Dakota took the cowardly road out.

"But it'll be easier if you've already agreed." Peyton painted on a wide grin—practiced to manipulate her parents for years.

"Your granny's going to be upset if you don't show up."

Clearly this was not an argument to persuade her kids. It was even clearer that what they really wanted was an unsupervised evening home alone, although all three of their parents could go upstairs at any time to check on them. There wouldn't be any wild parties with friends, just the two of them on their phones all night long, doing whatever they did without adult supervision.

"If it's okay with your dad, it's fine with me," Dakota acquiesced. It was hardly the best parenting, but she didn't want to listen to their pleas for the rest of the afternoon, not when she had to prepare for Jack coming to dinner, and introducing her to Chase.

"Thank you so much, Mom." The girls wrapped her in a hug Dakota hadn't seen coming.

"We want you to find someone as well, you know," Peyton said, surprising Dakota even more. "Like Dad has."

"Thanks." Funny how the girls could gang up on her one moment and be all sweet and lovely the next.

"Is she coming tonight? Is that why you're so tense?" Aubrey asked. *She.* Aubrey said it as though it was the most normal thing in the world.

"Yes," Dakota confirmed. "I'm introducing her to your dad." Dakota believed she'd hidden her nerves from her daughters, but kids picked up on every little thing that was out of the ordinary—no mean feat when they were glued to their phone most of the time. Her girls would make excellent detectives.

"Why does she need to meet Dad?" Aubrey asked. She furrowed her brow. "Because it's getting serious? Like when he introduced you to Corey?"

Dakota could barely imagine Jack meeting her kids, let alone something like that.

"No, darling. Your dad's just curious, that's all." Things with Jack had certainly gotten more serious than the experiment it had started as, but Dakota wasn't going to tell her children that. It was bad enough they knew Jack existed in the first place. In a perfect world, the girls wouldn't have a clue yet, but the world was hardly perfect —and her girls weren't born yesterday. And then Aubrey had walked in on her and Jack in bed.

"Let's go ask him." Peyton tugged at her sister's sleeve.

"Wait," Aubrey said, then fixed her gaze on her mother. "When do we get to meet her, like, properly? I'm curious too."

A nervous chuckle escaped Dakota's mouth. "I don't know, darling," she said, truthfully. "If and when the time is right."

CHAPTER 32

Jack knew what Chase Van Ness looked like—his picture was all over the internet—and she'd googled his life and ancestry extensively. He held a law degree from Yale and an MBA from Columbia. He'd taken over as CEO of Van Ness Holdings four years ago. He wasn't just dashing, but intelligent and, obviously, a billionaire as well. He was a catch in every single way and Jack could understand why a straight girl like Dakota would have fallen for him like a ton of bricks. She could even kind of imagine what it must have felt like for Dakota to have been Chase Van Ness's chosen one. Although it was all a lie. Yet, here they sat together, in this stunning living room with its couches that probably had cushions costing more than Jack's entire wardrobe—shoes included—and its artwork that was more valuable than Jack's apartment. But Chase was the reason why Jack was breaking one of her rules again—the first time was when she'd met some of Dakota's friends a few weeks ago. But she had to see how Dakota and Chase interacted. She had to find out what was the glue that kept them together, apart from their children.

Chase towered over Jack, his perfectly graying blond hair nearly falling into his eyes, but trimmed just so it didn't.

"I'm not going to lie." Chase sent Jack a wide smile. "Never in a million years did I see this coming."

Jack would love to get him alone and subject him to some of her more advanced interrogation techniques. Because how could a man who had promised a woman the world, but turned out to be nothing more than an emotional fraud, still hold such sway over her? Dakota wasn't stupid or naive, but she was clearly under the influence of something. Jack's best guess was money, but maybe there was something else at play as well. She was here to find out.

"Neither did I," Jack replied—not a word of it a lie. Jack had come here with an open mind. She didn't want to pre-judge Chase, because he still meant so much to Dakota. She liked Corey, who didn't exactly strike her as an idiot either. A memory flashed through her mind of their very first date, when Dakota had, jokingly, admitted she'd been fruitlessly scouring Tinder for a replica of her gay ex-husband. It was much too late for Jack to heed that warning now, although, in hindsight, it should have been another red flag. At the time, Jack had just thought it was funny. Something to chitchat about over a glass of wine on a date.

Corey's phone buzzed. With an exasperated sigh, he pulled it out of his pocket. "The girls keep texting me."

"What do they want?" There was a slight hint of panic in Dakota's voice.

"Don't worry," Corey assured her. "I'll deal with them."

"They successfully manipulated us," Chase said, "into letting them stay home alone upstairs instead of going to my mother's."

Us? Did he mean him and Dakota? Or him and Corey? Or all three of them? Jack had only been here fifteen minutes but the family dynamics of this weird throuple were already giving her a headache. She sipped from her champagne and took a deep breath.

"I thought they had a nanny," Jack blurted out.

"They're thirteen. They don't want a babysitter on a Saturday night any longer," Chase said as though that was the most logical thing in the world.

"I'm going upstairs for a minute. Have a much-needed chat with our little darlings." Corey rose. "Please excuse me, Jack." He shot her a quick wink that Jack didn't know how to interpret. Oh, boy. All she could do was take another sip of champagne.

A loud beep came from somewhere in the house. Dakota rose. "My kitchen timer. I'll be right back."

"Is she actually cooking dinner?" Jack was starting to believe she had landed in an alternative reality.

"Oh, no." Chase chuckled. "Milena prepared us a feast. All we have to do is keep it warm and pretend we made it ourselves."

Again with the *we*. Jack wasn't only breaking the biggest rule she'd lived by all her adult life—no emotional entanglements—she'd also, apparently, got herself involved in some sort of semi-platonic three-way relationship.

"So, you and Dakota, huh?" Chase smirked at her. "Why the hell not?"

For once, Jack wanted her phone to ring with a work emergency on a Saturday night. Her discomfort grew by the minute. Not so much because of how Dakota, Chase, and Corey interacted with each other—what had she expected? For them to be at each other's throats in front of her?—but because of how much she had lied to herself. She was the fool here.

Just like Dakota had been lured into a relationship with Chase all those years ago, Jack had let herself be lured into something with Dakota. Against her better judgement. She'd been blinded by Dakota's beauty, all her defenses torn down by their chemistry between the sheets. But this was not what Jack wanted. In fact, to sit face-to-face with the person who had hurt the woman she might fall in love with—might very well already be in love with —the most and, worst of all, be somehow judged by him, was the very last thing Jack wanted.

"We can all be merrily gay together," Chase said.

Jack knew he was only saying it to make conversation, yet it irked her. This whole setup annoyed her. She didn't belong here. Most of all, she didn't have to be here.

Corey barged back into the room. "They're being a nightmare. I don't know what's gotten into them."

"Are they all right?" Chase asked.

"They're agitated like when they were little and had too much sugar—"

"Please excuse me." Jack went to the bathroom with a plan. She stopped by the kitchen to get a glimpse of Dakota. She was studying something on the panel of the oven. Jack felt a twinge of remorse already for what she was about to do. Maybe—and it was a huge maybe—if it was just Dakota, without the twin daughters and live-in ex-husband, they could be something, although Jack didn't know what exactly. Jack didn't know anything, except that the time had come to put a stop to this. She should never have let it come this far, but that was another lesson learned—a painful one she wouldn't easily forget.

Jack went into the bathroom and texted Nico, asking him to call her as soon as possible, feigning an emergency.

When Jack emerged from the bathroom, Dakota had joined Chase and Corey again in the living room and they were chatting. A silence fell when Jack walked in—they were talking about her, then.

Dakota beamed her a smile—the kind that would almost make Jack text Nico again and call the whole thing off. What Dakota hadn't yet done, apart from a quick kiss on the cheek upon arrival, was engage in any display of affection with Jack in front of her ex-husband. Something she hadn't had a problem with in front of her other friends.

A noise in the stairwell startled them. In the hallway, a door busted open. Seconds later, Dakota's daughters appeared in the living room. Just then, Jack's phone rang. Right on time, Jack thought, as she turned away from the hubbub and took Nico's fake emergency call. Jack could always count on her partner.

———

"I'm ghosting her," Jack admitted. "I want out."

Nico shook his head. "I'm just a simple middle-aged cis-het white guy, so I obviously don't get it."

They both stared at Jack's phone, lying between them —like the most damning piece of evidence—on the Formica table of the diner. "But as far as I know, ghosting someone is heavily frowned upon," Nico said.

Despite Dakota's pleas, Jack hadn't returned to her house after tending to her pretend emergency. The last message she'd sent her had been on Sunday morning, saying she'd been up all night working and she needed to catch up on sleep before dinner with her mother. It was a blatant lie and not very nice, but Jack wasn't ready for the confrontation yet. She was deflated and embarrassed and felt like a complete idiot.

"What happened?" Nico asked. "Did the Van Nesses treat you badly?"

Jack shook her head. Nothing much had happened, except that, somehow, she'd landed with her feet back firmly on the ground for the first time since laying eyes on Dakota that fateful Saturday night a few months ago.

"I got a glimpse of the kind of life I absolutely don't want. Ex-husbands. Teenagers. So many blurred boundaries." Jack huffed out some air. "All I wanted was a bit of fun with a hot lady. Nothing serious. Which it says in black-and-white on my Tinder profile." She shrugged. "I got a little carried away, but I'm back to myself now. I don't need all this. I like a simple life." Marley would be pleased. "I certainly don't want to get involved with the Van Nesses."

"That bad, huh?"

"It's not them, per se." Jack had barely spent any time with Chase. "It's just not a good match." If anything, Jack should feel vindicated, relieved even, that she'd done right by herself by living by her rules, no matter what anyone else thought about them.

Her life; her rules. It had been so easy all these years, until Dakota came along, with her complicated life and history. Yet, Jack didn't feel an ounce of relief. She did know that she had to face Dakota sooner rather than later.

She would ignore both her messages and calls for today, but then she'd need to have *the talk*. She'd have to find the words to explain how sitting in the same room as Chase had freaked her out so much, all she'd wanted to do was flee the situation like a coward. Because Jack had been a coward, but sometimes that was the only option.

"You owe me big time, partner." Nico grinned at her.

"Thanks for having my back." Jack nodded. "Drinks on me tonight."

CHAPTER 33

"I'm beginning to think that was not a real work call." Dakota paced through Jamie and Mac's living room. "Why else would she refuse to speak to me for this long?"

"Hey." Jamie stood in front of Dakota and put her hands on her shoulders. "Take a breath. You're getting yourself all worked up."

"I don't know what I've done wrong." Dakota took that recommended breath, but it didn't help. "At least she had the courtesy to let me know she's okay. At first, when she didn't get back to me, I thought something had happened to her on the job." She blew out more air through her nostrils. "I know I need to get a handle on myself, but it's hard when you don't have a clue of what's going on."

"Did something happen with Chase?"

Dakota shook her head. "Jack was barely there for half an hour before she got called away." At least the previous time that had happened, she'd come back—and they'd had an amazing night together. "According to Chase, they hardly spoke."

With the girls rushing in, Dakota hadn't been able to say a proper goodbye to Jack. One moment, they were sitting comfortably in the lounge, about to start the evening; the next, it was all chaos, and then Jack was gone.

"You need to speak to her," Jamie said.

"It's kind of hard when the other party doesn't want to speak to you."

"How about you try calling her one last time and if she still doesn't answer or get back to you within a reasonable time frame, you show up at her door," Jamie suggested. "Come on." She held out her hand to Dakota and ushered her to the kitchen island, where she sat her down. Jamie poured Dakota some water. "Do you want me to stay while you make the call? Or do you want some privacy?"

"Stay, please." Dakota glanced at her phone, then at Jamie. "This is not how I had expected this experiment to end," she said, mostly to postpone that sinking feeling she got when she called Jack and she didn't pick up.

"You clearly have feelings for her," Jamie said, her voice soft and warm. "That's a good thing. It really is."

Dakota scoffed. "Not if this is how my feelings make me feel."

"Talk to her," Jamie repeated.

Her friend was right. Dakota dialed Jack's number. As the phone beeped in her ear, her heart hammered in her chest. Jamie was also right about that other thing—Dakota did have feelings for Jack. For another woman, who refused to pick up the phone when she called.

Dakota was about to hang up, when she heard a click, followed by Jack saying, "Hey."

Dakota was so stumped by Jack actually answering

I HOPE THAT I DON'T FALL IN LOVE WITH YOU

that, for a second or two, she didn't know what to say. Jamie put a hand on her arm, nudging Dakota in action.

"Can we talk, please?" Dakota said.

"Yes," Jack said matter-of-factly. "We should talk."

"What's going on, Jack?" Dakota couldn't help herself. She'd gone over every minute of Jack's visit to her house last Saturday, trying to find a reason for Jack's behavior afterward, but she hadn't found any. Granted, the girls barging in like that was a bit much, but it still wasn't a reason for Jack to not be in touch. If it bothered her, she could just say so.

"Let's go for a walk," Jack suggested. "I can be in Prospect Park in an hour."

A walk? That was new. Dakota felt as though she had to take what she could get, that she had to grab whatever little Jack was willing to give.

"I'll be there."

"Thank you," Jack said, then hung up.

———

Jack didn't want to meet Dakota in private because she was pretty sure that if there was no one around, all she'd want to do was kiss her instead of break up with her. She'd been pacing alongside the lake for the past ten minutes, trying to find the right words to tell Dakota they should stop seeing each other. It was difficult because one of the biggest perks of not doing relationships was the total absence of breakups in Jack's life. All Jack knew about breaking up with someone, she knew from TV—and if romantic TV was anything like cop shows, it wasn't much like real life.

From the corner of her eye, she spotted a tall, elegant

figure in a bright red coat heading toward her. Jack's stomach clenched because even though she couldn't see the person's face, Jack just knew it was Dakota. She had to stop herself from rushing over to her and wrapping her arms around her. That was not why she was here—quite the opposite.

Dakota's strides were much longer than Jack's and Jack had barely moved when Dakota walked up to her. Her hair was slicked back in that way that made her look so irresistible, but her eyes looked sad, and her face weary.

"Hey." Did you still kiss someone you were about to split up with? Once again, Jack had no idea.

Dakota made the decision for them by keeping her distance. "Hi." Her voice was cold, and as distant as the few yards between them felt.

"I owe you an apology for how I handled things," Jack blurted out. "I know that and I am really sorry."

"Handled what exactly?" Dakota asked, stuffing her hands deep into her coat pockets. "I don't know what happened or what's going on. Please, enlighten me."

"Shall we walk?" Jack couldn't look Dakota in the eye while doing this.

"Jack, please. I'm worried. What's going on?" Dakota didn't budge.

"Last Saturday at your house, I totally freaked out." Jack could only tell the truth. "To see you with Chase and Corey, talking about your kids like that." Until then, Dakota's kids had not been much more than an abstract notion to Jack—apart from that time one of her daughters had walked in on them, an event Jack had eagerly pushed to the outer regions of her mind. "It all of a sudden hit me that..." Jack paused. "That's just not what I do. It's not what I want. It has nothing to do with you. I'm crazy about you, but I can't deal with all the other stuff. It's too much."

"You drew that conclusion after half an hour at my place?" Dakota's voice was defiant.

"You and Chase..." Jack shuffled her weight from one foot to the other. "For the life of me, I just don't get it."

"I'm sorry you can't understand that the father of my kids is also one of my best friends."

"Can we go back to the beginning of all this, please? That night at the bar, when we both were very clear about what we wanted to get out of our date." Jack brought a hand to her chest. "It's my bad for, um, believing it could be more than that. I'm sorry if I led you on. I really am."

"Are you serious?" Dakota towered over her. "Are you really walking away from this because of... I don't even know. Because you don't like Chase?"

"I never wanted this. Neither did you, if I remember correctly."

"Then what are we doing here? Why are we standing here right now? Saying all these things?"

"Do you really want to bring me into your life?" Jack asked.

"That's what I was trying to do, before you just left." She spat out the words. "Was that even a real work call you got?"

Jack waved off Dakota's question. She didn't want to reply because she was guilty as charged. "We are so different, you and me. We could drag this out a little longer, but to what end?"

Dakota blinked slowly, her eyes filling with tears. Oh, fuck. Jack most certainly didn't know how to deal with that kind of escalation. In her job, she comforted crying people often enough, but in her personal life, it was not something she had to deal with.

Dakota wiped a tear from her face. "Because we fell in love." Her voice was nothing more than a cracked whisper, yet Jack heard her loud and clear.

"I'm sorry," Jack whispered back. "This is on me. I'm not capable of this. I tried, but…" She shook her head, then looked away from Dakota. That grimace on her face was too much to bear.

"I can only hope not all NYPD officers are cowards like you." Dakota's voice had regained some of its strength and her words cut Jack like the sharpest knife. "Goodbye." Dakota turned on her heels and walked away.

CHAPTER 34

"The worst part of it is that I know she's in love with me. She told me, although she didn't have to. I felt it and, for a minute there, it was so wonderful." Dakota sucked on the straw of the Aperol spritz Chase had made her.

"I'm so sorry," Chase said.

"You should be. It's all your fault."

"I'll take the blame if that's what you need right now." Chase could be so infuriatingly good-natured.

"Seriously though… Don't you ever wonder about our arrangement? That we still live in the same house?"

"Why wouldn't we? If we get along like we do?"

"Perhaps I can't see it because I'm in it, but maybe this isn't how it's supposed to be."

"Would you rather we argued all the time about how to raise the girls?"

"It's easy for you to say. You have everything you could possibly need, including an ex-wife at your beck and call."

"Do you feel like you're at my 'beck and call'?" He

curled his fingers into air quotes. "Because if you do, then I agree we have a problem."

"You have Corey and that's the big difference between us."

"You can have a Corey too."

"Oh, please. This is not the time to be condescending." Dakota waved her hand about. "How can this whole setup we've got going on not scare off other people?"

"You're right." That was the first surprising thing Chase had said all day. "It scared Corey off at first as well."

"It did?" Dakota had known Corey for years and he'd never told her about that.

"Of course it did, Dax. It's an intimidating situation. *You* can be rather intimidating."

"Me? Intimidating?" Dakota scoffed, then shook her head. "I don't think so."

Chase tilted his chin and gave her a look. "Surely you know that about yourself. Have you walked into any room lately? Have you noticed how all heads turn or are you that used to it by now?"

"Are you?"

Chase was being such a man about this.

"It's not the same," Chase said.

"What are we even talking about?"

"All I'm trying to say is that maybe Jack's got a teeny tiny little point." Another surprise. What was happening? "Despite her best intentions, she fell for you. You're hard not to fall for."

"Oh, no. Don't go there." Dakota did not need to hear how Chase had fallen for her as well, even though he was gay. That was the last thing she wanted to be reminded of right now.

"Fine. Got it. But we agree that Jack fell for you even though she doesn't do relationships because… remind me again?"

"Because…" Dakota buried her face in her hands. "Her dad, also a cop, died in the line of duty when Jack was seventeen and she doesn't want anyone she loves to be at risk of experiencing that kind of devastating loss."

"What?" Chase did a double take. "You didn't tell me that."

"I'm not sure I was supposed to tell anyone about that." Jack had told her this very private fact about herself in confidence.

"Poor Jack. She was only seventeen?" Chase's father had died not long before he came out of the closet—two events that were, in Dakota's opinion, very much related.

Dakota nodded.

"Damn. That's tough." He nodded as though he understood Jack better.

"I wasn't supposed to fall for her either."

"Yet you did." Chase fixed his gaze on her.

"I did," Dakota admitted before averting her eyes. "It doesn't even bother me that she's a woman." That probably came out all wrong. "I hadn't expected it. It really did start as kind of a joke with Jamie and Mac, but it all just snowballed from there." She looked at Chase again. "Am I bisexual now, or what?"

"That's not a question anyone else can answer for you. Only you know how you feel."

"The prospect of doing this all over again with another woman who isn't Jack doesn't exactly excite me."

"That's only normal because you're totally smitten."

Dakota huffed out some air. "I so am, but she doesn't want to be with me." She added another sigh. "It's not just you and our living arrangement. It's the girls as well. Jack doesn't want all of that in her life." Her shoulders sagged with deflation.

"I'm sorry, Dax." He flashed her a smile. "We could always send them to boarding school."

"Yeah right. You can hardly go a day without them."

"Not just me."

"No." Dakota attempted a smile. She might have lost whatever she and Jack might have become, but she still had—and would always have—what was most important to her. Her beautiful daughters. But it somehow felt like Dakota had lost something she didn't have to lose. Because of how she and Jack had been together. Still, she could say that about Chase as well, and losing him had also been inevitable—at least in the role of her husband.

"Is there anything I can do to make this better?" Chase asked while cupping her hands.

"There are some things that money just can't fix," Dakota said.

"Who knew?" Chase repeated an inside joke they'd had between them for decades.

"Fuck." Dakota bit back a tear. She freed her hands from Chase's grasp so she could have a big gulp of her drink. "I guess you'd better make me another one of these."

"Your wish is my command, Mama." Before he made her another cocktail, Chase slid off his chair, and wrapped his arms warmly around Dakota's shoulders. Although comforting, Chase's wasn't the hug Dakota wanted—or needed—most.

CHAPTER 35

"To what do I owe this rare but welcome privilege?" Jack's mother said as she pulled her into a hug.

"Beats me." Jack grinned at her mom as she let go, although she could stay in her embrace a good while longer. Maybe that's why she'd inadvertently ended up at her mother's place in Staten Island. Because certain hurts can only be soothed by a parent's presence. Marley's would have been the obvious shoulder to cry on, but Jack could do without a possible lecture on the Van Nesses and their one-percent-ness. "What's cooking?" Even though she'd turned up at her mother's out of the blue on a Wednesday evening, Jack wasn't the type to spill her guts. Just being here, sharing a meal with her mom, was enough.

Despite going through the worst, the Russos weren't a family who dissected their innermost feelings with each other. They ate, had a glass of wine, and joked around together. It was how they did things after Jack's dad had so suddenly passed away, after the first few years of absorbing the shock of his unexpected absence, and the ramifications it had on their lives. Even though they would forever miss an integral piece of their family's unique puzzle, simply spending time together was comforting.

"Leftovers from yesterday," Jack's mom said. "If I'd known my only daughter would be gracing me with her presence, I'd have made something special."

"Leftovers are fine." Jack wasn't very hungry. "How are you, Mom?"

While she poured them a glass of excellent Primitivo, her mother rattled on about a day trip to Atlantic City she'd been on with her friends. Jack did her best to listen, to take in the words and process them, but her brain was still too full of Dakota to give her mother the attention she deserved. She nodded and tried to give the impression of listening while images of Dakota flashed through her mind. And the last words she had spoken to Jack, calling her a coward. She'd been right about that.

"What's going on with you? Did something happen at work?" her mom asked.

Jack shook her head. "Work's fine. Nico's a pain in the ass, as usual," she replied, just to say something.

"Then why are you sitting here, staring into space, not listening to a word I'm saying?" Her mom slanted her head. "Don't contradict me because I just said your brother has joined Donald Trump's legal team and you didn't bat an eyelid."

"Excuse me? Matty's doing what?"

"It's not true, obviously. I just said it to test if you were listening."

"Thank fuck!" Jack exhaled dramatically.

"Language, please." Eyebrows arched all the way up, her mother gave her a faux death stare.

"Sorry, Mom. For swearing *and* for not listening. I just —" Oh no. Jack's eyes became itchy. Her throat swelled. What was happening? She hadn't come here to cry. She'd just come to be with her mother and soak up some of her unconditional motherly love. She tried to take a deep breath, hoping it would magically make the tears that were threatening to spill over disappear. Unfortunately, the body didn't work like that, and Jack's eyes grew moist. She hadn't cried in front of her mother since her father had died. She quickly wiped the tears away. "Sorry. Must be hormones."

"Hey, come on." Her mother put a hand on Jack's elbow and it was enough to completely unlock the flood-gates—surprising Jack as much as her mother. Where did these tears come from? What had she suddenly turned into? One of those women who foolishly cried over a one-night stand? But Dakota was hardly a one-night stand. And Jack was the one who had ended their affair. She had no right to cry over something she'd caused herself. But as much as she tried to get herself together, and stop those damned tears from drenching her cheeks, she simply couldn't keep from sobbing.

Her mother reached for a roll of paper towels on the countertop and handed it to Jack. She didn't say anything, just kept her hand on Jack's arm, and let her cry for as long as she needed to in silence.

Eventually, after what felt like hours, but was really only a few minutes, the tears dried up. Jack blew her nose and wiped her eyes. If she was going to cry like this, she should have stayed in her apartment. But this was unforeseen. So much was unforeseen.

"You don't have to tell me what's going on if you don't want to, but I do need to know that you're okay. That it's not a medical issue or anything like that." Her mother's voice trembled.

"It's nothing like that. It's something really silly. Nothing for you to worry about."

"Doesn't look very silly to me, sweetheart." She gave Jack's elbow one last squeeze before retracting her hand.

"It's this woman. I met someone and it's all turned to shit. That's all."

"That's all, huh?"

"Yeah." Jack blew her nose again. "I should be over it soon enough."

"Did she break your heart?"

Jack shook her head. "Of course not. I would never let…" Let that happen? *Yeah right.*

"Jackie, no matter how hard you try to pretend otherwise, you have a heart, too. A heart that can be broken."

"No, Mom, you don't get it. I broke up with her."

"Looks to me as if that was the very last thing you wanted to do."

"I had no choice. I don't want…" Jack made a dismissive gesture with her hand. "All of that."

"All of what?" her mom asked, as though she had suddenly procured a police badge and was trying to pry the truth out of a suspect.

"She has kids and an ex-husband—a *gay* ex-husband, by the way—she's still too involved with." Jack huffed out some air. "You know that's not what I want. I've told you a thousand times."

"What you tell me and what I conclude from that are two very different things."

"What do you mean?"

Her mother squared her shoulders and cleared her throat. "Do you really want me to tell you?"

Jack's eyes grew wide. "Why wouldn't I want that?"

Her mother scoffed. "Because you've always made it clear to me that your love life, or lack thereof, is none of my business. I've respected that. It's your life. You do whatever you want. But when you show up at my door more upset than I've seen you in years, perhaps I can say something that you've never allowed me to say."

"Please, be my guest." Jack braced herself.

"Do you know what made your father happiest of all?"

Jack's gut clenched. Her mother was going down the daddy-route—straight in for the kill.

"You and your brother. His family. Me. The four of us together. It was what made his life special. Love made his life extraordinary every single day. Not being a cop, but coming home to his family. *That* was everything to him." She paused. "Your father dying has left a deep mark on you, but it's been twenty years, Jackie. You've almost got twenty years on the job yourself and nothing has happened to you."

"Doesn't mean it can't happen tomorrow." Jack swallowed a lump out of her throat.

"Your father never let his life depend on a 'what if.' Not for a single minute. How I wish you could see that. But I know you're scared. You've been petrified for so long, it has become a part of you. It's who you are."

Jack pursed her lips while trying to digest her mother's unusual candor. "What I don't get is, if family was the most important thing to Dad, why he didn't get another, far less dangerous job. A job where you're not expected to run toward danger every single day."

"I could say the same of you. Being a police officer

was in his DNA. You're the last person I'd need to spell that out to."

"Of course, I'm scared, Mom," Jack admitted.

"Or maybe you think you're scared of one thing, but you're actually scared of something else." Her mother bit her bottom lip, a sure sign she was going in for another home truth. "Because after what happened to your father, you still chose to go to the academy, to become a cop. You're not afraid to go out there every day, because you know, in your heart, that the actual risk of something happening to you is very small."

"Becoming a cop was *my* choice, just as living life according to my rules is *my* choice. I don't want to be with someone to have them live in fear every day, wondering whether I'll make it home from my shift in one piece."

"What about me? What about my fear?"

"You're my mother."

"Exactly. I've never had a choice, nor did I stand in the way of you becoming a cop because I know what it means to you, just as I know what it meant to your dad. But believe me, the first couple of years when you were a beat cop, I was terrified. I always feared the worst when the phone rang. But nothing happened. And I got used to it."

"I'm sorry, Mom." There was nothing else Jack could say.

"You don't have to apologize to me for who you are. I just wish you could also have what made your father so happy, that you wouldn't stubbornly stick to all those rules you made to protect something that doesn't even exist, because you won't let it." While she sighed, a small smile appeared on her mother's face. "The past can never be undone. What's done is done. But we can change how we deal with the past, how we let it affect our life right now.

You don't have to stay the same for the rest of your life. Things change. We meet certain people who knock us sideways. People whom it's worth changing for." Her mother reached for Jack's hand. "Who doesn't want a life with more love in it?"

Jack shook her head. "I hear you, Mom, but... I don't think I can do it. Because in my life, I've already been through the worst. And in my head, I go through the worst every single day."

"If that's the case, it's my job as your mother to tell you that's no way to live. That kind of constant anxiety will eat you up from the inside."

Jack couldn't tell her mother that she had ways of breaking the cycle of anxiety she got trapped in. She had Tinder and one-night stands and sex with hot ladies. "It doesn't," she just said. "I have my own ways of coping."

"That may be so, but..." Her mother let go of her hand. "You fell in love with this woman regardless. What's her name?"

"Dakota," Jack said, and saying her name instantly softened something inside her.

"She has kids?"

"Thirteen-year-old twin girls," Jack said on a sigh.

"What about the gay ex-husband you mentioned?" Her mother chuckled, lightening the mood.

"Chase Van Ness," Jack said slowly, as though it explained everything.

Her mother's eyes grew wide. Gina Russo being lost for words was not an everyday occurrence, and it made her silence all the more deafening. Jack's mother had to take a sip of wine before she could speak again.

"You picked up Dakota Van Ness on one of your dating apps and then you fell in love with her?" She said it as though she was reading this information from a sheet of paper in front of her. "What about, um, Dakota? You said you broke it off with her? Does that mean she's in love with you, too?"

Jack shrugged, as though it was the most normal thing in the world to have a Van Ness-adjacent woman have a crush on her.

"My god." Her mother took another sip of wine.

"Do you regret that little speech you just gave me now you know who I'm so cut up about?"

"Of course not. I just wasn't expecting that."

"Sorry, Mom. That sounded so unkind after everything you just said. I appreciate you telling me those things about Dad," Jack said. "I really do."

"Thank you," her mother said matter-of-factly. She was clearly still processing the revelation of Jack's object of affection's name and affiliation. "How long did you date her?"

"About two months," Jack said, not adding that she'd met Isabel Adler along the way—and stayed at her opulent vacation home upstate.

"Two months, huh," her mom murmured. "You must really like her." She gave a short shake of the head. "What was it like being in that world for a couple of months?"

"I didn't spend much time in Dakota's world. We mainly met at my place. And it's not her being a Van Ness, by former marriage, that I have an issue with. The ex-husband lives upstairs from her in the same house. The girls go from their father's to their mother's all the time. Chase has a husband who's all up in Dakota's business as well. It's a madhouse, as far as I'm concerned, Mom. They're all so close. It's not… normal."

"According to you."

"I've seen a thing or two on the job." Jack just shook her head.

"What's normal, though?" Her mother leaned back in her chair. "What's normal to you might be completely abnormal to someone else. You know that."

"It's not normal to me and I don't want any part of it."

"All I know, Jackie, is that you're not the type of daughter to come crying to your mother. Dakota must mean a lot to you for you to break down like that.

"It was hardly a breakdown. Just a couple of tears for a few minutes as I'm trying to come to terms with it. Nothing more than that."

"If you say so."

"I say so," Jack said, more than ready to talk about something else.

"You could be rich." Her mother shot her a grin.

Jack grinned back, because she could do with a laugh. But her eyes were still itchy and her throat still swollen from stifling tears. She would need some more time to get over Dakota Van Ness.

Her mother was, perhaps, right about something else as well. That for someone so fearless, Jack was awfully scared of certain things.

CHAPTER 36

D akota had quit working for Van Ness Holdings after her divorce. She now ran a small firm specializing in luxury residential architecture, which made for a lot less red tape—and hassle, in general—with the city. Gigantic property development projects were a thing of the past, except for today. Because Chase had asked and while Dakota had quit VNH easily, without giving her former employers—and in-laws—an explanation she didn't owe them anyway, she still had too hard a time saying no to Chase when he asked her for a favor, because 'no one currently working at VNH had an eye like her.'

Dakota had another appointment in less than an hour. She rushed into the construction site trailer, looking for the latest blueprint revisions before inspecting—with her 'special eye'—the latest massive VNH build. Stacks of large blueprint sheets covered every surface of the cramped office.

Balancing two hefty binders in her arms, she navigated through the clutter with urgency, her eyes scanning the mess, when her foot snagged on something on the floor.

Dakota stumbled, trying to regain her balance, but her heel skidded across a loose sheet of blueprint and her foot slipped forward. Her ankle rolled painfully as she crashed to the ground amid the scattered papers.

Dakota's lower leg hit something incredibly hard. She heard a chilling snap as her leg buckled beneath her. A searing pain shot through her limb. She cried out in agony, knowing instantly that something was very wrong.

The contractor ran into the trailer. Dakota sat on the floor. She looked down at her leg. She saw blood and protruding bone. She felt queasy at the sight of the bone jutting out at an unnatural angle through the skin. Fuck. It hurt so much, she nearly passed out from the pain.

"I'm calling an ambulance," she heard the contractor say. "Don't move."

Fucking Chase. What kind of site was VNH running here? Whatever happened to strict tidiness and safety measures being put in place to prevent stupid accidents like this?

"The ambulance is coming." The contractor crouched next to her. "Hang in there, Miss Van Ness." Miss Van Ness? Argh. If she wasn't in such agony, she'd give him a piece of her mind—an ugly one. A siren sounded outside. A bit quick for the ambulance to arrive, but it made Dakota think of Jack.

"Call Chase," she said through gritted teeth. It was still a reflex to call Chase when something happened—and Dakota could hardly contact Jack.

"Of course." The contractor—Dakota didn't even know his name—looked down at her. "I'm so sorry about this, Miss Van Ness. I was in the process of tidying up, making things look spic-and-span for your visit. I must have got the time of your arrival wrong."

He was babbling—and possibly worried about getting sued.

Dakota's leg throbbed like hell. She was afraid to really look at the damage—she didn't have to examine it closely to know it was really bad.

"Just call Chase. Tell him what happened and have him meet me at the hospital." If it weren't for Chase, Dakota wouldn't even be at this site—let alone lying on the floor with what very much looked like a broken leg.

———

Dakota blinked her eyes open. Her head was fuzzy and her entire body felt like it was wrapped in the softest cotton. The painkillers were doing their job. She tried to look at her leg, but she could barely move.

"Hey." She recognized Chase's voice. "You had surgery," he said. "It went well."

It went well? How dare he say that? But Dakota was too tired to be furious right now. Her muscles had no strength. Her body didn't feel like it belonged to her.

"Wh-where are the girls?" she whispered.

"With my mother," Chase said. "Corey's with them, as well."

"I want to see them." Dakota's mouth was so dry, she could barely speak.

"Absolutely. I promised I'd let them know as soon as you were awake." He put a hand on her arm. "I'll text them right away."

While Chase was busy on his phone, Dakota let the memories of what happened rush back. That stupid fall—who slips on a sheet of paper at a building site? The ambulance. The fracture to her tibia the paramedics talked about. Her arrival at Mount Sinai was a blur. As far as Dakota remembered, she'd had surgery almost straight-away, which might be the general anesthesia playing tricks on her memory, or simply how Van Nesses were treated at this hospital.

"Corey's bringing the girls over. It's late and they won't be allowed to stay long, just so you know. You have to rest." He held up a plastic cup. "The nurse said you're only allowed ice chips for now. Do you want some?"

Dakota shook her head. "How bad is my leg?"

"It's going to be okay," Chase said.

"Just tell me." Dakota was becoming more alert and aware of her reduced mobility. She glanced down at a monstrous contraption around her right leg.

"You have a compound fracture of your shinbone. They'll have to keep you here for a few days to keep an eye on the wound, but we'll get you home and as comfort-able as possible in no time. I promise. I'll take care of everything." He squeezed her shoulder. "I'm so sorry, Dax."

Dakota closed her eyes and sank into the pillows. In the end, it had been an accident and accidents happen all the time. It wasn't even Chase's fault that she'd been there —she could have said no. She *should* have said no. But she hadn't.

"Hey, um," Chase said softly. "Is there anyone else you want me to call?"

Dakota opened her eyes and looked into his soft gaze. "You mean Jack?" She was still sufficiently sedated to be able to say that out loud.

"For instance." Chase smiled gently.

Tears pressed behind her eyes. How Dakota would love for Jack to turn up at her bedside.

"Do you think she'd come?" Dakota asked stupidly, because how would Chase know the answer to that? He'd barely met Jack. He was the reason Jack no longer wanted to see her—on the surface, at least.

"I'd like to make that call for you. Can I do that?" Chase reached for her hand and wrapped his warm fingers around it. "Can I try to make this right?"

Under normal circumstances, with access to her full faculties and simply going about her life, Dakota would never agree to something so ludicrous—but nothing about today was regular. Moreover, she'd be laid up in this hospital bed for days, and then chained to her couch at home for much longer. She'd have too much time on her hands to think about Jack and to wonder what might have happened if she had let Chase make this call. So he might as well make it. He might as well try.

Dakota nodded. "Okay. Please, call Jack," she said.

CHAPTER 37

"I know," Jack said, "it's ridiculous to be so cut up about a Van Ness." She didn't want to use the word heartbroken because the only time that Jack had experienced true heartbreak was when her father had died—and her heart had never fully recovered.

"It's not ridiculous," Marley said. "You clearly liked her if you gave up all your stupid rules for her, if only for a couple of months. But look on the bright side. There's hope for you yet."

"What do you mean?" Jack asked.

"I mean that you're not as coldhearted as you'd like to be. You need *love-sweet-love* just like the rest of us mere mortals."

Jack expressed her disagreement with a vigorous shake of the head. "Nu-huh. I'm done with that."

"Done? You've barely even started."

"If this is what it feels like, I can most definitely do without."

"Now you're just being obtuse. Obviously, it's not

supposed to feel like this. With the right person, it will feel divine."

What will feel divine? Jack wanted to scream. The sex? Because that had been out-of-this-world with Dakota. Waking up next to her? One of the best feelings in the world. Getting an impromptu text message? That made Jack's stomach erupt in a fountain of dizzy butterflies.

"With someone more like you, without the complex family life," Marley said softly. At least she didn't add 'without the billions in assets'.

Jack huffed out some air.

"Maybe you should get back on the horse as soon as possible," Marley offered.

"The horse? Really?"

"You know what I mean," Marley said.

Jack did know, but she didn't think Marley knew how much this breakup had hurt her. This wasn't Marley's fault. Jack didn't feel she could show her best friend the full depth of her pain—which was, perhaps, the most ridiculous of all.

"I think that, um, I was really, um… in love with her," Jack admitted.

"Duh." Marley surprised her. "Of course, you were in love with her. Any fool could see that."

"I broke down in front of my mom last night," Jack admitted.

This earned her an inquisitive stare from Marley. "In front of Gina? This really is a month of firsts for you, babe." Marley rose from her chair and sat next to Jack. She put her arm around her. "I'm sorry for giving you a hard time about dating her. I can see you're hurting. She really got under your skin and I'm sorry it didn't work out."

"It was never going to work out. That was never my intention."

"Then what did you want? What were you doing spending all that time with her? Falling in love with her?"

"I was being a fool," Jack said, although she felt the much bigger fool now that it had all come to an abrupt end. "I let myself be intoxicated by—" Jack was interrupted by the loud ring of her phone. Deflation ran though her. She didn't have the energy for a work emergency, but she was on call so she had no choice.

"Yes," she said curtly, without even looking at the number.

"Um, hi. Jack? It's Chase. Um, Van Ness."

"Oh, Chase. Hi." What the hell? "Is everything okay?" Why was Chase calling her? Jack's heart nearly burst out of her chest with anxiety.

"Dakota had an accident at a building site and she broke her leg. It's a pretty nasty compound fracture, which will keep her in the hospital a few days at least. She just had surgery and it went well. I'm with her now and..." He paused.

"Which hospital?" Jack asked, even though she had no right to ask that question.

"Mount Sinai," Chase replied. "Eleven West."

The premium patient accommodations. Of course. Jack tried to take a deep breath but her lungs refused to expand fully. What was Chase really trying to say? She should let him finish his sentence. It was hard with a million questions running through her mind, and her heart full of worry for Dakota.

"Do you think you could maybe stop by some time?" Chase asked, his voice calm and confident. "Dakota would like to see you."

She would? She didn't think Jack was a coward any longer?

"Can I come by tonight?" Jack blurted out, her voice taking over.

"There's around-the-clock visiting hours in Eleven West," Chase said. "She's in suite 406. I'll let her know to expect you."

———

Forty-five minutes later, Jack was running into Eleven West as though for an emergency. She slowed as she reached suite 406. She tucked a few loose strands of hair behind her ear and smoothed out her blouse. She still had that distinct image in her head of Dakota walking away from her in that wretchedly bright red coat. She knocked softly on the open door. Chase appeared in the doorway.

"Hey, Jack," he whispered. "I'll give you some privacy. Let me just say goodnight." He gestured for Jack to step farther into the room.

Jack's heart sank when she saw Dakota lying there, her right leg immobilized in an elaborate steel frame that looked like a medieval torture device.

She watched as Chase said goodbye and kissed Dakota softly on the cheek. It was obvious he was so much more than Dakota's ex-husband—he was her best friend.

On his way out of the room, Chase touched his hand gently against Jack's arm and whispered a quiet "thank-you" to her in passing.

"Hey, you." Jack had a hard time moving her body.

"You came," Dakota said. For the first time since they'd met, she didn't glow with good health and fortune.

Her skin was paler than usual and her hair matted against her head.

"Of course. What happened?" Jack shuffled closer.

"Freak accident," Dakota said. "I'm glad you're here." Her voice broke a fraction.

"Do I need to make an arrest?" Jack tried to lighten the mood. "Whose fault is this accident?" She cast another glance at the intricate contraption Dakota's broken leg rested in and didn't find a lot of room for humor. "Jesus. It's not just a sprained ankle, then." She looked back at Dakota's tired, ashen face. "Does it hurt?"

"They have good meds here." Dakota's smile didn't even come close to reaching her eyes.

"Can I sit?" Jack pointed at the chair next to the bed.

Dakota nodded and Jack pulled the chair closer, but not too close.

"Can I get you anything?" Jack asked.

Dakota's eyes seemed to moisten. "Just… sit with me. Please."

"Of course." Jack suddenly had a hard time keeping her eyes dry as well.

Dakota extended her arm and offered her hand to Jack.

Jack took it in hers without thinking.

"I'm… just so glad you're here," Dakota whispered. She held on to Jack's fingers for dear life. "I—" Tears dropped down her cheeks, but Dakota didn't seem to care. She didn't try to wipe them away. "Fuck. It's been a day," she said on a sigh that transformed into a sob.

Jack understood that her only job right now was to be here for the woman she had left, and to hold her hand, until she felt a teeny tiny bit better.

CHAPTER 38

Dakota opened her eyes and blinked into the semi-darkness of the room.

"Sorry to wake you," a voice said. "Just giving you a new dose of painkillers." A nurse she hadn't seen before stood next to her bed. "I think you'll need them." While the nurse fiddled with her IV bag, Dakota looked to her right.

Were those drugs working really quickly or was that Jack, fast asleep in an awkwardly slumped over position, in the chair next to the bed?

"She doesn't want to leave," the nurse said. "Apparently, you need very close police protection."

For the first time since her fall, something resembling a chuckle rose in Dakota's throat.

"Push the call button if you need anything," the nurse said, and left.

Dakota must have fallen asleep while Jack was still there. She couldn't believe she had, so easily, let Chase call Jack, and, even harder to believe, that Jack had come. What was that all about? Still, she was so grateful Jack had showed up—and that she was still here. Although she should probably go home and get some proper sleep. Jack most likely had to work tomorrow. She couldn't catch criminals on a few stolen hours of sleep in a hospital chair.

Before she tried to wake her, Dakota fixed her gaze on Jack and wondered what it meant that she was still sitting in that chair—if it meant anything at all. Dakota had been too exhausted and emotional to ask before she fell asleep.

"Jack," she called into the darkness. She must be in a deep sleep if she hadn't heard the nurse come and go. She must be worn out. "Jack!" Dakota tried raising her voice a little. Jack's chair stood too far away for Dakota to reach and she couldn't move with that frame around her leg.

Jack stirred. Her head snapped upward and she smacked her lips in the most adorable way before opening her eyes. She looked dazed, but only for a split second.

"Hey." Jack's face was as crumpled as her blouse. Her legs were short enough to tuck underneath her in the chair and find a comfortable enough position to sleep, but still. "You should get some sleep in a proper bed," Dakota whispered.

"You fell asleep," Jack said. "I didn't want to wake you, but I also didn't want to leave without saying goodbye."

"I'm awake now." Dakota tried a smile.

"Are you in pain?" Jack glanced at her leg. "Is that why you woke up?"

"No. A nurse came in. I'm still pretty high on meds." Dakota surprised herself by making light of the situation. Maybe she could only do that because Jack was here.

"I'd say good for you, but it seems a little inappropriate." Jack stretched her arms and legs. "When I come back tomorrow, you're going to explain to me exactly how this happened and at which building site. I'll have those incompetent assholes shut down, I swear to you."

"Believe it or not, I tripped on a piece of paper and landed very unfortunately. It could have happened anywhere." While perhaps not entirely true, Dakota didn't feel like defending a Van Ness building site against Jack's scrutiny. "Hey." Dakota reached out her hand again. "Thank you so much for coming after... um, what happened." After dumping me, she thought.

"I was surprised to get the call." Jack accepted Dakota's hand and looked at it as though it was an object from outer space. "To say the least."

"I'd just woken up from general anesthesia and was on a lot of pain meds when Chase suggested it." Dakota slid her fingers in between Jack's.

"Chase suggested it?" Jack tipped her head and lifted her gaze from their intertwined hands to Dakota's face.

"Yeah." Dakota looked into Jack's dark eyes.

"Why?" Jack's voice was soft but inquisitive in the semi-darkness of the room.

"I don't know." Probably because Dakota's ex-husband knew her better than anyone, but she wasn't going to tell Jack that. "I know that you don't, um, want any part of my life anymore." Had Jack not just said that she was coming back tomorrow? "I respect that, even though Chase calling you on my behalf might not make it seem that way. I wasn't myself yesterday. I'm in the hospital and I can barely move. I was emotional and I just wanted to see you, even though I now realize how selfish that was." This time last week, Dakota had still been dating Jack—having the hottest sex of her life—and both her legs were fully intact. Look at her now. Look how it could all turn on a dime.

"Hey." Jack softly stroked Dakota's palm. "It's okay. I'm glad Chase called. I'm sorry that it's under these circumstances, but I'm…" Jack swallowed hard. "It's good to see you."

"Did you miss me?" Maybe those newly administered drugs were starting to do their job already. Dakota had surely missed Jack—and she'd never been more entitled to feel sorry for herself than right now, which apparently included asking her ex-lover impertinent questions in the middle of the night as she sat next to her hospital bed.

"Of course," Jack said, then mumbled something Dakota couldn't understand.

"What was that?" she asked.

"Like fucking crazy," Jack whispered quietly but perfectly audibly this time.

Dakota sank into the pillows. "You don't have to come back tomorrow if it's too hard."

"I'm coming back. I don't care if it's hard." Jack held onto Dakota's hand a little tighter, before dropping it. "I need to know you're okay. I need to see it with my own eyes."

"In that case, I'd love it if you visited me again." Dakota could only express what she so clearly felt. She wanted to see Jack again. It was all well and good to forget about someone you were crazy about when going about your normal life, but Dakota's life as she knew it had been abruptly put on hold.

"Okay." Jack rose from her chair and towered over Dakota's bed. She smiled down at Dakota. Her hair was mussed and she looked more disheveled than Dakota had ever seen her. "Get some rest," she whispered, as she brought her hand to Dakota's forehead and smoothed back a strand of her hair. Dakota might have been dead tired, hurt, and drugged up, but Jack's touch reverberated in every single one of her cells.

———

Jack didn't bother trying to get more sleep when she arrived home from the hospital. Her shift started in less than four hours and she'd be a zombie if she fell asleep now and her alarm clock woke her in two hours—if she'd be able to sleep at all after seeing Dakota like that. Instead, she took a long shower, turning the water from scalding hot to freezing cold slowly, so she barely noticed it, but emerged feeling as fresh as possible on the few hours of broken sleep she'd got in that chair in Dakota's room.

She remembered the conversation she'd been having with Marley when her phone had rung—when Chase Van Ness had called her. Chase had been polite, friendly, and every inch a gentleman. Then again, Jack's issue wasn't with Chase as a person, but with his role in Dakota's life. He might be the friendliest, warmest, most fun person in the universe, it still wouldn't make a difference. It would still be too much for Jack to deal with.

"Get back on the horse," Marley had said. So Jack reached for her phone, because that was the only way she knew how to do that. If she swiped right a couple of times now, in the middle of the night, there might be a few promising matches waiting for her when she checked her phone on a break from work later—and she might be able to get her mind off Dakota.

The problem was that none of the women in the pictures on Tinder even remotely came close to Dakota. But it was high time for Jack to get her feet back firmly rooted to the ground. Dakota had been out of her league, in more ways than one. Not only physically, but emotion-ally as well. For someone who was new to dating women, Dakota had shown very little fear about dating Jack. She'd simply gone for it, without asking herself too many ques-tions—what a novelty—whereas Jack had ruined it because of the doubts that permanently lived in her heart.

She swiped and swiped and her thumb didn't even come close to veering right once. Screw getting back on the horse. Screw even trying. Jack wasn't ready to date anyone else yet—let alone have a one-night stand—when her mind was still so full of Dakota, especially after seeing her again.

They hadn't really talked. They'd just sat together, Jack's company seemingly enough for Dakota in that moment. She ran her fingers through her wet hair and let her head tilt backward. Against her will, her eyes fell shut because Jack was bone-tired. She hadn't been sleeping well since the break-up, because that sense of relief she'd anticipated—she'd so desperately craved—had never materialized. Her eyes flew open as her phone rang. The panic was real and instant. Had something happened to Dakota? Maybe she'd been hurt in a less obvious place than her leg and the doctors had missed it. Maybe her leg had become infected. What did Jack know? She wasn't a doctor. She was a cop with nerves like a live wire because the woman she was in love with was in the hospital. But it was only Nico calling.

"Hey, partner," he said. "You up? We caught one."

Thank fucking god, Jack thought, which really was the very last thing she should think when being notified of a homicide.

CHAPTER 39

"I'm a little confused," Leila said, because she was that kind of person. "Why did you have Chase call Jack?" Leila didn't care that Dakota was in the hospital, her leg trapped in what very much looked like a cage, with months of recovery ahead of her.

"Because… it was what I wanted at the time." Dakota couldn't come up with a better explanation.

"Are you two back on?" Leila tapped her fingertips against each other.

"Of course not." Dakota rolled her eyes. She was getting sick of lying in this bed already. She couldn't even go to the bathroom. She couldn't move from the waist down and she was pretty sure the nurses were dialing back her pain meds already because her leg was starting to hurt more.

"Are you friends then?" Leila didn't let up. Where was Izzy and her calming influence when Dakota needed her most?

"No. I don't know." Dakota tried to shift her weight a little, sending a pang of pain down her leg. "Argh," she groaned. "I don't know. Okay? Neither of us do," Dakota snapped. "Sorry." She gave up on trying to find a more comfortable position.

"You don't have to apologize," Leila said. "I can imagine this ordeal is terribly inconvenient, but..." She leaned a little closer to the bed. "Maybe it can facilitate some kind of truce between you and Jack."

"Truce?" Dakota shrugged, and even a small gesture like that was becoming uncomfortable. "Nothing has changed. I still have kids and, frankly, I'm pleased as punch right now that Chase and I live in the same house. I'm not going to be able to walk for weeks. If she can't accept all of me, and how I've arranged my life, then so be it."

"But she did come." Leila remained unperturbed by Dakota's outburst. "Rushed to your bedside, more like. Doesn't that mean anything?"

"We only just broke up. There are still a lot of feelings involved. It doesn't just all go away because she decided that she doesn't want... me." Damn. Dakota was feeling mighty sorry for herself again. She was glad it was just Leila in her room.

"My point is that Jack might change her mind. What if she does?"

"Leila, please stop with your hypotheticals. I just can't right now. Tell me something about your life. Preferably something fun."

"Hey." Leila grabbed Dakota's hand. "This will pass. I know you're in pain, but you won't always be."

Dakota didn't know if Leila was referring to her leg or her break-up from Jack. She didn't have time to ask because there was a sudden rush of noise outside her room. Dakota checked the clock on the opposite wall and a wide smile spread on her lips.

Seconds later, Peyton and Aubrey stormed in followed by Corey.

"Easy, girls," Leila said as they rushed toward Dakota.

Her daughters hugged her much tighter than they had since turning twelve—and, coincidental or not—receiving mobile phones for their birthday.

Corey kissed her affectionately on the forehead.

"Bad news," he whispered. "Chase did everything he could to stop it from happening, but Grandma Van Ness will be visiting later today."

"Please stay until she has come and gone," Dakota pleaded.

"You got it." Corey shot her a wink, then kissed Leila hello.

———

Jack arrived at the hospital, hoping to catch Dakota alone. She had texted before taking the subway, but hadn't received a reply.

When she approached, she saw the door to suite 406 was closed, which she took as a good sign. Before she knocked, she put her ear to the door. She heard hushed voices. It could be the TV or, more likely, Van Nesses. Should she turn around? But she was here. She'd had a hell of a long day—and she really wanted to see Dakota.

Jack softly knocked on the door. An instant later it flew open, and Jack stood face-to-face with the girl who had walked in on them that one fateful morning.

"Mom," the girl said. "It's your ex-girlfriend."

"Hi." Jack offered the girl her hand. "I'm Jack."

The girl eyed Jack's hand as though it was made out of the most disgusting material, but then gave it the lightest of shakes anyway. Maybe Jack should have opted for a fist bump instead—she had no idea.

"You broke up with my mom," the girl said, then promptly walked away, as though that was the only possible follow-up to that statement.

Chase hurried toward the door and quickly closed it behind Jack, ushering her in.

"Sorry about that," he said to Jack in a low voice. "The girls are all over the place because of their mom being in hospital."

Jack finally got a good look at the room and the people in it. Corey was there, as well as a regal, older lady dressed as if she was going to tea with the King of England.

"This is my mother," Chase said. "Eleanor Van Ness."

"Nice to meet you, Mrs. Van Ness." Jack painted on her most professional smile.

"And you are?" Eleanor Van Ness knitted her perfectly sculpted eyebrows together.

"I'm Jack. A friend of Dakota's."

"You must be a very devoted friend to show up this late."

"I am, indeed." Jack had never wanted to flee a room so badly. "But you're having family time, so I should go."

"No, no." Chase put his hand on Jack's shoulder. "We're going." He put his other hand on Eleanor's elbow. "Come on, Mother. I'll take you home."

Eleanor raked her gaze over Jack, her face expressionless. "Lovely to meet you, Jack," she said, her voice all fake sweetness.

Jack watched as the girls hugged Dakota gingerly but with surprising affection in their gangly limbs. Chase and

Corey kissed Dakota on the forehead. Eleanor just waved at her ex-daughter-in-law from a respectable distance.

"Worst timing ever," Jack said when the Van Nesses had filed out of the room. She shuffled closer to the bed.

"Sorry about Eleanor. I don't even know why she came to visit. Probably because, in her view, it was the only right thing to do. At least now that she's been, she won't come again." Dakota looked tired and the lines in her face had deepened.

"How are you?" Without thinking, Jack gently touched her hand against Dakota's arm.

"So much better now you're here." She tried a grin, but it failed so miserably, it broke Jack's heart a little.

"Did you hear what your daughter said?" Jack asked. "Does Eleanor know about us?"

Dakota sighed. "In the state I'm in, I really couldn't care less what Eleanor knows or thinks about me."

Jack shot Dakota a small smile. She couldn't possibly know if that was really true, but it didn't matter. All that mattered to Jack was making Dakota feel better than she looked. She found it hard to retract her hand from Dakota's arm—so she just left it there, lightly swiping her thumb back and forth.

"I texted you to see if the coast was clear." Keeping her hand firmly in place, Jack pulled up a chair.

"Sorry. It's been total pandemonium since the girls arrived after school."

"You look exhausted. I won't stay long."

"Thank you for coming." Though still weary, Dakota's smile definitely looked more genuine.

"Is it not too confusing that I'm here?"

"It's a real treat, if I'm being honest," Dakota said. "Can I ask you something?"

"Of course." Jack maneuvered her chair a little closer to the bed.

"What was it like being in a room with all those Van Nesses?"

"Between your daughter throwing shade and your ex-mother-in-law looking at me as though I'm in dire need of an extreme makeover?" Jack grinned. "Truly wonderful."

Dakota chuckled for an instant, then a grimace appeared on her face.

"Are you in a lot of pain?"

"I think they took me off the good drugs already." The skin around Dakota's eyes crinkled.

"How long do you have to stay here?" Jack asked.

"A few more days. Chase will set me up with the best home care. Nurses around the clock." She pursed her lips in another attempted smile. "Will you, um, come by the house? Once I'm home?"

Jack didn't really want to make the promise, but she also couldn't say no. "Whatever you need," she said.

"Leila asked if we were back on."

Jack sighed. Now that she'd gotten over the shock of Dakota ending up in hospital, it was time to look reality in the eye. She could sit next to Dakota's bed, holding her hand, all she wanted, but it didn't fundamentally change anything about their situation.

"Sorry. I shouldn't have said that," Dakota whispered into the silence that had fallen. "I keep blurting out the most inappropriate things. I just... I'm so fucking annoyed by this stupid accident. By having to lie here with my leg stuck in this god-awful contraption. By having my life come to a stop. But"—she took a breath—"on the flip side, knowing that my leg will heal, and I'll be okay in the end, also gives me pause. It made me reassess some things about my life. Take that scene with Eleanor earlier. I shouldn't have to stand for that. She shouldn't even be here. But there are other things about my life that are important to me, like Chase. And I know you don't get that. It might be completely incomprehensible for anyone who's not me or Chase. Except for Corey, maybe. But Chase will always be a part of my life."

"I don't have to get it," Jack mumbled. Dakota was right. She simply couldn't wrap her head around that kind of intimate relationship with an ex.

"And my kids, well, they're my kids." Dakota sounded as though she was running out of steam. "They're a vital part of me. What else can I say?"

"What *are* you trying to say?" Jack wasn't sure if she was being scolded or having something spelled out to her that she already knew.

"I am who I am and you are who you are." Dakota's voice had grown into a whisper again. "Can we really not meet somewhere in the middle of all that?"

Jack didn't know what to say, so she didn't say anything.

"Why are you here?" Dakota asked, breaking the silence.

"I'm here because… I don't know. I didn't think about it when Chase called. I just rushed over. I wanted to see you. I had to—I—"

"You're here again today," Dakota pushed. "Surely you've had some time to think about it by now."

"I don't know what you're trying to get me to say or admit to. I was so worried about you and, um, of course I still have feelings for you, but…"

"But what?"

Jack wondered what kind of drug Dakota was on tonight.

"What are you so afraid of? Really?" Dakota sighed. "Look at me, lying here. I had an accident. Because accidents happen. They're part of life. Not one single person gets away scot-free. No matter how much money you have or what you do for a living. We're all at risk of something, all the fucking time. Don't you see that?"

"I think I know that better than anyone."

"I have kids, Jack. That makes me afraid every single day. But I can't let that paralyze me. And I most certainly don't let it stop me from enjoying my life. From making the most of it. From falling in love."

"Um." Jack was tired and overwhelmed and, frankly, a little shocked by this impromptu speech. "I didn't come here to get a lecture. I came here for you. To…" To what? Jack didn't know the answer to that either. "What do you want from me?"

"I want you to stop being so afraid," Dakota said.

In response, Jack finally let go of her hand. "If only it were as easy as you telling me that." Jack's voice broke. "I should go." She cleared her throat. "We should keep our distance again."

———

Helplessly, Dakota watched Jack hurry out of the room, as though she suddenly had somewhere urgent to be. Dakota could hardly run after her. She could only lie there and do absolutely nothing but regret her own words.

It was foolish to ask Jack to change this thing about herself that she so clung to, this fear that she—ironically—wrapped around herself like some sort of safety blanket.

But Dakota had nothing to lose—and, despite all the painkillers, the lack of sleep, and the discomfort she found herself in, she could see a few things much more clearly because of this freak accident.

She pushed the call button to ask the nurse for something to help her sleep. She'd had enough of all the thoughts swirling around her head. Most of all, she wanted to stop thinking about Jack—and what they could have had, if only Jack would let herself.

CHAPTER 40

"No more visits from the hot cop?" Leila asked. She and Mac and Jamie formed Dakota's welcome home committee, trying to soften the blow of Dakota having to remain in bed for another week, her leg bolted to the frame as though it was a part of her body. But at least she was in her own home—albeit not in her own bed. Chase had procured a hospital bed that was easy to maneuver and had it put in the middle of Dakota's living room.

The TV played on mute in the background. Dakota had been watching a re-run of *King & Prince*—Jack's reluctant favorite—and had found herself unable to switch it off.

"I was too hard on her." Dakota'd had plenty of time to think it through, and to replay the conversation she'd had with Jack—perhaps more of an accusatory monologue than a dialogue. "I really wasn't myself when I was in the hospital."

"That's totally understandable." Mac shot her a

worried look. "Don't underestimate what you've been through."

"I think that," Jamie offered, "what should also not be underestimated is the hot cop showing up at the hospital. She didn't need any persuading. Just a short phone call, from Chase of all people. Doesn't that tell us something?"

Dakota refused to be hopeful about that. She'd seen Jack's face before she left the hospital for the final time. It was not the kind of facial expression that elicited a lot of hope.

"She came on a whim. I get that. If something had happened to her and someone had called me, I would have rushed to her bedside as well." In a heartbeat, Dakota thought.

Leila rolled her eyes at what Dakota had just said.

"You're not usually one to hold back." Dakota grinned at her friend, then caught a glimpse of Sadie Ireland as Leona King on the TV screen behind her.

"I am holding back," Leila said. "Because I understand that kind of fear. The kind that lives so deep inside of you, it's always there, informing every decision you make. But—" She narrowed her eyes. "I also know it's a fear that's possible to overcome. Because that's what Izzy did for me. It was one of the hardest, but also one of the best things she's ever done."

"I think I know a thing or two about that kind of fear as well," Mac said.

"We're all afraid of something," Jamie added. "Making love so much more complicated than it needs to be."

"What are you watching?" Leila admonished Dakota. "If you'd rather watch TV, we can leave you in peace, you know?" She followed up with a big smirk, indicating that she wasn't really angry at Dakota for paying attention to the screen instead of the conversation they were having.

Dakota wasn't paying attention to the comforting words her friends spoke for good reason because a crazy idea had taken root inside her. "Izzy's still in LA, right?" She asked Leila.

"For a few more days," Leila confirmed.

"Do you think she'd be willing to do a most unfortunate friend—we're talking about a poor woman who has screws attached to her shinbone, on top of a broken heart —a humongous favor?"

"We can always ask," Leila said. "What do you have in mind?"

————

It had been almost a week since Jack had stormed out of Dakota's hospital room. Dakota must be home by now, but Jack hadn't been in touch. She thought it best to, as she'd said in her final words, keep her distance—before they started getting silly ideas in their head again.

She and Nico were on their way back to the precinct when Jack's phone buzzed with a message.

"Oh," she said when she saw who it was from.

"What's up?" Nico asked, keeping his gaze on the road ahead.

"It's from Dakota." Jack's heart hammered in her chest.

"See what she has to say then, partner."

Jack sighed. "I don't want to get sucked in again. It's too easy for her to make me feel things I don't want to feel."

"Whoa." Nico glanced at her sideways now. "Should I pull over for a heart-to-heart?"

Dakota's unexpectedly harsh words from that last evening in the hospital still stung. Jack was used to Marley talking to her like that, but then her mother had said something along those same lines, and now Dakota as well? God knows what this text message was all about. It could easily be more of Dakota calling Jack out on all her infinite flaws. She was getting fed up with that. Her life had been just fine before she'd met Dakota.

Jack put her phone facedown so she didn't have to look at Dakota's name. She could ask Nico to delete the message, but the window of opportunity for that was quickly passing. Because of course Jack wanted to know what Dakota had to say—she was just afraid of how it might make her feel. Again.

By the time they arrived at the precinct, and Nico had parked the car, Jack was more than ready to read the message. Dakota had a hold over her that was much stronger than Jack's flimsy willpower—that much was clear.

"It's a video message," she said to Nico.

"How about I give you some privacy." It wasn't a question. Nico was already exiting the car. Jack sat alone in the passenger seat in the precinct's parking lot. Nervous sweat pearling on her forehead, she opened the message.

That was not Dakota on the screen. She clicked the play button.

"Hi, Jack. This is Sadie Ireland," Sadie Ireland said into the camera. What the hell? "You may know me better as Leona King from *King & Prince*. I hear you're a big fan of our show." Sadie Ireland grinned into the camera and it felt as though she was looking directly into Jack's eyes.

"Coming from an NYPD detective, I take that as a huge compliment." Sadie Ireland actually winked. She put her hand in her blazer pocket. "I still have the badge." Sadie Ireland took a visible breath. "Anyway, enough about me, Jack. I have a message from Dakota." Jack's stomach did a funny flip-flop. What on earth was happening? Sadie Ireland cleared her throat. "Dakota is sorry for how she spoke to you the last time you saw her. It was the wrong way to go about it and she would like to apologize to you for that, Jack." Every time Sadie Ireland said Jack's name, a shiver ran up her spine. This was too much. Jack didn't know if she should laugh or cry. "Dakota would love, and I really mean L.O.V.E, as in she would be utterly beside herself, if you would visit her at her house. She would like to talk to you and clear the air. That's it. Nothing is required from you, only your, as I'm told, very attractive physical presence." Sadie Ireland was in full Leona King mode, meaning her face looked as though saying no to this request was not an option. "If you were to drop by any day this week between eight and nine in the evening, Dakota will make sure you can be alone, without any family members present." Sadie Ireland nodded. "Okay, Jack? How about it?" She grinned the most irresistible grin. "Cop to cop. What do you think?" Sadie threw in the most delightful chuckle. "Best of luck and lots of love." To end the video, she blew a kiss.

"Well, fuck me sideways," Jack said to her phone, as though Sadie Ireland was in the car with her. She watched the video again a few more times, until there was only one more thing left for her to do. Jack had no other choice. Sadie Ireland had told her so.

CHAPTER 41

B y the time Jack rang Dakota's bell, at eight o'clock on the dot, she was so worked up, she cursed Sadie Ireland and her persuasive fake cop ways. A woman she hadn't met before opened the door—it had to be Milena, of the delicious pierogis.

Dakota was lying in a state-of-the-art hospital bed in the middle of her living room. She could still barely move, but she looked much better than the last time Jack had seen her. Her cheeks had more color, and her hair was combed properly. Jack still felt sorry for her—and like an asshole for walking out on her that evening.

"My devious ploy worked," Dakota said. "You came."

Jack shook her head, an inadvertent smile tugging at her lips. "What a move." She held up her hands. "I have no counter move."

"Being here is your move."

"How are you?" Jack kept a respectable distance from Dakota's bed.

"I'm home, that's something. And you're here."

"When Sadie Ireland tells me to come over, I simply must obey," Jack said.

"Because you have a crush on her." Dakota's eyes twinkled.

"Yeah." Jack dug her hands into her pockets to keep herself from touching Dakota. "It must be that."

"Do you want a drink? Coffee? Water? Something stronger?" Dakota asked.

"I don't know," Jack said. "Depends how long I'm staying."

"I hope you stay a while." Dakota fixed her gaze on Jack's, and a pang of lust shot through Jack's flesh. How long was she going to torture herself by trying to resist Dakota?

"In that case, I'll have some water." Jack could do with a glass of wine, but being in the same room as Dakota was intoxicating enough.

Milena brought them a bottle of water and a couple of glasses, then closed the door discreetly behind her.

"Time to spill the beans," Jack said after she'd pulled up a chair. "How much did you pay Sadie Ireland to record that video?"

"Millions and it was worth every single cent." Dakota shook her head. "Nah. Izzy asked her for me."

"Wow. Really?"

"Izzy has a lot of sway."

Jack took a sip of water. "It was a very pleasant surprise, even though you didn't have to apologize to me for what you said."

"How else was I going to see you again?" Dakota sunk her teeth into her bottom lip.

"You could have called."

"Would you have answered?"

"I don't know. Either way, I'm sorry for walking out on you—again. Especially in your current situation. Aren't you going nuts lying here? Confined to your bed?"

"Hell yeah. Mobility is so underrated. I have all this energy I don't know what to do with. And my brain keeps whirring and whirring." Dakota painted on a grin. "I can only watch so many episodes of *King & Prince.*"

"You could watch something else."

"Yeah, but watching *King & Prince* makes me think of you." Dakota held out her hand, and Jack felt herself being sucked in again. Who was she kidding? Being here was once again drawing her into Dakota's mesmerizing orbit. And she kept coming back for more.

Jack took Dakota's hand, although she'd like to touch much more of her, but that was out of the question—and not just because of that frightening brace around her lower leg.

"I'd like to say something." Jack looked into Dakota's green-blue eyes. "But I'm warning you up front that I don't really know how to say it."

"That's okay." Dakota stared right back at her.

"My biggest problem is that I can't stop thinking about you."

"Quite the first world problem to have."

Jack tilted her head. "It would help if you'd let me speak." She added a smile.

"I'm sorry." Dakota looped her fingers through Jack's. "I'm anxious and excited at the same time."

"I'm, um, in love with you and I don't know what to do about that." Jack knew how completely inadequate she sounded. "Falling in love is not…" She shrugged. "It was never part of the plan I had for my life. Then you came along and I swear, it only took that one night for me to fall for you." Jack averted her eyes. "I've thought about you non-stop since, as if you've taken over my brain or something. And that scares me. You were right. I *am* afraid. I'm petrified because I don't know how to do this. How to be vulnerable. How to fall in love without seeing all the doom and gloom that may come from that. I'm a cop. I'm a protector. That's how I've dealt with the trauma of my dad dying. By shutting everything and everyone else out."

Dakota wrapped her fingers tighter around Jack's.

"Hey," Dakota whispered softly after a while. "We're all damaged in our own way," she said. "To live is to be damaged." Dakota pointed at her leg with her free hand. "Look at me."

"Are you saying your gorgeous leg will have a big scar on it?"

Dakota nodded. "Like that scar you got on your heart when your father died."

Jack let the tears well in her eyes.

"I'm scared too, Jack," Dakota said, her voice a mere whisper. "But it's a fear I can live with."

"That's easy enough when you have a cop as your girlfriend."

"My girlfriend?" Dakota chuckled. "We'll have to see about that."

"I'd like to try," Jack said, her eyes moist but her heart open. "Being your girlfriend. Your daughter called me your ex-girlfriend, so it's not that big a leap." Jack grinned and it felt good. It felt right.

"Come here." Dakota pulled Jack closer. "Put your ear to my mouth," Dakota said.

Jack rose from her chair and hunched over Dakota.

"Let me love you in all your damaged glory already," she said, then pressed her lips against Jack's cheek.

"Is there room for one more in that bed of yours?" Jack asked.

"There's plenty of room, but I can't move," Dakota said. Her leg hurt a little less now that Jack was here—now that what had seemed like the craziest idea ever had worked like a charm.

"I'll be very careful." Jack kissed Dakota on the lips and Dakota desperately wanted to invite her into her bed, but it was not possible.

"You're going to need some patience, officer," Dakota said on a sigh. "But look on the bright side. It will give us plenty of time to talk."

"Haven't we done enough of that already?" Jack kissed her again, but then softly pulled away. "Just for the record, I want you, but of course your recovery comes first."

"I want you too." Dakota swallowed something out of her throat, a lump made of pent-up lust and frustration and all the feelings she'd had to keep at bay. "But I can't fucking move." A soft glow burned inside of her. "An orgasm might very well loosen a screw, and then what?"

"I guess more conversation it is." Jack pulled her chair closer and put both hands on Dakota's arm. "What do you want to talk about?"

"Maybe we should discuss the fact that you're my girl-friend now, apparently." Dakota relaxed into the pillows. "All because you value Sadie Ireland telling you something more than you value the same message coming from me."

"That's not true," Jack said. "Unless you're referring to Sadie calling my physical presence very attractive?"

Dakota grinned at Jack—at her *girlfriend*. Jack wasn't the only one who would need more patience. Dakota knew it would take time for Jack to truly open up to her, and to not automatically turn everything into a quip in order to avoid discussing her feelings, but they'd made it this far. It hadn't been easy, but it had been worth it.

For now, Dakota was happy to play along. "For someone who so vocally dislikes *King & Prince*, it sure was easy to make you listen to Leona King."

"She did flash her badge at me." Jack caressed Dakota's arm. "I have to respect the badge."

"Maybe I should get one, then."

Before Jack could reply, there was a loud knock on the door—not the discreet kind Milena specialized in.

"Must be the kids," Dakota said. "Even though I asked them for privacy." She rolled her eyes.

Jack nodded, the expression on her face understanding enough. She retracted her hands from Dakota's arm.

Another loud knock.

"Come in," Dakota said.

"We always knock now," Aubrey said as she waltzed into the living room, Peyton hot on her heels.

"I appreciate that, darling."

Aubrey and Peyton stood at the foot of the bed, staring at Jack.

"Girls, it's time you properly met Jack." Dakota had never thought she'd see this day. She glanced at Jack from the corner of her eye. Formally meeting her daughters had not been on the agenda for tonight, but when you had kids, so many unplanned things happened all the time—and her kids were an integral part of Dakota's life.

"Hi, girls." Jack rose and walked toward Dakota's daughters. "It's good to see you again." It sounded a little awkward but it was mostly endearing to see Jack try so hard.

The girls said their names and waved at Jack. It was a bit too soon for the three most important people in Dakota's life to start exchanging hugs, but it was a good start.

"Are you back together?" Peyton asked.

Jack nodded, a smile appearing on her lips.

"We are," Dakota said.

"Okay." Aubrey glared at Jack. That word could mean many things when spoken by a teenager. "I guess we'll see you around then."

"What should we tell Granny when she asks?" Peyton said. "Because she's been asking."

"Don't tell Granny anything. It's none of her business."

"We just came to say goodnight, Mom." Aubrey moved closer to the head of the bed. "How's the pain?"

"It's okay," Dakota assured her daughter—it had become more manageable since Jack had arrived. "Nothing for you to worry about, darling." She stretched out her arm and caressed Aubrey's hand. "I'm going to be all right."

Aubrey gave her a small smile, then kissed her mother's cheek. "Goodnight, Mom. Love you. See you in the morning."

"You too, sweetie."

Peyton followed suit and Dakota hugged her daughter as tightly as she could.

Then the girls huddled together the way they'd done since they'd been born. They glanced at Jack. Peyton was the first to speak.

"Night, Jack," she said.

"Goodnight, girls," Jack said.

"Night." Aubrey raised her hand for another stilted

wave, cast one last glance at her mother, then dragged her sister out of the room.

Dakota took a breath. "Are you okay?"

"They're children, not criminals," Jack said.

"You're a cop. Maybe you can deal with criminals better than you can with children."

"Teenagers do have their own special way of being intimidating." Jack approached the bed again. "But I think I can handle it."

"Good thing I didn't let you crawl into bed with me." Dakota pulled Jack closer.

"Do you want me to stay?" Jack nuzzled her nose against Dakota's neck. "That couch looks a whole lot more expensive than my bed." She pressed her lips against Dakota's skin. "We can watch *King & Prince* together."

Dakota shook her head. "No way. I can't have you sleep so far away from me. Let's wait until we can have a proper sleepover."

"A sleepover?" Jack's lips grazed Dakota's earlobe as she chuckled.

"We are girlfriends now," Dakota stated.

"We are." Jack looked into Dakota's eyes. "We should really let Sadie Ireland know."

They both burst out laughing.

CHAPTER 42

"Dakota had an accident and I just rushed over there, without thinking," Jack said to her mother.

"Maybe that's what you needed. To not overthink it." Her mother poured them both a cup of coffee. "Is she okay?"

"Her right shinbone is broken and strapped into a steel brace, but she should be fine." To think of Dakota in that hospital bed in her living room, all delicate and vulnerable, moved something inside Jack. It touched her in a deeper way than seeing Dakota all made-up and dressed in designer clothes, ready to take them off for Jack. "She has the best medical care money can buy."

"Are *you* all right, Jackie?"

"Oh, Mom. I don't know. I don't know what's come over me. Sometimes I don't feel like myself but other times I feel more myself than I've ever done before."

"How do you feel when you're with her?" Her mother shot Jack a warm smile over the rim of her cup.

"Like a million bucks." Jack chuckled. "But also terrified."

"It's perfectly normal to feel that way, you know."

"Is it?"

Her mother nodded and put down her cup. "It's okay to be scared. Remember?"

She did. It was what her father used to tell her when she was anxious about something.

"Yeah." Jack's turn to nod. "Just as long as you don't stay scared forever," she and her mother said at the same time.

"Scared or not, right now I feel as though I have no other choice than to be with her. Like my feelings for her are stronger than my fear."

A wide smile bloomed on Jack's mother's face. "That's love, Jackie. That's what love does." She briefly shook her head. "I'm so happy you can finally let this kind of love into your life."

"Even if it's with a Van Ness?" Jack asked.

"They must be human like the rest of us. Dakota's laid up with a broken leg and I'm sure her teenagers are just as obnoxious as you and your brother were at that age." Another smile.

"At least they have a nanny to deal with the worst of that," Jack joked. "Apparently Corey's pretty good with them as well."

"The ex-husband's new husband." Her mother grinned. "I looked them all up on the internet."

"You did?"

"Of course. When my daughter tells me she has the hots for a Van Ness, I'm going to do some research." She blew some air through her pursed lips. "They own a *lot* of property."

"I own my apartment," Jack said defensively, which

wasn't even technically true, because her mortgage was far from paid off.

"And you're a Russo," her mom said. "That's worth more than any fortune."

Gina Russo couldn't be more right.

———

Jack had taken a rare day off to be with Dakota as she got the frame removed from her leg and a closed cast put on instead.

Chase was there as well. Didn't he have a property empire to run? Dakota's accident had happened on a Van Ness building site and maybe he felt guilty. Or, more likely, this was just how things were between him and Dakota.

While Dakota was in the treatment room, Jack and Chase were let into a private area that Jack didn't even know existed in hospitals.

"Now that we're alone," Chase said, "I've been meaning to ask." He fixed an unwavering stare on Jack. "Did we get off on the wrong foot?"

"No," Jack replied.

"That time we were meant to have dinner and you were called away for a work emergency—was that really an emergency?"

"No, it wasn't. I ran away, but it wasn't because of you." Sitting by Dakota's bed, not being able to touch her in the way she wanted, had given Jack ample time to do some soul-searching. Chase had been an easy scapegoat for the fear that ran rampant inside of her. "It wasn't because of Dakota either. I was very confused and it took me a while to figure out what I really wanted."

"Dakota told me about your dad," Chase said.

"I know." It was one of the first things Dakota had told her after they'd gotten back together.

"I'm so sorry you had to go through that. It must have been so hard for you and your family."

"We made it through." Jack shuffled in her seat.

"I know we have a bit of a strange arrangement, and it can be daunting for someone new in our lives, but Dakota means the absolute world to me. She has done for a long time."

"You clearly mean a lot to her as well," Jack said.

"So do you." Chase's smile was so warm, it felt almost impossible to push him harder. But Jack hadn't acquired her gold shield by being easily influenced by other people's charms.

"I get that she's important to you and you have kids together, which overrules everything else, but"—Jack was probably about to offend a Van Ness—"you hurt her so much and yet you're still so close. It completely baffles me sometimes."

"I did hurt her, but that doesn't mean I didn't love her. I still love her."

But you used her, Jack thought. She didn't voice this particular thought because it was always better to let someone speak than to judge them.

"You may think that because I'm a Van Ness I grew up in a perfect world, but I didn't. There's always been a lot of pressure on me to be a certain way, a prescribed way —the Van Ness way—and I wanted to try. Honestly, when I met Dakota, she blew my mind."

At least Jack knew what that felt like, although it could hardly have been the same.

"She was the answer to, if not all, then at least most of my prayers." Chase exhaled slowly. "I truly believed that if there was one woman who could help me overcome who I really was, it was her."

Jack was far from naive. Even though she had come out of the closet less than twenty years ago, she was lucky to be able to live her life as her true self—she knew that wasn't the case for everyone.

"I'm sorry that being gay was something you felt you had to overcome."

"And I'm sorry that I hurt someone I truly loved so much in the process of finding myself. Although it's impossible for me to claim that it shouldn't have happened, because then she wouldn't be in my life, and we wouldn't have the girls."

The door to the waiting area opened and the male nurse who'd been fawning over Chase since they'd arrived walked in.

"You can go in now." He fluttered his eyelashes at Chase.

"I'll wait here," Chase said to Jack. "You go in."

Although Jack was pretty sure the nurse would rather stay in the waiting room with Chase, he took her to the treatment room where Dakota was waiting.

"I can almost walk," Dakota said from a wheelchair, a cast covering her right lower leg from just beneath her knee to her toes.

Jack crouched down next to her and found her ear. "A walk is so not what I have in mind," she said.

CHAPTER 43

The girls were upstairs with Chase and Corey—under strict instructions to stay put. Dakota and Jack were alone. Although Dakota still had the clumsy cast, it was a huge improvement because—at last—she could move around. She had to use crutches for another few weeks, but right now, it was the biggest gift of freedom to be able to stumble around her living room and simply sit in an ordinary chair instead of being confined to the bed. She could also sleep in her own bed again and—even better—Jack could sleep right next to her.

Since their bedside reunion, they'd only kissed and hugged in awkward, unfulfilling positions. Not only did the leg brace make it impractical and too painful for them to do anything else, but Dakota had hardly felt like her sexiest self while laid up in that hospital bed. On top of that, she had around-the-clock care and a nurse was always on shift, staying in one of the guest bedrooms.

But Dakota didn't need twenty-four hour care any longer and there was no one else in the apartment. Jack had already made it crystal clear what she thought they should do tonight. They'd still need to be careful—and certainly no strap-ons could be involved—but Dakota's skin tingled at the prospect of their postponed reunion sex. Or should she call it lovemaking now?

"What can I get you, Ms. Van Ness?" Jack asked.

"The promise that you can't get called away, for starters," Dakota said.

"I'm on leave and most certainly not on call," Jack said. "Look." She reached for her phone and pushed the off button ostentatiously hard. "I'm unreachable, except to you."

"How will the city of New York survive the night without its finest detective on call?" Dakota reached out her hand.

"My services are needed elsewhere." Jack crouched next to her.

"In that case, I think I'll have an orgasm." It made Dakota think of their very first date, when Jack, with all the swagger in the world, had promised her multiple climaxes—and made good on that promise, and then some.

"Your wish is my command." Jack stood and helped Dakota up. She handed her the crutches.

They made their way to the bedroom where Dakota found a comfortable position she could lay in for a while— that extra weight around her leg didn't allow for much leeway, let alone freedom of movement.

Jack sidled up to her. "Hey," she said. "Welcome back to your bedroom. I'm your welcoming committee." She brushed a lock of hair away from Dakota's forehead.

"Can't wait to discover all the delights a Jack Russo welcoming committee entails." Dakota twisted her body to fully face Jack.

"You're about to find out." Jack kissed her and gingerly pressed her body against the side of Dakota that was not partially wrapped in a cast.

When they broke from their soft kiss, Jack said, "I'll be very gentle. I promise."

Dakota could only smile. Because Jack was there despite all the odds stacked against them. Despite all the obstacles they'd had to overcome. As Jack kissed her again, Dakota thought about what Corey had said, weeks ago, about her and Jack being in lust and it either becoming something or not—most likely not. Yet here they were. Because sometimes there's an undefinable something hooking you to another person and, no matter how hard you fight it, you can't let go. Just maybe, Dakota could have more than one big love in her life—and Jack could be the second, perhaps even last one.

Dakota couldn't predict the future, that much she knew for certain. She'd already tried that once, when she'd said "I do" to Chase and believed, with every fiber of her being, that it was forever. Nothing was forever. That was the only conclusion Dakota could draw. This also included her only being attracted to—and falling in love with—men.

Dakota was still completely in lust—but she was also completely in love. That was all she knew. It was all she needed to know.

Jack's hand skated underneath her top. Her fingers were light as a feather on her skin. It was enough to make Dakota delirious with desire. Especially because Jack's fingers didn't hesitate on their way up, and were soon sweeping across her bra.

Jack's touch was like magic on her skin. Dakota didn't

know how it was possible to miss something so much that she'd barely known before.

They kissed and kissed, their lips soft against each other, their tongues meeting gently. The tenderness in Jack's touch wasn't new, but maybe the degree of it was. In her heart, Jack was such a softie—that much Dakota knew as well. Otherwise, it would have taken a lot more than a Sadie Ireland video to get her back. She was a tough nut to crack, but she was also caring and kind and had so much love to give—all that love she had decided to lock away somewhere deep inside of her.

Jack's finger traveled down, hooking under the waist-band of the cut-off sweatpants Dakota was destined to wear as long as her leg was in that cast. They came in very handy now because they allowed Jack's finger easy access to Dakota's throbbing center.

Jack pulled back from the kiss and looked in Dakota's eyes as her hand dipped lower, and her fingers floated into Dakota's panties.

"I'm so crazy about you," Jack said, as her finger touched against Dakota's pulsing clit.

"Ditto," was all Dakota could reply, as Jack worked her magic on her body again. As she, with the simple brush of a finger, drew another inevitable—and very much announced—orgasm from her.

———

"There's only one position in which I will be able to return that favor." Dakota gazed into Jack's eyes, a satisfied smile on her lips.

"You don't have to return the favor," Jack said, although her body was screaming the opposite.

Dakota rolled her eyes. "What do you think I've been doing the past two weeks with all that time on my hands? I'm an architect. It's my job to figure out structural issues."

Jack chuckled. "Can't wait to hear what you've come up with." She had a pretty good idea what Dakota was about to suggest.

"Well, babe." Dakota pulled at Jack's blouse and drew her near. "The only option is for you to sit on my face."

"It took you two full weeks to come up with that?" Despite the wisecrack coming out of her mouth, heat bloomed inside Jack.

"You try having sexy thoughts with your shinbone bolted to a metal frame," Dakota whispered. "And I'm also discounting the days you didn't want to see me."

"I'm so sorry." Jack couldn't stop a grin from splitting her lips. "For talking back. That's no way for a welcoming committee to behave."

"Damn straight. You've got a real mouth on you, Detective Russo." Dakota grinned back. "How about you shut it and find out what *my* mouth can do."

"My pleasure." Jack's clit throbbed like a second heart. She kissed Dakota again. This had become about so much more than sex—it certainly was a whole lot more than the one-night stand Jack had tried to cling to. But Dakota lit her up inside. She shone such a bright light on the bitter darkness Jack didn't know she'd been living in for so long.

Dakota pulled away from the kiss and gave Jack a look —one she couldn't possibly misunderstand. For once, Jack did exactly what she was told. Exactly what the other woman in her bed requested from her. She stripped off all her clothes, carefully maneuvered her way to where Dakota wanted her, her body ready and her heart more open than it had ever been.

CHAPTER 44
SIX MONTHS LATER

Dakota raked her gaze over the people she loved most in the world. The twins sat in a corner of the couch with their phones, on TikTok or texting with their friends. Chase was in deep conversation with Curtis, a fireman, about something building-related. Jack's brother Matty, also a lawyer, was explaining something to Corey. Jack, her sister-in-law, and her mother perched on the edge of the couch, all three of their bodies intently angled toward Izzy and Leila. Jack had told Dakota that Gina had been so nervous about meeting Isabel Adler, she'd almost bailed on coming to this party, to their celebration of Jack moving in with Dakota.

Jack's best friend, Marley, was the only person not talking to anyone, even though Dakota knew for a fact that Marley loved to talk. She walked over to her—her right leg completely pain-free now.

"I don't know why it took Jack so long to come and live here with you," Marley said, casting an appreciative gaze about the place. Clearly, she wasn't referring to the time span Jack and Dakota had been dating, but to the difference in their living situations. "I'd have moved in here with you in a heartbeat."

Dakota grinned at Marley. It had taken a while before Jack's friend had warmed to her, but now they could banter like this.

"We haven't decided yet if we'll stay here in the long run, or get a place of our own," Dakota said. Who knew what the future might bring?

"Hm," was Marley's only reply while she mulled something over. "I'm still processing that she's actually moving in with you, regardless of this place being straight out of some high-end architecture magazine." She held up her hand. "Don't get me wrong. I'm really happy for Jack. But moving in with someone is another huge step for her."

"She spends most of her time here already." Jack's job was so absorbing, her hours long and unpredictable, that if she kept on living in her own place, the time they spent together wouldn't be nearly enough. Getting to see each other as often as they could was something both Dakota and Jack wholeheartedly agreed on.

After Dakota and Jack had started seeing each other again, Jack had, naturally, spent more time at the house than at her apartment. Dakota had negotiated clear boundaries with the girls as well as with Chase and Corey regarding privacy, knocking, and the utmost respect for a locked door. So far, it was working.

"How are your kids taking it?" Marley asked.

Dakota glanced at the girls. They were probably waiting for Mac and Jamie to arrive to put their phones down. Her neighbors had an uncanny ability to get the girls to engage with them. It was through Mac and Jamie that Dakota knew for sure that the girls were ready for their mother to take the next step in her relationship—a step that very much impacted their lives as well.

"They get along better and better." A small smile spread on Dakota's lips. "Jack's not as bad with the kids as I expected her to be." She chuckled. "God, did that sound terrible?"

"Hell no. I feel you," Marley said. "But if I've learned one thing since Jack swiped right on you, it's that wonders never cease."

"You can say that again." Dakota held up her glass to Marley and they clinked rims. Because Marley was right. This afternoon was, if not a miracle, then at least the result of some sort of magic. Of a chain of events that could have been interrupted at multiple occasions and gone awry. Yet here they were. Jack was officially moving in.

When Dakota opened her eyes in the morning, Detective Jack Russo was the first person she saw. Jack, who was a woman.

Mac had called Dakota's coming out 'adult-onset lesbianism' the other week, claiming, with the authority of a TV news anchor, that Dakota wasn't the first woman to discover that she had feelings for another woman after having been married to a man, and she certainly wouldn't be the last. That she was far from alone in this. But Dakota didn't feel alone. She had Mac and Jamie by her side, and Izzy and Leila, and of course, she had Chase and Corey. She was anything but alone. And now, she also had Jack.

———

"I do apologize for my brother talking your ear off," Jack had joined Corey and Matty. "It's kind of his specialty." She shot Matty a loving grin.

"I'm going to check on my wife," Matty said. "Before she falls completely in love with Isabel Adler." He sauntered off, leaving Jack alone with Corey.

"Welcome to the Van Ness residence." Corey raised his glass of champagne. "I'm over the moon it's official now."

When Dakota had asked her to move in, to her own great surprise, Jack had said yes immediately. She didn't want to mull it over and think it to death again. Because she knew, without a shadow of a doubt, that she wanted to be with Dakota. Even if that involved part-time living with two teenagers and Chase and Corey upstairs. Besides, it hadn't taken Jack long to fully grasp how convenient it was that the girls' dad and stepdad lived in the same house.

After Jack had dropped her defenses and looked at the arrangement from Dakota's point of view, it was easy enough to see why it worked so well—provided that everyone got along, which they did. Because Jack had also learned that, despite everything, Dakota and Chase had a deep mutual respect and enduring love for each other. That they somehow still belonged together—not just for their daughters, but for themselves as well—and this was the form their relationship had taken.

"Cheers, roomie," Jack joked. She'd liked Corey from the start. He had an easygoing manner and had always made Jack feel incredibly welcome.

Jack took a sip from her drink and looked around the living room—*her* living room from now on. It was a far cry from her shoebox apartment in Williamsburg but, in the end, it was also just a living room. It was the place where she and Dakota came together after a long day, and once Jack laid eyes on Dakota, she no longer registered the plush furniture and abundant works of art.

"I sure hope it doesn't go to your head, partner," Nico, who couldn't be here today, had said when Jack had told him she was moving in with Dakota. "Expecting me to fetch your coffee from now on."

But Jack had also learned that having a lot of money doesn't automatically make you a jerk. She only had to look at Dakota—and Chase and Corey—to be reminded of that. She glanced at Marley, who had given Jack her best-friend blessing after spending some actual time with Dakota instead of judging her from afar. She and Dakota looked over at her and a shot of warmth burrowed its way through Jack's core. She blew her best friend and girlfriend a kiss.

Most of all, Jack had come to realize that you can't possibly cure heartache in advance. That change is the only certainty in life, no matter how hard you try to keep it at bay by controlling the emotional aspects of it. She dealt with that on the job every day, but she'd never before been able to accept it in her personal life, because she was so afraid to get her heart shattered into pieces again. But today, she was certain—because her mother had told her —that her father would be proud of her. That he would want this for her. And Jack wanted this for herself as well, oh so very much.

The bell rang, announcing more guests. Jamie and Mac were yet to arrive, so it was probably them. But Izzy surprised Jack by jumping out of her seat.

"I'll get it," she said. "It must be my housewarming present." She shot Jack a wink as she walked to the hallway.

"Izzy's opening the door?" Jack looked at Corey to check if he knew why this extraordinary thing was happening. "Izzy never even opens her own front door."

"Must be some present." Corey grinned at her.

Dakota and Marley walked over to Jack and Corey.

"What's going on, babe?" It only took one look into Dakota's eyes for Jack to be sure she was in on this mystery present.

Dakota put her arm around Jack's shoulder and pulled her close. "You'll see," she said.

Izzy walked back into the living room, followed by an extremely attractive, dark-haired woman whose face Jack knew all too well.

"I've been told I'm fully responsible for all of this romantic happiness," Sadie Ireland said, filling the room with her magnetic presence. "So I figured I'd better check it out for myself."

"Surprise," Dakota whispered in Jack's ear.

Chase and Corey whooped. There was even a small round of applause.

Jack was utterly stumped for words. Sadie Ireland wasn't dressed like her character, yet it felt like Jack's television had come to life.

"Congratulations." Sadie opened her arms to Jack. "To *King & Prince*'s biggest fan."

Jack giggled like a true fangirl and giddily stepped into Sadie Ireland's embrace. As Sadie closed her arms around her, Jack realized that the biggest lesson she'd learned was, perhaps, that you just never knew what delights life had waiting for you around the next corner. If only you weren't afraid to turn it.

GET THREE E-BOOKS
FOR FREE

Building a relationship with my readers is the very best thing about writing. I occasionally send newsletters with details on new releases, special offers and giveaways.

And if you sign up to my mailing list I'll send you all this free stuff:

1. An e-book of *Few Hearts Survive*, a Pink Bean Series novella that is ONLY available to my mailing list subscribers.
2. A free e-book of *Hired Help*, my very first (and therefore very special to me) lesbian erotic romance story.
3. A free e-book of my first 'longer' work, my highly romantic novella *Summer's End*, set on an exotic beach in Thailand.

You can get *Few Hearts Survive* (a Pink Bean Series novella), *Hired Help* (a spicy F/F novelette) and *Summer's End* (a deeply romantic lesfic novella) **for free** by signing up at www.harperbliss.com/freebook/ or scanning the QR code below

ABOUT THE AUTHOR

Harper Bliss is a best-selling lesbian romance author. Among her most-loved books are the highly dramatic French Kissing and the often thought-provoking Pink Bean series.

Harper lived in Hong Kong for seven years, travelled the world for a bit, and has now settled in the Belgian countryside with her wife, Caroline, and her photogenic cat, Dolly Purrton.

Harper loves hearing from readers and you can reach her at the email address below.

www.harperbliss.com
harper@harperbliss.com

Printed in Great Britain
by Amazon

36765582R00179